Mira Robertson is an award-winning screenwriter who
has also published short fiction. She has written feature
films, documentaries and short films; her feature-film credits
include *Only the Brave* and *Head On*, co-written with
director Ana Kokkinos. She has taught screenwriting at the
University of Melbourne, RMIT and Victoria University,
and currently teaches in the University of Melbourne's
Master of Arts and Cultural Management. She grew up
in the western Wimmera and lives in Melbourne.
The Unexpected Education of Emily Dean is her first novel.

The UNEXPECTED EDUCATION of EMILY DEAN

The UNEXPECTED EDUCATION of EMILY DEAN

MIRA ROBERTSON

Published by Black Inc.,
an imprint of Schwartz Publishing Pty Ltd
Level 1, 221 Drummond Street
Carlton VIC 3053, Australia
enquiries@blackincbooks.com
www.blackincbooks.com

9781863959728 (paperback)
9781743820346 (ebook)

A catalogue record for this
book is available from the
National Library of Australia

Cover design by Jo Thomson
Text design and typesetting by Marilyn de Castro

Printed in Australia by McPherson's Printing Group

For my mother
(1927–2014)

1

PASSENGERS MOVED ALONG THE PLATFORM, opening
carriage doors and saying their goodbyes. Emily leaned out of the
train window. She gave her father an especially pleading look.

'There are snakes and spiders and I'm allergic to sheep. Please
don't make me go.'

She knew it was hopeless – the train was due to leave at any
moment – but she had to make one last attempt. If nothing else,
she wanted her father to feel guilty for bundling her off against
her will.

'Don't be silly,' he replied, impervious to her tragic
countenance. 'No-one is allergic to sheep. Fresh air, sunshine and
the splendours of nature. You've always enjoyed it.'

But that was on her last visit, *ages* ago. She'd been thirteen
then and knew no better.

'I can't go. Mummy needs me.'

She wished she hadn't said *Mummy* as it sounded immature, and now it was she who felt a twinge of guilt, knowing that it wasn't about helping her mother at all, but the thought of spending weeks with ancient relatives in the middle of nowhere.

Further up the platform, the stationmaster blew his whistle. Carriage doors slammed shut as her father reached out and patted her arm.

'Send my love to your grandmother and the others,' he said, ignoring her last words. 'Make yourself useful and don't be a burden. And don't forget to collect your suitcase when you arrive at the station. As soon as things are back to normal, I'll come for you.'

When would that be? There were still five weeks to go before school began again; she could not possibly stay that long. But there was no time to ask – her father had already begun to hurry away. She leaned further out of the window, catching a glint of his clerical collar. Although there was no hope of a reprieve, she still longed for him to turn and give her one last wave, but he passed through the gate without looking back. Tears stung her eyes, and she had to blink twenty-three times to stop them. She hoped that the counting thing had not begun again; she was far too old for that sort of nonsense.

It was a relief when nobody entered her compartment. She did not want strangers staring at her reddened eyes or asking dull questions in their attempts to make polite small talk. Nor, on the other hand, did she want the journey to be filled with interesting conversation. She was, after all, travelling against her will. Nevertheless, she was surprised to have the compartment on her own for there had been quite a crowd on the platform. Perhaps they were all in the second-class carriages.

The train shunted forwards, causing her head to knock against the back of the seat. A headache began to throb, and she embraced the pain with the fervour of a martyr. *See what you've done.* It was a silent accusation to her father and she hoped that he felt it.

When the train had left the city behind, she leaned out of the window again, feeling the air whip against her face. Once more tears leaked from her eyes, but this time it was only an effect of the wind. Her hair flew up, twisting and flapping as if it had a life of its own. She felt something stick to her cheek and discovered a fleck of sticky black soot. She closed the window and sat down.

There were hours to go before the train reached her station. She thought about getting *Middlemarch* from her satchel in the overhead luggage rack. It was the perfect opportunity to make a start on the book, despite the disappointing reality that it was not *Jane Eyre*. Since that day at school when Dorothy had rapturously declared it to be the best book ever written, and Mr Rochester the most romantic hero of all time, she'd been desperate to read it. Dorothy hadn't told her directly of course; she'd been addressing her friends, a group in which Emily, hovering nearby, was not included.

Leading up to Christmas she'd made it quite clear to her parents: all she wanted was a copy of *Jane Eyre*. Seeing a book-shaped present under the Christmas tree – a sawn-off branch from a garden shrub that her mother had propped up in the corner of the living room and decorated with balls of cottonwool 'snow' – she'd been convinced it was the longed-for novel. But it was not to be. Worse still, the copy of *Middlemarch* did not even look new. She was sure it had come from her father's study. He did not believe in unnecessary expenditure, especially with a war on and so many in need.

At the third stop, a woman in a green dress entered her compartment. Emily knew the name of the station even though it was blocked out to confuse the Japs in the event of invasion. To date no such invasion had occurred, but she had heard Father on the telephone mentioning the possibility to his friend, the Very Reverend Eric Simons. Father was only a Reverend and although Emily had never asked him, it sounded like an inferior title. Talking to the Very Reverend, her father had muttered the words *last line of defence*. They had an ominous ring.

'Would you mind closing the door, dear?' the Green Dress asked her. 'I'm susceptible to draughts.'

She rose to shut the door, feeling rather put upon as it was the Green Dress who had failed to close it properly in the first place. She murmured the word *susceptible* to herself, feeling the s's slither on her tongue. Her fellow traveller caught her eye and smiled, but Emily looked away, determined to remain aloof.

Barely a minute passed before the woman spoke again. 'Would you like one, dear?' she said, holding out a large square tin. 'Lovely corned beef and pickle. Awfully tasty.'

They did sound tempting, particularly as she'd forgotten to take the sandwiches her mother had made for her. Father had been calling out from the car. They were going to be late. In any case, her mother's sandwiches were often unreliable, spoiled by incompatible fillings like jam and gherkin. But how could she accept the *awfully tasty* corned beef and pickle when she was

4

travelling under protest? It would undermine her suffering.

Half an hour later, as they approached another station, the woman packed away the tin and prepared to get off. How Emily wished she could change her mind. All she could think of was sinking her teeth into the fresh white bread, her tastebuds tingling with the mustardy sharpness of the pickle and the saltiness of the corned beef. But after rejecting the initial offer of sustenance, she didn't have the nerve to ask.

Hoist with your own petard, her mother would have said, as the sandwiches departed.

There was nothing left to do but try to begin *Middlemarch*. Putting off the moment once again, she gazed out of the window and watched a tractor trundle across a paddock. A horse took fright near the fence line and bolted along beside the train briefly until it was left behind. Two boys hung off a gate, waving. Then the paddocks ended and bush took over. Gum trees with their drooping leaves, and flashes of red from the bottlebrushes. She closed her eyes, listening to the sound of the wheels, the train rushing onwards, delivering her to her fate.

George Eliot's masterpiece remained unopened in her satchel when the train pulled up at a small country station some hours later. Emily was the only one to get off, and she had scarcely stepped down onto the platform before the whistle blew and the stationmaster waved the all clear. The station name, *Garnook*, had not been blocked out, a sign, she thought despondently, that not even the Japs wanted to invade such a remote spot.

She collected her suitcase from the surly stationmaster who soon decamped to his office, leaving her alone on the platform. Had they forgotten she was coming? she wondered, feeling like Anne of Green Gables – except that Anne was a mere child of eleven, whereas she was fourteen. It was an annoying comparison, and she wished she hadn't made it. Perhaps they were waiting for her outside in Uncle Cec's black Packard. Of course, that was it, and with a feeling of relief, she picked up her case and hurried out of the station.

There was no sign of the black Packard. Heat haze shimmered in the distance; there was not a soul about. Fresh air, sunshine and the splendours of nature had never felt more desolate. Even worse was the recognition that, while not wanting to visit was one thing, not to be wanted was another altogether.

Perched on her suitcase, she was beginning to feel panicky. Mount Prospect farm was ten miles away. 'We don't say *farm*, Emily,' she heard Grandmother correct her. 'The word is *property*. Or *station*. We are not farmers, we are pastoralists.' Grandmother was a stickler for doing and saying things correctly. There was nothing more important than keeping up standards. *Putting on airs and graces more like it*, her mother would say sarcastically.

She thought about going in search of the morose stationmaster but noticed, some distance away, a cloud of dust rising into the air. A few minutes later, the black Packard crunched to a halt beside her. Uncle Cec waved through the dusty windscreen, and she waved back, as if she hadn't a care in the world. The car door opened and he got out.

'By Jove,' he said, 'you must be Emily.'

'You must be Uncle Cec,' she replied, aware this was his little joke, and kissed him on the cheek, while attempting to avoid his nose, which was enormous. He was no oil painting and also quite ancient, being Grandmother's bachelor brother and sixty-two.

He did not apologise for being late. Instead he picked up her suitcase and put it in the boot of the car. 'Rightio,' he said, 'we'd better get a wriggle on.'

The afternoon sun was just beginning its slow descent towards the horizon as they drove along the gravel road towards Mount Prospect – the *property*, not the mount, which was fifty miles away. Her mother thought it was a cheek, calling the property Mount Prospect when its namesake was so far away. *Why not Rabbit Flat, or Vue de Swamp?* she'd say. Emily knew how much it offended her father. She never wanted to hurt his feelings and always tried not to giggle.

'Good joke, eh.'

Uncle Cec's voice came as a shock, alerting her to the fact that she must have laughed out loud.

'Oh, it was nothing really,' she said, feeling flustered. To divert him from enquiring further she tried to think of something to say. 'Gosh, I suppose it's been hot.'

'Too right,' Uncle Cec said. 'Cool change should be here in a few hours.'

'How do you know?'

He pointed at the roadside trees. 'Wind's moving round to the south.'

She looked at the flapping leaves, feeling uncomfortably responsible for keeping up the conversation, and began to chatter on about the weather. 'Of course it's summer, so it's not unusual.

7

Being hot, I mean. If it was cold, that would be unusual. Although sometimes it can be quite cold.' The words poured out until she saw that Uncle Cec was tapping his fingers on the steering wheel as if accompanying a tune only he could hear. He was not listening to her, and how could she blame him? She subsided into an embarrassed silence.

After a while Uncle Cec began to talk about a mare called Rivette who was a champion of the turf. Now it was her turn to stop listening, and she abandoned herself once more to the satisfactions of self-righteous misery. *Oh, cruel fate, to be sent so far from home.* Thus absorbed, the time passed quite quickly and it did not seem long before they turned in through the Mount Prospect gates. A short time later they pulled up on the circular driveway at the front of the homestead.

Grandmother stepped out from the shade of the verandah to greet them. 'At last. I was nearly going to send out a search party.'

It was what she always said, and she offered her cheek for a kiss. It was soft and white like Della's scone dough, and Emily just had time to wonder whether Della was still the cook when Cousin Eunice appeared. It was always like that: first Grandmother, and then Eunice a step or two behind, a tall skinny shadow who had the annoying habit of echoing Grandmother's words.

'There you are at last,' Eunice said, on cue.

Emily felt the scratchy peck of dry lips on her cheek and tried not to flinch. According to Della, Eunice had arrived at Mount Prospect twenty-two years ago to help Grandmother with the birth of her last baby. 'Course, after Lydia was born, she never left. Had a sob story about nowhere to go. Penniless, they reckon,' Della had said with a certain relish. It was hard to imagine

Eunice as the willowy young bridesmaid who Emily had spotted in Grandmother's wedding photograph – the one on the mantelpiece in her father's study.

Grandmother told Uncle Cec to take the suitcase to the white room. Emily watched him set off around the verandah. He was wearing outdoor boots, which meant he was not allowed inside.

'Come along, my dear.' Grandmother ushered her into the entry hall and, with Eunice bringing up the rear, they made their way to the other end of the house.

On entering the white room, Emily saw that nothing had changed since her last visit. Everything was still white, including the chest of drawers and the dressing table. A white bedspread covered the single bed.

She plopped down on the bed feeling weak from hunger and thirst. Uncle Cec arrived at the French doors, delivered the suitcase and departed again. Outside the white room, a punching bag hung from a rafter on the verandah. She remembered how William – her father's younger brother – and his friend Harry were always dancing around it, jabbing with their boxing gloves. In her memories, William's chest was pearly white, his arms burned brown from working in the sun. Now he was stuck in a hospital in Brisbane with no-one to visit him.

What had happened to him? Her father had been so vague: 'Wounded in action.' Yes, but what exactly did that mean? He'd been in hospital for months. At first in Port Moresby and then in Brisbane. Father refused to speak about it except to say that she was not to worry, everything would be alright. She knew her father; there was no point in pressing him. But if it was alright, why couldn't he tell her what had happened? She wondered how she would feel if it was her little brother. But that was absurd; unlike Father, she didn't have a brother.

'Emily?'

She looked up to see both Grandmother and Eunice peering at her.

'Goodness me, someone's away with the fairies,' Grandmother said. 'You must be starving. Let's go and find you something to eat.'

Emily stood up and allowed herself to be shooed from the room and along the various passageways, with Grandmother and Eunice nipping at her heels. They reached the kitchen where she expected to see Della the cook and her assistant, Florrie, but they were not there. A glass of milk and a plate of oatmeal biscuits had been laid out for her on the table. She'd been hoping for a cup of tea. Had they forgotten she was no longer a child?

'Plenty of time to unpack once you've had afternoon tea,' Grandmother said.

'Plenty of time to settle in,' Eunice added, before they both departed.

After drinking the glass of milk and eating the oatmeal biscuits, Emily returned to the white room to unpack. She opened her suitcase and picked up the dress that lay on top. Holding it up, a hot blush rushed up her neck, spreading to her cheeks. Thank goodness she was alone, the only witness to the pink gingham monstrosity with its lace collar and puffed sleeves. How could her mother have chosen it? But she knew anything was possible when her mother was on a high. Sometimes it meant cleaning the house from top to bottom. Or abandoning housework altogether in order to campaign on behalf of the orphans of the world and the rights of merchant seamen. Or, as in the case of the dress in question, arriving home from the city in a taxi with too many parcels.

'I've bought you a present from that divine little shop in the city,' her mother had said. Ripping off the tissue paper, she lifted it up, and Emily had tried to smile while her heart sank, Dorothy's merciless laughter already ringing in her ears.

In the days before her departure to Mount Prospect, when everything was unravelling, her mother had insisted she take it with her. 'Just the thing for dinner at the Mount,' she'd declared.

Emily knew that it was not suitable and that she would look ridiculous. She stuffed it back into the suitcase and closed the lid before throwing herself onto the bed. Five weeks. How could she possibly endure it? She felt her eyelids begin to droop from ennui.

2

SHE DIDN'T NAP FOR LONG, and when she emerged from the white room she found Grandmother, Uncle Cec and Cousin Eunice sitting in wicker chairs on the front verandah, catching the start of the cool change that Uncle Cec had predicted earlier. She refused Grandmother's offer of a chair in their immediate circle, preferring instead the canvas swinging seat. From there she could vaguely hear their voices although she could not have said what they were talking about – in any case, it was sure to be dull. She suppressed a sigh and slumped back on the seat, determined to feel utterly bored, when Lydia suddenly appeared from the other end of the verandah wearing a yellow silk dress, a shotgun slung casually over her shoulder. She passed Emily without so much as a glance in her direction, heading across the lawn towards the orchard.

Lydia was her aunt – the baby whose birth had led to the arrival of Cousin Eunice – and only twenty-two. Everyone said it was a miracle, Grandmother having two more children so late in life. It was all because of the ones in between who had never been born. Three miscarriages, her mother had told Emily when she'd wondered how it could be that her father was so much older than William and Lydia. The unborn babies were between her father, who was the eldest, and William who came next. Lydia was the youngest. That was why Lydia and William – but especially Lydia – were more like cousins. Although she didn't mean cousins in the sense that Eunice was a cousin. She wasn't even sure what that sense was and suspected that Eunice wasn't actually related at all. She meant cousins in the sense of confidantes. Perhaps even sisters. Despite not wanting to be at Mount Prospect, she had always yearned for Lydia's friendship. But Lydia seemed determined to withhold it. At least Emily hoped that was the case. It was too crushing to think that the word *withhold* might be wrong and that her aunt had simply never considered the possibility of friendship at all.

Once out of sight, Lydia began to sing, and the sound drifted through the evening air.

'*O hear us when we cry to thee for those in peril on the sea ...*'

'I don't know why she's singing about peril at sea,' Grandmother said with a hint of irritation. 'Harry's in the jungles of New Guinea.'

Now that the conversation had turned to Lydia, Emily's hearing sharpened.

'Quite,' Eunice added.

'Blasted Japs,' Uncle Cec said, giving vent to his outrage by aiming a kick at the fox terrier, Mrs Flynn, who was sniffing about nearby.

Grandmother frowned at her brother. 'There's no need for that sort of language, Cecil, even if they are barbarians. And there's no need to kick the dog either.'

Emily rose from the swinging seat and began to walk across the green expanse of the lawn and into the orchard that encircled the house. She wasn't following Lydia; she was just stretching her legs. If they happened to meet it would be quite by accident. A flash of yellow silk between the fruit trees was enough to set her in the right direction, and soon after she saw Flea, the tabby cat, winding his way through the layered straps of a row of agapanthus. Fat buds swayed at the top of their long green stems. The agapanthus flower heads were ready to burst and the shape of the buds, the way they bulged against the green skin that enclosed them, gave her a tingling sort of feeling. She pressed her legs together and felt her thighs touch. Her skin was hot and damp despite the fitful arrival of the cool change.

Pausing beside a cherry plum tree, she contemplated the possibility of joining Lydia, who was loading her shotgun some distance away. *Divine evening.* She repeated the phrase a few times, hoping to perfect a suitably casual intonation. She was still practising when she saw that Flea had stopped and was crouching down, his tail stretched out straight, just the tip of it vibrating. She watched as Lydia raised the shotgun to her shoulder in line with Flea's tail. There was a hollow boom followed by an echoing crack, and the strappy green skirts of the agapanthus flapped wildly. When the leaves settled, something in the hidden centre of the plant went on thrashing. Lydia moved towards it, and now

Emily noticed she was carrying a lengthy piece of wire with a hooked end. Lydia poked it into the agapanthus and lifted out a long brown snake, still twisting in its death throes.

'Well done, Flea, good puss.'

The cat rubbed himself proudly against the legs of his mistress.

The sight of the writhing reptile had instantly obliterated all thoughts of the divine evening and, if her legs had not felt so suddenly weak, Emily knew she would have hurried back to the verandah. Instead she leaned against the trunk of the cherry plum for support, as Lydia carried the snake to the fence that marked the boundary of the orchard. She witnessed her aunt hang the snake over the top rail of the fence beside a row of similar carcasses. Some had dried out and were fluttering like crepe streamers in the evening breeze while, from more recent additions, she caught the odour of rotting flesh as it mingled with the sweeter scent of windfall cherry plums. She watched as Lydia slid her fingers over the sleek, scaly body of the newly dead snake, before running the same fingers over her cheek, as if, for some mysterious reason, she was comparing the texture of the two surfaces.

Then the bell rang out calling them to dinner, as it always did just before seven. Lydia picked up the gun where she'd rested it against the fence and began walking towards the house. Too late, Emily saw that her aunt was veering towards her.

'Hello, Emily.'

'Oh, hello.' She smiled, pretending to be surprised, as if she had been absorbed in a moment of solitary contemplation and had not noticed Lydia's approach. 'Divine –' But she got no further, for Lydia continued on without breaking stride.

At seven o'clock on the dot everyone was gathered in the dining room. They sat down in their usual seats: Grandmother at the head, with Lydia to her left, then Eunice beside Lydia; Uncle Cec at the opposite end, with Emily on his left. Between Emily and Grandmother was William's spot.

As Emily pulled out her chair to sit, she noticed the place setting beside her. 'Is William here?' she asked with surprise.

She expected Grandmother to answer, but it was Lydia who spoke first. 'I don't know why you keep setting his place,' she said, addressing Grandmother. 'He'll let us know when he's discharged from hospital.' She sounded irritated, and Emily felt sure they'd had this conversation before.

Grandmother did not respond, but Emily saw her flinch. Neither Uncle Cec nor Eunice spoke. It seemed the mention of William elicited only silence.

The door between the dining room and kitchen flew open, and Della came in carrying a leg of mutton on a large serving platter, her arrival saving everyone from the awkward hush that had befallen the room.

Emily couldn't help staring. The cook was even more enormous than last time. Was there a point at which she would simply explode? Della put the platter down on the sideboard with a bang and retreated to the kitchen. Seconds later, she returned with two covered silver serving dishes.

Uncle Cec rose to do the honours with the meat. On a ledge on top of the sideboard sat a row of pewter beer mugs, and the effect of his vigorous carving made the mugs jiggle against one another. A small clinking sound echoed through the otherwise still-silent room. Emily counted the mugs. Sixteen, the same as always. The clinking continued as her thoughts drifted, and she recalled hiding under the sideboard. It was years and years before, and all to do with the crumbed brains that she would not eat. 'Beggars can't be choosers,' Eunice had scolded, giving her a good shake. That's when she'd bitten Eunice on the wrist to make her let go, and then Eunice had become hysterical and Grandmother had to slap her cheek. In the kerfuffle Emily had scuttled under the sideboard and refused to come out. It was quiet down there, with just the occasional sighting of shoes passing by. When hunger finally drove her out, Della gave her a slice of lemon cake and there was no further mention of the brains.

Now Uncle Cec had finished carving, and Della began to serve everyone, moving round the table like a ship of state, her plain cotton dress straining at the seams. '*I will love thee, O Lord, my strength,*' she intoned, setting down a plate with a slice of dark mutton, boiled onions in white sauce, and a small mound of peas in front of Grandmother. '*The lord is my rock and my fortress, and my deliverer,*' came next as Eunice was served. '*My God, my strength, in whom I will trust.*' A plate for Lydia. '*My buckler, and the horn of my salvation. And my high tower.*' The plate slid onto the placemat in front of Emily. Della tapped her on the head and gave her a nod in greeting before moving on. She delivered the last plate to Uncle Cec just as he sat down. '*I will call upon the Lord, who is worthy to be praised: so shall I be saved from mine enemies.*' Della paused, surveying the room as if daring someone to speak. Nobody did. 'Psalm 18, verses 1 and 2.' With that, she sailed off, back to the kitchen.

Grandmother gave a great sigh. 'What a blunder.'

Eunice sighed in sympathy.

Emily waited. 'What blunder?' she asked when nothing more was forthcoming.

'The King James Bible,' Grandmother said. 'I should never have given it to her. Quoting it day and night as if ...' She shook her head, unable to find the right words.

'As if it's the Bible,' Lydia added with an ironic smile.

Grandmother frowned. 'Don't be snide, Lydia. The Catholic Church thrives on keeping its flock ignorant. All that Latin nonsense. The priests have far too much power.'

'Damn right they do,' Uncle Cec said from the other end of the table.

'Then I don't see why you're complaining,' Lydia said. 'It's been a raging success. Della's become quite the biblical scholar.'

Emily wasn't sure she was following. She knew that Grandmother couldn't abide Catholics. For one thing, they were mostly Irish, or at least their parents or grandparents were; being Irish was forever – like being Scots except that the Scots were superior of course. Della was a Catholic and Irish too. But she had also heard Grandmother describe Della as a treasure. And formidable.

'One believes, but in moderation.' Grandmother's voice rose a notch. 'Della's taking it all far too literally.'

'Quite so.' Eunice nodded with approval.

'Moderation. Like your father, Emily,' Grandmother went on. 'It was a shock when he decided to enter the church, however Protestants don't prey on the gullibility of the poor and uneducated.'

This, she knew, was a reference to the Catholic practice of confession, which Grandmother saw as both immoral and theologically wrong. There were so many things wrong with the Catholic Church: the power of the priests, confession, the Pope, and an irrational and unpatriotic refusal to eat meat on Fridays. In Grandmother's opinion, the Catholics showed far too much enthusiasm for religious behaviour outside of the church walls. It was all quite unnecessary.

And deadly dull. She fiddled with her serviette ring. Were they ever going to eat? Fortunately, Grandmother must have read her mind and announced that grace should be said before the meal was stone cold.

Everyone mumbled, '*For what we are about to receive may the lord make us truly grateful, Amen.*'

She looked up to catch Uncle Cec winking at her. '*Eat away, chew away, munch and bolt and guzzle. Never leave the table till you're full up to the muzzle.*'

The words belonged to Albert, the magic pudding. It was a book her mother had often read to her, and she remembered how shocked she'd felt at Albert's desire to be eaten. It seemed wrong, like wanting to be smacked, although of course he was a pudding and not a person. Albert's words popped and fizzed in such a pleasurable way, it was almost as if they were food to be eaten too, and she smiled back at Uncle Cec.

'Really, Cecil,' Grandmother scolded.

'I see we're to have the pleasure of your company for the rest of summer, Emily,' Eunice said, surprising everyone by introducing a new topic.

Emily felt a jolt of alarm. 'Only for a week.' Father had said just until things got back to normal, and she'd managed to convince herself that it would be no more than a week. She could not endure the thought that it might be longer.

A glance slid between Eunice and Grandmother, followed by Eunice's treacherous little smile. 'Of course, dear. It's important to keep your hopes up.'

A hot hard lump got stuck in Emily's throat, and she wished something terrible would happen to the fake cousin. Tears pricked in her eyes. As an emergency measure, she began to count the peas and, on reaching twenty-five, was able to lift her head again. A fleeting yet sympathetic look from her grandmother surprised her, knowing that Grandmother believed feelings of any sort were an extravagance. But then she wondered if she had imagined it, for Grandmother was already addressing Lydia.

'Lydia, dear, I see you had a letter yesterday from Harry.' She turned to Emily. 'Did you know that Lydia and Harry are engaged?'

Emily nodded.

'The war effect,' her mother had commented on hearing the news. 'A rush of blood to the head – and other regions. Let's hope she doesn't rue the day.'

'Why would she?' Emily had asked, but her mother simply laughed and raised her eyebrows at her father as if he knew what she meant.

Grandmother continued, 'Do tell us Harry's news.'

Lydia's eyes were glittery, and there was a spot of red on each cheek. 'Harry's news?' she said in a strained voice. 'Oh, he's having a wonderful time, Ma, living the jungle high life and waiting for a Jap to stick a knife –'

But that was as far as she got before Uncle Cec banged his fist on the table.

'This damn war,' he boomed. 'Everyone knows the Boche are a treacherous lot, but the bloody Japs are even worse. Ruthless bloody murderers. They haven't evolved like us. One thing's for certain, if the worst comes to the worst, I'll do what has to be done. They won't get their filthy paws on any of you, I'll make sure of that.'

Emily tried to control a rising sense of panic.

Across the table Lydia caught her eye. 'Uncle Cec plans to kill us. The women, that is. Mercy killing.'

'Mercy is right, Lydia,' Uncle Cec replied, pointing his knife at her, a transgression of table manners almost as serious as the topic under discussion. 'Better that than let the Nips get hold of you. Mark my words.'

Emily's eyes flicked nervously from Lydia to Uncle Cec. She had never met a real Japanese person but she had seen the official posters warning of their imminent invasion. They looked quite terrifying. On the other hand, the thought of Uncle Cec carrying out mercy killings was hardly comforting.

'How?' The word popped out before she could stop it.

Lydia smiled. 'I expect he'll shoot us.'

Grandmother could contain herself no longer. 'Enough! What on earth has got into you, Cecil? And you too, Lydia. Is there to be no civilised conversation at this table?'

Uncle Cec lowered his head in a suitably chastened way, while Lydia shrugged as if she couldn't care less. Dinner proceeded in silence until Della came in to gather up the empty plates and bring in the pudding, a lemon meringue pie that she placed in front of Grandmother for her to serve. Emily heard something about the *lilies of the field* before Grandmother artfully interrupted Della's recitation with praise for the perfect swirls of snowy white meringue and the delicate aroma of lemon wafting from the pie.

The conversation was able to restart with a discussion of the merits of Della's puddings. Grandmother took the lead, closely seconded by Eunice, with grunts of affirmation from Uncle Cec. It was not in the first rank of dinner conversations, but at least it had Grandmother's 'civilised' seal of approval. Emily was just relieved that there was no further talk about the duration of her stay or of Uncle Cec's plans to eliminate them in the event of the Japanese invasion.

3

AFTER DINNER EVERYONE GATHERED IN the sitting room to listen to the eight o'clock BBC news on the wireless. Emily lingered in the doorway, reluctant to enter. She did not want to hear any more about the war. Far more pressing was her desire to ring home and establish how soon she could return. She simply could not stay for the rest of the summer. But to use the telephone she needed permission. Trunk calls were expensive and only to be made on special occasions or in the event of an emergency. The telephone was on a party line. Grandmother had gone over it with her on earlier visits: an incoming call for Mount Prospect was signalled by two long rings followed by one short ring; Pleasant Springs, a nearby property, was two short and one long; and the next-door neighbours at Rose Park, by three short rings. If one made a mistake and picked up the wrong call, one was duty-bound to indicate the error and hang up immediately. Continuing to listen to the conversations of others was quite beyond the pale. Everyone agreed on the rule, although the speed with which private information spread through the district was an indication that agreement did not mean adherence.

'Come in, don't dally in the doorway,' Grandmother said, now settled into her armchair.

'I thought I'd just ring home and let my father know I've arrived.' She heard herself say 'my father' as if she was talking to a stranger.

'I'm sure he knows,' Grandmother replied with a smile. 'There's nothing so urgent that it can't be conveyed in a letter.'

'It's hardly an emergency,' Eunice said, fanning Emily's desire for Eunice to meet a violent and untimely end.

'*The good news grows by keeping, and you're spared the pain of weeping over bad news when the mailman drops the letters in the creek*,' Uncle Cec recited, tamping a plug of tobacco into his pipe. 'Banjo,' he added, in case she had not recognised the signature style of the Bard of the Bush.

Lydia remained silent. She was flicking through a copy of the *Illustrated London News* and did not seem to be listening.

'Come along. There's room on the couch with Lydia. The news will be on soon and meanwhile Uncle Cecil's been showing us a most interesting artefact.'

Uncle Cec held up a smooth black stone. 'Greenstone axe head. Found it this afternoon in the spring paddock. By jingo, those old blackfellas knew how to sharpen a stone.'

'You ought to show Roy. He'd be interested,' Grandmother said.

Emily knew that Roy was an Aboriginal stockman who

worked on and off at Mount Prospect. She couldn't help a secret flutter of interest in the axe head but a splinter of rebellion had formed. If she wasn't allowed to ring home, then she was not going to join them in the sitting room. Her father's last-minute instructions came to her aid: *Make yourself useful and don't be a burden.*

'I thought I'd help in the kitchen if you don't mind.' She lingered, half hoping someone would notice her frosty tone and persuade her to stay.

Grandmother, however, had moved on. 'Pass it here, Cecil, I'd like to examine it myself.'

Now that she was being ignored, Emily had no choice but to carry out her stated intention. She tried not to feel as if it were a defeat, and hurried back along the passage. She slipped into the kitchen through the connecting door to see Florrie at the sink scrubbing pots and Della peeling sheep's brains in a tin dish at the kitchen table. Della was holding forth while Florrie listened with rapt attention.

'*For without are dogs, and sorcerers, and whoremongers, and murderers, and idolaters, and whosoever loveth and maketh a lie.*' Della let the words roll off her tongue with relish. 'Revelation, chapter 22, verse 15. The devil's gaining ground, you mark my words.'

Florrie had stopped scrubbing and was nervously squeezing the steel wool. 'But we'll be alright, won't we?' She stared at Della, her shiny moon face surrounded by stiff black hair.

'It's moral drift, that's what it is,' Della said, ignoring Florrie's plea for reassurance.

Emily gave a little cough to announce her presence. She didn't want them to think she'd been eavesdropping.

Della jerked round, the slimy brains almost slipping from her grasp. 'Blimey, you shouldn't sneak in like that.' She gave Emily an appraising look. 'Thought so. You've shot up. Still a skinny malink, mind you. We'll have to fatten you up, won't we.'

Florrie had gone back to scrubbing pots, but at this her head bobbed up and she grinned.

'A good feed of brains for tomorrow's breakfast is just what you need,' Della continued. 'That's if the men leave any.' She wiped her bloodied hands on her apron.

Emily felt queasy. The thought of eating brains for breakfast was as revolting as ever, although the days of biting Eunice to avoid it were probably over.

'Who'd have thought we'd be feeding the enemy?' Della added.

'What enemy?' The cook's conversation was often hard to follow even without the biblical digressions.

'Where's that blinking Roy?' Della said, changing the topic. 'He should have been here for his dinner hours ago.'

'You shouldn't swear, Della,' Florrie piped up from the sink.

Her rebuke was received with a snort of contempt as Della beckoned to Emily, still loitering beside the passage door. 'There's a tea towel going spare if anyone's got the inclination.'

Emily hurried across, grabbing a tea towel from the stove rail and set to work, drying up. Meanwhile Florrie turned away from the sink, a dripping saucepan in one hand. 'Swearing's a sin, Della. Father O'Gorman says so.'

Della gave a long-suffering sigh. 'How many times have I told you that blinking's not swearing. If I wanted to swear, I wouldn't blinking well say blinking, would I?' She pointed to the saucepan. 'You're dripping all over the floor.'

It was enough to distract Florrie and she swivelled back.

'If you don't get on with it we'll be here all night,' Della added. 'No more gasbagging.'

When all the pots and pans had been washed and dried and put away, Della and Florrie bade Emily goodnight and retired to the servants' quarters behind the house. It was a mysterious realm in which she had never set foot. Grandmother always said that everyone had a right to privacy – meaning the servants. Years ago Emily had climbed onto the table next to the meat safe where Uncle Cec butchered the carcasses in order to see into the servants' living room. The window was dusty and partly covered with Virginia creeper, but inside she saw Della lying on a couch in her underwear. She hadn't thought about that for a long time – the sight of Della's big fish-white thighs.

With Florrie and Della gone, there was no point loitering in the kitchen. She left, stopping outside the sitting-room door and wondered whether to go in. Classical music was playing on the wireless. It was all too tedious for words.

Middlemarch by George Eliot. She'd been staring at the cover for quite a while – ever since returning to the white room. She knew she ought to unpack but she couldn't face that tonight and had decided instead to begin reading George Eliot's classic novel. So far, she had tried and failed to get past the first page. Reading it was essential if she was ever to achieve her goal, which was to have finished the classics of English literature by the time she turned twenty. She couldn't remember exactly when this ambition had formed but it gave her a sense of purpose and, when she was feeling particularly dispirited about her friendship prospects at school, a secret sense of superiority.

She was staring at the cover of the book, and yet her thoughts were about Dorothy. It was the last day of term. 'See you next year,' Emily had called, waving gaily, and Dorothy, surrounded by her acolytes, had waved back. As she walked past, Dorothy had turned to the girl beside her and stage whispered, 'God, I hope not.' Their laughter had followed her out of the school gates, her face burning with shame.

Since then, she'd made a vow never to seek Dorothy's friendship again. But she knew that the test of the vow was still in the future and required the new school year to begin. The infuriating thing was how often her nemesis kept appearing in her thoughts. Even now, while staring at the cover of *Middlemarch*, she was escorting her on a tour of the homestead, showing her the four bathrooms and all the bedrooms, the piano room and the billiard room. *There's the servant's quarters too*, she imagined telling her, making it sound as if there were squadrons of servants, and not just Della and Florrie, who were not only lacking in numbers but also the qualities expected of a servant, such as humility and obedience.

Emily shook her head to clear her mind of the silly fantasy. Why did she want Dorothy to see Mount Prospect anyway when all she wanted herself was to go home? With a yawn, she put *Middlemarch* on the bedside table. Taking her sponge bag out of the suitcase, she set off for the bathroom.

Just as she was passing Lydia's bedroom, the door flew open and Lydia emerged.

'Oh good, you're here,' she said, grabbing her by the arm and pulling her into the room.

Emily was still off balance when the door closed behind them with a decisive click.

'The zip's stuck,' Lydia said, turning away to present the half-undone yellow dress.

She put the sponge bag down on the floor. Up close, Lydia's perfume smelt musky and mysterious. Her glossy dark hair was pinned up in a loose coil, exposing the back of her neck, which was pale and smooth and seemed to fill the whole of Emily's vision. She took hold of the zip and tugged.

'Be careful, don't tear it.'

'I'm trying not to,' she replied. It wasn't her fault that the zip was stuck. She could see where the material had got caught, but her fingers were sweating from the pressure of Lydia's impatience, and damp marks were appearing on the yellow silk. She was beginning to panic when at last it came free.

The dress slithered to the floor, lying there like a puddle of molten gold. Lydia stepped out of it and turned to face her.

'It's gorgeous. I wish I –' Emily stopped herself just in time. She had been about to wish that she had a dress like that too. How wet it would have sounded.

If Lydia had heard and guessed at the unsaid part, she gave no indication. She unhooked her bra and tossed it on the bed, before stripping off her knickers. It was clearly time to leave, but instead Emily found herself staring at her aunt's perfectly shaped breasts and rosy nipples, the gentle swell of smooth stomach and the smudge of springy dark hair between her legs. At the alarming sight of Lydia's pubic hair, her eyes skittered upwards. Lydia was surveying her with amusement.

'Haven't you ever seen a naked body?' she said, crossing the room to where a satin dressing gown had been thrown carelessly over the curved cherry-wood bedstead. Lydia laughed, slipping on her dressing gown. 'Safe now, you can look.'

She tried to laugh too, in a casual way, as if naked female bodies were something she was all too familiar with. To cover her discomfort, she picked up the framed photograph of Harry on the bedside table and examined it with what she hoped would pass for genuine interest. In fact, she felt far too frazzled to see anything of Harry at all.

Lydia was taking no notice of her anyway. She was opening a drawer in her dressing table and, as Emily glanced over, she took out a silver cigarette case and lighter. Flicking open the case, she held out the neat row of unfiltered cigarettes. 'Want one?'

Emily quickly put down the photograph and shook her head. Nobody had ever offered her a cigarette before. But then she allowed herself to feel a kind of thrill, thinking that Lydia had identified a maturity in her, and considered her someone to whom cigarettes might be offered.

Lydia moved to the window and opened it. She perched on the sill, lit a cigarette and blew the smoke outside. 'So they've dumped you here.'

'Only for a week,' she replied swiftly, repeating her earlier words to Eunice.

'What a little odd bod you are,' Lydia said. 'You might as well get used to it. You're stuck here, just like me.'

Emily felt herself frown and the emerging bond over the offer of the cigarette evaporated.

'I wouldn't be surprised if you're still here at Easter,' Lydia added.

'What do you mean?' She blinked at her aunt in horror. 'I have to go home before school starts.'

'Oh, I wouldn't worry. Eunice can give you lessons. She was a governess once.'

The idea of months at Mount Prospect with Eunice taking over her education was so appalling that she emitted a sharp shocked cry. It sounded horribly like a bark, and she quickly cut it off and tried to look unconcerned, but Lydia was laughing again. It was too awful and, with as much dignity as she could muster, she grabbed her sponge bag and stalked out.

Once in the bathroom, she gave the tube of toothpaste a vicious squeeze. 'I won't stay, I will not,' she muttered to herself before shoving the toothbrush into her mouth, scrubbing with a furious intensity. After she had finished rinsing out her mouth, she caught sight of her scowling face in the mirror above the basin. *Watch out the wind doesn't change*, she heard her mother say, and tried to let her features relax. Even without the scowl, it was no good. Her mouth was far too big and her face too long. She was hideous.

Back in the white room Emily opened her suitcase and rummaged around for pyjamas. She slid between the crisp white sheets and lay flat, listening to the regular chug of the generator, yet to be turned off by the last person to bed.

'Now I lay me down to sleep, I pray the Lord my soul to keep. If I should die before I wake, I pray the Lord my soul to take.'

It was ages since she'd said that prayer as, to be perfectly honest, she was no longer sure she believed in God. But she couldn't tell her father that and, now, so far from home, it was a connecting thread.

Her eyes closed, but instead of drifting into peaceful sleep, her mind was awhirl with all kinds of tormenting thoughts. She would be stuck here forever, with Eunice forcing her to conjugate irregular French verbs or, worse, something to do with mathematics. She was hopeless at algebra and geometry. If only she could think about happy things. Home.

With her eyes shut tight, she imagined her dear little bedroom with the row of books in the bedhead bookcase. But then her thoughts took a different turn and she saw herself standing once more beside the open suitcase as she tried to delay the moment of packing. Was it only twenty-four hours ago that her parents' voices had echoed through the house?

'You want to get rid of me.'

'I don't, Sybil. I want you to get better.'

'Better, better. *Good, better, best, never let it rest, until the good is better and the better best.*' Her mother began to chant, louder and louder, 'I am better best, better best, better best.'

She'd heard her father trying to calm her. He spoke low and soft, and she couldn't make out the words. There was a lull before her mother's laughter rang out, a manic series of high sharp hoots that went on and on, and then her father was shouting, 'You can't go on like this. I can't go on.'

Back in the white room Emily grabbed the sheet and pulled it over her head. '*Now I lay me down to sleep, I pray the lord my soul to keep.*' She said it over and over until none of the words made sense anymore. Until she couldn't hear any other words in her head. Until somehow she fell into an uneasy sleep.

DAWN LIGHT FLICKERED THROUGH THE grapevines hanging along the verandah eaves and through the open curtains that she had forgotten to close the night before. The warmth on her face woke her, and for a second she did not know where she was. Then a rooster crowed and memory flooded in. A dog began to bark and a flock of cockatoos passed overhead, trailing their raucous cries. Emily lay there, loneliness pressing down on her chest like a brick.

Every sound was alien. She longed for the familiar rattle of the tram as it reached the corner of her street and continued down Wattletree Road. She even missed the irritating sound of Mr Boothby's tuneless whistling as he pottered in the garden next door, remembering her mother's opinion that whistlers really ought to be shot; nobody should have to put up with them.

She was beginning to feel tearful at the thought of home when a bang like a gunshot startled her. The Japs! She leaped out of bed and was scrambling for clothes when it happened again, followed by the sound of something rolling and bouncing on the corrugated iron roof. How could she have forgotten that noise? Not the Japs after all, but parrots pecking unripe pears from the tree where the branches hung over the roof. Thankful that nobody had witnessed her panic-stricken behaviour, she nevertheless made a conscious effort to continue dressing in a casual sort of way. As she buttoned up her blouse, she heard Lydia's words: *I wouldn't be surprised if you're still here at Easter.*

By the time she had slipped on her sandals, her mind was made up. She stuffed her spongebag and pyjamas back into suitcase, picked it up and left the house through the French doors.

Outside, the dawn air was cool. The sun, already lifting from the horizon, was staining the fairy-floss strands of cloud a vibrant shade of pink. Before long it would be a fiery disc in the blue sky, sucking the moisture from every living thing.

She crossed the lawn – lopsided because of the weight of the suitcase – passing beds of roses and lavender. At the laden apricot tree, she paused and plucked three fragrant ripe orbs, shoving them into the pocket of her skirt. It was a long way to the train station and she was bound to get hungry. Not that she expected to walk all the way: it was too far and too hot for that, and her case was already weighing her down. Someone would be sure to see her on the road and give her a lift. She couldn't be late. There was only one train a day and it left Garnook Station at ten o'clock in the morning.

She continued on through the orchard and through the little wooden gate that led to the gravel drive. It was half a mile to the main road. Mrs Flynn, Lydia's fox terrier, appeared and trotted behind her. The foxy's wet nose bumped the back of her ankles, and she tried to remain calm, knowing that foxies could be snappy. After a while Mrs Flynn seemed satisfied with her investigation and detoured away, her nose now glued to the ground, scurrying after a scent that only she could detect.

With each step, the suitcase banged painfully against her leg. She swapped hands and tried not to think of how far there was to go. Overhead, yellow-tailed black cockatoos flapped up from the pines that lined each side of the drive, their haunting cries ringing out in the dawn air. Uncle Cec had told her that the black cockatoos only arrived once a year to eat the pine nuts. She wondered where they came from and where they went next. Like her, they weren't from around here.

Little clouds of dust puffed up around her feet with each step. Shadows from the pines created a pattern of light and dark across the drive. In the distance she could see the wrought-iron archway over the cattle ramp where the drive ended and the road began. How would she ever get to the railway station when even the arch at the end of the drive was so far away? Perhaps she should give up and return to the homestead? She heard Father's voice telling her: *If at first you don't succeed, try, try and try again.* Yes, she would keep going, although thinking of Father made her nervous. Would he really understand her effort to return as the triumph of *try, try and try again*?

Putting one dusty sandalled foot in front of the other, and with the suitcase growing heavier with each step, she let her eyes wander past the pines to where the redgums grew thickly along the edge of the swamp. Further in, many were dead from waterlogging, their stiff scarecrow branches stark against the blue sky. At dawn and dusk, cockatoos and galahs swirled and screeched over the swamp, heralding the beginning and end of each day. With the setting of the sun they came to rest in sentinel rows along the dead branches of the waterlogged gums. They hadn't always been dead – and it hadn't always been a swamp. At one time the water had run through freely and the trees had flourished.

'That was before we came and changed the watercourses,' Uncle Cec had explained to her once. 'Back when the blacks roamed the land.'

She had wanted to know what had happened to the blacks. Where were they now? Uncle Cec had gone vague and mumbled something about progress and civilisation before changing the topic, warning her not to go swimming in the swamp. 'The first layer's warm enough but underneath it's cold as charity, and there are holes you can't see, big enough to swallow a cow.' He made her promise to be careful.

At last she came to a stop beside the cattle ramp. Nearby grew a twisted old peppercorn tree and she sank down in its shade, feeling weak. Why hadn't she brought water? At least she had the apricots. If she was careful, they should last until she reached the station. Or until an obliging farmer with a bottle of water and a bag of crisp apples stopped to pick her up. She took an apricot from her pocket and bit into it, the sweet juice flooding her mouth. The second and third apricots went the way of the first, as she imagined herself in the comfort of the farmer's truck, the fence posts whizzing past. She leaned against the trunk of the peppercorn, her eyes closing. She must get up and keep walking, the sooner the better. She couldn't be late. Whatever happened, she mustn't be late for the train.

It rattled along with a clackety-clack. *Home soon, home soon,* she sang in time to the train wheels turning. Her throat was burning and dry; she had nothing to drink. A woman came in and offered her a glass of water but, when she took it, the glass was empty and the woman gave a harsh laugh and vanished. After that she found herself walking along the passage peering into all the compartments. Two schoolgirls were drinking tea from china teacups with roses on them, but the door to the compartment was stuck, and when she tapped on the glass one of the girls gestured angrily for her to go away. It couldn't be? Was it … Dorothy? She tried to call out her name but no sound emerged. In desperation she banged on the glass with her fist. Dorothy turned away just as the glass shattered.

Emily woke with a start and sat up. Beads of sweat ran down her face and neck, and her heart was thumping. At first, trapped in the dream world where people appeared and disappeared at random, she thought that the young man standing a few feet away was just another apparition.

'I'm awake,' she said aloud, to check that it was really so, and to see if he would vanish. But he was still there, and she felt her stomach lurch. Adrenaline shot through her system and she leaped up, ready to run. But which way to go? He was standing in the way, saying something that she couldn't understand. Was she in a dream after all? One where people babbled in strange languages? She grabbed the suitcase and held it against herself like a shield.

'Stay away from me.' It was meant to sound authoritative, but her voice let her down and the *me* came out as a squeak.

The young man was making calming gestures with one hand, and she noticed that he had a long-handled shovel over his other shoulder with a canvas waterbag hooked on the end.

'Is okay, is okay. No need for fright.'

He was wearing what looked like an army uniform but, instead of the usual khaki, it was the colour of a blood plum. A curl of black hair poked through the hole in his old felt hat. He put his free hand on his chest and smiled at her. It was hard not to smile back.

'My name is Claudio. And you?' He gestured towards her.

She shook her head, knowing her voice would betray her with another squeak, and anyway she wasn't at all sure she wanted to reveal her name. The monologue in her head continued. *What sort of name was Cloudio? Like a cloud with an io, like cheerio. And didn't he know it was rude to stare at people?* She realised she'd been staring at him ever since her abrupt awakening, but that was different somehow. *She* might be in danger.

Suddenly he swept off his hat and the shovel on his shoulder swung precariously. 'My name is Claudio,' he repeated. 'I am from *Italia.*'

He continued to speak, reverting to the earlier foreign babble, which she now recognised as sounding like Mr Donati, the Italian greengrocer from whom her mother bought their fruit and vegetables. What was he saying, and why, when it was clear that she couldn't understand? She took the opportunity to examine him. His hair was black and curly, and his eyes were almost black too. Mysterious, unlike the pale cornflower blue eyes of the boys on the morning tram. She wondered how old he was. Older than the pimply schoolboys, she was sure. He must be at least twenty. She was forgetting that she might be in danger.

'Prison of war.'

The words jolted her back into the present. 'What?'

'Prison of war. Me,' he said.

What had Della said? Something about *feeding the enemy*. Was this who she'd meant? It must be him. She was alone with the enemy.

Claudio pointed to himself and repeated his name for the third time. 'And you?' he asked again.

Perhaps she ought to play along. After all, what did it matter if she said her name?

'Emily.'

He smiled. 'Emilia.'

She smiled too; it seemed like the safest thing to do even though he had mispronounced her name.

'Where you wanna going?'

She looked down at the suitcase, still clutched to her stomach, and tried, as casually as she could, to lower it into a more natural position.

'Train.'

Claudio nodded. 'Long way, no? How you are walking?'

Emily detected a note of scepticism in his voice and wished that she did not feel so dizzy. She hadn't even left the farm – *property* – and the train wouldn't wait. She had to go now, immediately. She took two steps and then her legs gave way and she slumped down like a bag of oats falling off the back of the cart.

Claudio dropped his shovel and ran forwards with a cry. 'Emilia!'

'Water,' she whispered.

He unhooked the waterbag, pulling the cork from the spout and, with a supportive arm around her shoulders, drizzled water into her mouth. She gulped it greedily – the cool musty water had never tasted so delicious.

By the time she had drunk her fill, the dizziness had passed and she felt quite normal again. It was time to continue her journey.

Claudio helped her up and held out her suitcase. She imagined her hand grasping the handle, her feet moving forwards through the arch. She saw herself marching along the road with iron-willed determination, repeating *where there's a will, there's a way*. But an opposing inner voice began to make itself heard. The station was miles off, and if nobody drove past, she'd never make it on time. The plan was childish. It wasn't even a plan; it was just running away. She was stuck between the impossibility of reaching the train station and the embarrassment that awaited on turning around. How could she explain her second arrival in the space of twenty-four hours – this time on foot, dragging her suitcase? There seemed to be no way out of her dilemma when Claudio spoke.

'Go back, eh? Too far, by jingo.'

Despite how gloomy she felt, hearing Uncle Cec's expression made her smile.

'I carry her,' he said, gesturing to the suitcase. He nodded as if to affirm his decision. And then without waiting for her to agree, he hoisted the shovel over one shoulder and, with the suitcase in his other hand, set off towards the homestead. She wanted to tell him to stop and that he had no right, but her feet were already in motion.

They walked together along the drive. She was surprised to find that the lack of conversation was not uncomfortable, and had just made a vow never to prattle on again, when the silence was broken by a sharp whistle from some way off. Claudio stopped. There it was again, followed by the sound of Uncle Cec calling his dog.

Claudio threw the shovel down in the long grass beside the drive, grabbed her hand and jerked her towards the nearest pine. They crouched down behind the tree. He put a finger to his lips, and she complied, for she dreaded having to explain her presence to Uncle Cec, and supposed that Claudio felt the same way even if she did not know why.

She pressed her cheek against the rough trunk and watched a row of ants as they marched past in single file. She felt the warmth of Claudio's body next to her and heard his breathing. He was still gripping her hand, and her fingers had begun to grow numb. When she pulled it away, he did not seem to notice.

They waited together. A minute ticked by. The ants began to abandon their original path for a short cut over the parts of her pressed against the tree. Then she heard the sound of hooves on the gravel drive. Peeping around the edge of the tree, she saw Uncle Cec and another man, riding along at a leisurely pace. A brown dog trotted behind them. As they got closer, she saw the other rider was Roy. When they were in line with the tree, Roy looked across and their eyes connected. She whipped back behind the tree, waiting for the inevitable.

'Emilia?' Claudio whispered. She shook her head, sure that they were about to be flushed from their hiding place. But it did not happen. Instead, the sound of hooves gradually faded.

When they could no longer hear anything, Claudio rose. He stepped around the trunk, and soon signalled the all clear. They hurried on, with Claudio striding out so that every few steps she had to break into a run to keep up. Nothing was said, and now that they were once more on their way, all she could think of was reaching the house before anyone had discovered her absence, if in fact it was not already too late.

Claudio opened the orchard gate. They wove across and reached the verandah where William's old punching bag hung. He put her case down by the French doors, smiled and then pressed a finger to his lips once more. She nodded and, before she could thank him, he was gone.

She was still thinking about how white his teeth were when she heard Grandmother calling her name. There was just enough time to enter the room, shove the suitcase under the bed and sit at the dressing table before Grandmother hurried past the open bedroom door. A second later, she reappeared.

'Where on earth have you been? We've been searching high and low for you.'

Emily heard in her mind her mother declaiming: *Oh, what a tangled web we weave when first we practice to deceive.* Often, just for good measure, her mother would add: *Remember, if you want to tell a fib keep it simple.* On one such occasion Father had been writing his sermon with the study door open and had interjected that teaching one's child to lie was thoroughly irresponsible.

'Emily?' Grandmother prompted.

'I went for a walk and forgot the time,' she mumbled, focusing on her feet, knowing that her lie would collapse under the scrutiny of Grandmother's sharp gaze. When she dared to look up, having arranged her face in a suitably innocent expression, something unexpected happened: more words tumbled out.

'I can't stay until Easter. I have to go back to school. I know Cousin Eunice was a governess but I'm too old for a governess, and she doesn't know any Latin, and anyway … I can't …' She sputtered to a stop.

Grandmother was staring at her. 'Easter? Eunice, a governess?'

'Did someone call my name?' Eunice arrived at the doorway, somewhat belatedly for her.

Grandmother turned to her. 'You never told me you were a governess.'

'A governess?' Eunice looked bewildered. 'Never.'

'What's all this nonsense? Really, Emily, I thought you had more sense. You can't possibly stay here until Easter – it's out of the question.'

For a second she felt offended. Why shouldn't she stay? And then relief flooded in as the full import of Grandmother's words took effect. Lydia had got it wrong. It was all a mistake.

'What a waste of a morning,' Grandmother added huffily. 'And you've missed breakfast too. Come along, perhaps Della can find something for you.'

Emily followed Grandmother to the kitchen where, to her great relief, the crumbed brains had all been eaten by the early risers.

'What about a cup of tea and a scone?' Della suggested. 'There might be a scrap of apricot jam going spare.'

Emily was dabbing her finger onto the plate to get the last crumbs of the scone when Lydia wandered in.

'So they found you,' she said, as she filled the kettle at the sink. 'Caused quite a kerfuffle.'

'It's not true.'

'Yes, it is. Everyone was worried.'

'Not that. I mean about Easter and Eunice giving me lessons. Grandmother says it's not true.'

Lydia put the kettle on the stove, pulled out a chair opposite Emily and sat down.

'Oh, that. You didn't believe me, did you? You knew I was joking.'

She stared at the empty plate. What a pathetic idiot she was.

5

FOLLOWING THE DISCOVERY THAT SHE would not have to stay until Easter, Emily abandoned her fantasies of running away and resigned herself to staying at Mount Prospect until the school year began. It was only five weeks anyway, which sounded quite manageable until she counted it out in days.

But after a week of Eunice's endless list of jobs, a day at Mount Prospect was beginning to feel like a month. Eunice was always on the lookout for idle hands and seemed determined that Emily should pay her way.

That morning when, expecting an ally, she'd complained to Della, the cook had been unsympathetic.

'It's like the chooks, there's got to be a pecking order,' she said. 'You're on the bottom.'

The chook comparison was apt as they were cleaning out the

chook yard at the time. Or at least she was; Della was sitting on a stump, instructing her, now that it was one of her morning chores. It used to be Old Stan's job – Emily recalled that he did the odd jobs and helped in the garden. But he was no longer around and, except for Roy, nor were any of the station hands and workmen who'd always been there in the background. Men with names like Mick, Ernie and Jim.

'Where are all the men?' she asked Della.

'War. Where do you think?'

'Even Old Stan?'

'Course not. He's too old and, anyway, he's got the rheumatism, poor bugger. Moved into town.'

Emily put the last of the clean straw in the nesting boxes, wondering why Roy hadn't joined up. Was it because he was black? She knew the Aborigines didn't have the vote. They were not citizens either, which was confusing. If they weren't even citizens, what were they? Her father said it was a disgrace, a stain on the whole country.

'What about Roy?'

'What about him?'

'He hasn't joined up. Aren't they allowed? Aborigines, I mean.'

'Course they are. Albie and Ray Fenton are blackfellas. Joined up quick smart.'

'Then why hasn't Roy?'

Ignoring her, Della heaved herself off the stump. 'Right. I can't stand around yacking with you all day. Make sure you clean out the trough, and don't forget the bucket.' At the chook yard gate, she stopped and looked back. 'Reckons he'll join up when blackfellas get treated right.'

Emily watched the cook head off to the house.

She swished the straw broom along the shallow trough, getting rid of the dirty water. Did Roy mean that he was not treated right at Mount Prospect? Or was he talking about Aboriginal people in general? Either way, it made her feel uncomfortable and she almost wished Della hadn't said anything.

Later the same day, she finally began *Middlemarch*. Reading at the kitchen table, with Della and Florrie busy around her, she was expecting Eunice to turn up at any moment with an additional task for her list; it added a nervous intensity to the whole endeavour. She turned a page, wondering how she would ever get to the end of such an enormous tome. She was only at chapter two and already there were things about the novel that were quite unnerving. For example, the heroine's name, Dorothea, was a constant reminder of Dorothy. And Mr Casaubon, for whom she had developed an instant dislike, was a reverend like her father. But Dorothea seemed nothing like Dorothy, and nor did Mr Casaubon resemble her father. If only she could stop thinking about them as she read.

It was a relief to find herself distracted by the conversation between Della and Florrie, who were rolling out pastry for jam tarts at the other end of the table.

'Whatsisname reckons he's going to show us how to make spaghetti the proper way.'

Della called Claudio *Whatsisname* or, sometimes, *Mussolini*, although not to his face. Claudio was no sort of name for a man.

Despite keeping an eye out for him, Emily had scarcely seen him since that first morning. She knew that sometimes he and Roy ate dinner in the kitchen with Della and Florrie, and she'd felt sure that by helping with the dishes each evening, she might run into him, but it had not yet occurred.

'What's the proper way?' Florrie asked, pressing a pastry circle into the tart tin.

'How would I know? The *Eye-tie* way I 'spect.'

'When?' Emily startled herself, having only meant to think the question.

Della and Florrie both swivelled their heads in her direction. She tried to smile nonchalantly.

'This arvo, if Mr Cec doesn't need him,' Della replied.

Emily shrugged and returned to her book. Her eyes moved across the page without taking anything in. 'I could help if you like,' she said without lifting her head. She continued her pretend reading, relieved when the cook agreed, on the basis of many hands making light work.

The conversation moved on to other things, and she let their voices recede into the background and picked up the thread of her novel again. It was clear that Dorothea was going to make a terrible mistake and reading of the heroine's wrong-headedness made her feel increasingly agitated.

After lunch, she found herself lingering near the kitchen door, having swept the back verandah without any prompting from Eunice. Della came out to empty the ash can just as she began to sweep it for the second time and she felt the cook's eagle eye on her. It was best to pretend not to notice. How could she admit to Della that she was awaiting Claudio's arrival with such anticipation? It was far too revealing.

A third sweeping of the verandah was out of the question and still he had not come. She sat down at the men's outdoor dining table and opened *Middlemarch* again, only to find that reading was impossible. She was about to count the number of words on the page when she noticed Claudio at the far end of the courtyard. But now that he was walking towards her, anticipation became anxiety. What would she say? Her cheeks were already burning. She stared down at the page, having decided to look up in surprise at the very last minute and greet him with a casual 'hello'.

The screen door banged, and her head snapped up to see him already behind it.

'*Buongiorno, signore,*' she heard him say cheerily.

She was stuck outside on her own, for entering the kitchen now would make it seem as if she was following him. How long should she delay? And could she trust Della not to comment on the fact that she had been hanging about for ages, waiting for Claudio to arrive? It was almost enough to make her give up. Should she go in, or should she leave? The dilemma was paralysing her. The screen door squeaked.

'Are you coming in or what?' Della stood in the doorway with one hand on an enormous hip.

Given her concerns, she was relieved when Claudio did not pay her any special attention. He put her to work at the kitchen table helping Florrie peel scalded tomatoes for the sauce.

He was in charge and everyone had a role to play but, beyond the giving of instructions, he barely seemed to notice her.

Della and Claudio had set up their stations side by side at the long kitchen bench. In front of both was a mound of flour. They worked in tandem, keeping an eye on each other as they shaped their mounds to create a well in the centre into which eggs were cracked. Della began to whisk the eggs with a fork.

Claudio put a restraining hand on her arm. '*Delicatamente,*' he said. 'Like this.' And he picked up his fork and whisked with a lighter touch.

'I know how to make dough,' Della grumbled.

'We make tagliatelle,' he told her.

'I thought we were making spaghetti?'

'Is little bit different. You will see. Is how my *nonna* is making.'

Despite her grumbling, Della followed his directions and watched how he drew the flour into the eggy well with his fingertips. Emily watched too, although she had to be careful as the tomatoes were hot and slippery and the paring knife sharp.

When the dough had been mixed, Claudio beckoned her to the bench. 'I am showing,' he said, and began to knead his lump of dough using the heel of his hand to press down into it. 'Now you turn.' He moved aside to let her try.

It was not as easy as he made it seem, but she was determined to persevere. It was her chance to make an impression.

'Is not bad. More, more,' he urged.

She repeated the motion over and over until her hand was aching. Della was doing the same beside her, sweat beading her meaty cheeks.

'Got us working like blooming navvies,' Della muttered. 'As if I don't have enough to do.'

Emily wondered if Della's complaint was really about giving up her role as the boss of the kitchen. After all, she was the cook and used to kneading – she made bread every week. Even so, it was a long time before Claudio allowed them to stop. Florrie stopped too. She had finished chopping up the tomatoes.

Once the tomato sauce was simmering on the stovetop, the dough was ready to roll out. Emily was keen to try, but Della shooed her and Florrie out of the way, while she and Claudio took over. She watched them working at the kitchen bench as they wielded their rolling pins, competing for the best results. At least it seemed to her that it was a competition, even if neither of the pasta makers had openly admitted it. After the dough had been rolled, Claudio took the lead again and loosely folded each sheet into a flat roll. Using a cleaver, he cut the rolls into quarter-inch ribbons.

'See. Is tagliatelle,' he said with a proud smile, unravelling one of the rolls so that the strips dangled from his hand.

Florrie looked suitably impressed, but Della made a *pffft* sound, as if it was nothing to write home about. Emily wondered if she was jealous.

It was no time at all before strands of tagliatelle hung drying from the broomsticks that Claudio had placed between kitchen chairs. The kitchen was filled with swirling floury specks that settled in their hair, and dusted their faces to a papery white. The tomato sauce bubbled on the stove, and there was an air of exhilaration in the room.

Claudio clapped his hands to get their attention. 'Time for smoko,' he announced, sitting down at the table. He took a packet of tobacco from his pocket and began to roll a cigarette.

Emily hurried across to the dresser to fetch the cups and saucers, while Florrie made the tea, and Della put out a plate of cinnamon biscuits. Florrie set the teapot down on the kitchen table and, turning to go back for the milk jug, slipped on the floury floor. She let out a squawk and Claudio leaped up, catching her before she fell. They staggered off balance until, regaining their footing, he turned it into a dance. Watching on, Emily felt a fizzy sort of feeling in her chest.

Claudio let Florrie go and took Della by the hand. 'You now,' he commanded.

Emily was sure that Della would bat him away like an annoying bug, but instead the cook let herself be whirled around the kitchen. The fizzy feeling grew. It was her turn next. In the general merriment she didn't hear the door to the passage open, or see the shadowy shape of someone entering, until Florrie gave a screech, bringing the dancers to an instant halt.

'What on earth is going on?' Eunice stood in the doorway staring in shocked amazement, not only at the culprits, but the floury strips of pasta dangling from chair backs and broom handles. 'Like a Chinese laundry,' she managed to splutter. She raised her hand and pointed a finger at Claudio. 'You,' she ordered. 'Out.'

Claudio hesitated; the joy drained from his face and his whole body stiffened. Nobody moved. Then he turned and walked unhurriedly to the back door.

After he had left, Eunice turned to Della. 'What madness has been going on? You of all people, Della.'

Emily cast a sideways glance at Della, whose word within the confines of the kitchen was generally treated as law, even where

Grandmother was concerned. She could not remember when she had understood it, but she knew that Eunice occupied a somewhat precarious place between family and the servants and to challenge Della in her own domain was a risky business. But, surprisingly, the cook did not respond with a well-chosen biblical quote and a belligerent glare, or even an outright demand that Eunice leave the kitchen. Instead she shuffled uneasily and said nothing at all.

'Letting him loose in here,' Eunice added, sensing her advantage.

'What does that mean? He wasn't loose,' Emily burst out, feeling outraged on Claudio's behalf.

Eunice pinned her with a beady eye. 'Perhaps you should read the Army's directions regarding the Italian prisoners, Emily. I believe they know more about the Italian mentality than you do.' And with that, she turned her attention once more to Della. 'You'll have to clean up this mess.'

Della had begun to look formidable again, and Eunice faltered. In a change of course, she gestured at Emily. 'As for you, come with me. I've some jobs that need doing.'

Feeling unable to defy Eunice, she allowed herself to be hustled from the kitchen and along the various hallways towards the other end of the house.

'You can start in the billiard room,' Eunice said. 'Everything needs a good dust. And not just a flick of the feather duster. I've left cloths and polish for you.'

6

WHEN EMILY ARRIVED AT THE billiard room she found
dusters and a tin of polish on a cedar trolley, but she ignored
them and moved along beside the billiard table, trailing her
fingers over the plush pile of the magenta dust cover. She was not
a slave. Nevertheless, she was unable to stop a nervous backwards
glance in case Eunice was lurking. The coast, however, seemed to
be clear.

The air in the billiard room was cooler than the kitchen and
smelled faintly of cue chalk and cigarette smoke. How long had it
been since the click of billiard balls and male voices had been
heard around the table? Thinking of this, Grandfather came into
her mind. Everyone said he was a first-class player before he'd
had a stroke and been confined to a wheelchair. Not that long
afterwards, he'd died. Whenever his name was mentioned

someone always said, *Poor Alf, felled in his prime*, which made him sound like a tree. Of course it all happened eons ago, before she was born. Lydia had only been four. It was awful to think that her aunt could not remember him.

She reached the mantelpiece and paused there to look at the stuffed mallee hen and her large pinkish-brown egg. The mallee hen always made her feel sad; perhaps it was the bird's eternal vigilance, guarding the egg from which no chick would ever hatch. Beside the hen lay the greenstone axe head that Uncle Cec had shown the others that first night when she'd wanted to ring home. She picked it up, and it felt cool and smooth in the palm of her hand. She ran her finger lightly along the honed edge and felt goosebumps rise. The axe was sharp enough to cut, and she put it back on the mantelpiece with a clunk.

She continued on, heading for the leather daybed at the far end of the room. Lying on the daybed, she could see the score on the roller board and wondered if it belonged to William and Harry, and who had won. 'Wounded in action,' she murmured to herself, imagining William leaning across the billiard table as he potted a ball. But she did not want to think about him. She closed her eyes and transported herself to the kitchen and Claudio's arms.

From somewhere in the house came the muffled sound of footsteps moving to and fro. And then the rise and fall of women's voices, Grandmother and Eunice. Unlike her, she knew they would be hard at work, emptying vases and rearranging fresh flowers, dusting mantelpieces and polishing the floorboards in the hallway. She sat up to listen. Grandmother was speaking.

'Patriotism is one thing, but working in a factory is quite another, even if it is war work.'

'Quite,' Eunice responded.

'Anything could happen.' There was a short period of silence before Grandmother added, mysteriously, 'Bees to a honeypot.'

'Bees to a honeypot,' Eunice repeated. 'Anything could happen.'

'Bees to a honeypot,' Emily murmured, feeling puzzled. Who and what were they talking about? She waited, hoping to hear more, but their footsteps became fainter and the sound of their voices faded. Even so, she knew her time was running out and that sooner or later Eunice would return to check on her progress.

Warm air swarmed over her as she stepped out onto the verandah from the billiard room. Where to go? With no destination in mind, she paused at the window to Lydia's room. The bed was unmade, the sheets all twisted up and two pillows lay strewn on the floor along with some clothes. The wardrobe door gaped open and more clothes spilled from it.

At the end of the verandah, she took the south path that led to the stables and machinery sheds, arranged around an open yard. She had no destination in mind, just the need to get away from the house and the prospect of a confrontation with Eunice.

She wandered past open-sided sheds filled with an orderly row of farm machinery, motor vehicles and horse-drawn conveyances. Her gaze swept over the yard. It was empty, and only then did she feel disappointment and recognise a half-formed hope of running into Claudio.

At the far end of the sheds, the orderly arrangement disintegrated into a jumble of miscellaneous objects. On the tray of a dilapidated cart Grandfather's wicker wheelchair listed at an angle. 'Felled in his prime,' she murmured, relishing the phrase. She moved closer to the wheelchair and saw that the wicker seat had collapsed and, in its place, someone had wedged an old side-saddle. A tangle of rusty wire and scrap iron surrounded the chair.

It all looked like the sort of sculpture her mother loved to praise in the presence of her father, who liked *proper art* – paintings by the old masters and the sculptures of Michelangelo. She suspected that her mother didn't really care about modern art and was only doing it to annoy her father. *Poking a stick down the ants' hole*, as her mother might say.

She had a pang of homesickness and tried to imagine what they would be doing. Her father writing sermons in his study, and her mother ... what? She scrambled for a comforting image but, instead, the disturbing sound of her mother chanting *good better best* intruded. No, she would not think of it and whirled around, setting off diagonally across the yard in an effort to leave behind her unsettling thoughts. She rounded the corner of the stables and hurried along the other side of the building where Virginia creeper had taken over, covering the outer walls in a shaggy coat of luminous green. A faded blue door, half hidden by tendrils of creeper, snagged her eye.

Inside, all was dark and silent. The smells of coal dust and musty old wheat bags and a faint menthol-y whiff of horse liniment filled her nostrils, and she remembered that it had once been the blacksmith's workshop. She waited for her eyes to adjust, and flinched when the silence was broken by the sharp crack of tin and timber expanding in the heat. From the far side of the room came the sound of something scuttling. Her toes curled inside her sandals, in tense anticipation of the scratchy tickle of mouse paws.

After a little while, shapes and shadows became visible. Dust motes swirled in a beam of watery light from a dirt-encrusted skylight in the roof. There was no ceiling, only sheets of corrugated iron over a skeleton of rafters. Old rabbit skins dangled from the centre beam, stretched over wire frames. As each second passed, she began to see more clearly. Along the wall to her left, tools lay abandoned on a long workbench. She trailed her fingers along the dusty surface, past riveters and rusty rabbit traps, saws, files and a pile of horseshoes.

'*For want of a nail a shoe was lost*,' she murmured.

At the end of the bench she looked across the room and, making out the bulky shape of an armchair, moved towards it. Wiry horsehair sprouted from rents in the leather. She peered further into the gloom. Where did the room end?

She crept forwards a little more and was already thinking about returning with a torch when a wall of books loomed up before her. Was it an hallucination based on her own desire, for what could be more wonderful than to discover a library? Tentatively, she extended her hand, half expecting to meet no resistance and for her fingers to pass through the ghostly apparition. But it – they – were real. Rows of books. Classics, she was sure of it.

Just as she was about to tug one from its place, she heard her name being called.

'Emily. Emily.'

It was Lydia, and each repetition sounded louder and more irritated. She felt a prickle of guilt. She did not want to be caught snooping. It made her think of her mother's frequent reprimand: *You're a sly little thing.* She heard it as the truth and not a passing comment, soon to be forgotten. The dreadful feeling of shame was as strong as ever. Shame, and the fear that it was true. She had things to hide even if she did not know exactly what those things were. Why couldn't she be like Lydia? Forthright and strong.

'Where are you?' Lydia's voice was fainter, and it came from a different direction. If there was a time to act it was now and, before she could change her mind, she ran back across the room to the blue door. She inched it open and sidled through, pulling it shut behind her. She was halfway across the yard when her aunt appeared from the shadow of the open-sided sheds ahead of her. A meeting was unavoidable. She tried to slow to a saunter, as if she had all the time in the world but, in executing such an abrupt change of pace, she lost her footing and was forced into an undignified hop. By the time she'd regained her balance, Lydia had reached her.

'Where have you been?' her aunt demanded. 'Didn't you hear me calling?' She did not wait for an answer and turned away. It was clear that Emily was meant to follow.

They walked back to the stables where Dapple was standing patiently, harnessed to the cart. Lydia climbed on and took the reins. Emily hovered, unsure what she was meant to do.

'Come on, hop up,' Lydia said. 'I need a helper.'

They set off, with Lydia regularly slapping Dapple lightly with the reins to keep him moving, as without encouragement he was inclined to slow to a stop. On the tray of the cart, Mrs Flynn ran back and forth, tongue flapping. They made good progress along a dirt lane, one of several that ran through the property and linked up with the main roads. After turning off at a gate, they began bumping their way across a tussocky paddock.

As soon as she'd encountered Lydia, Emily had noticed that her aunt was dressed in men's clothes and now, sitting next to her, she discreetly examined them, wondering if the faded blue shirt and khaki work pants held up with a plaited leather belt belonged to William. Even dressed like a man, Lydia looked – as Madame Dubois, the French teacher would have said – *très chic*. So far, she had still given no hint about their destination or what kind of help she needed, and Emily had decided not to ask, hoping to demonstrate a lofty sort of indifference that she thought Lydia would find appealing. It was proving impossible to maintain.

'Where are we going?'

'See the scrub.' Lydia pointed to a blur of bush in the distance. 'Rabbits. In plague proportions. I've got to check my traps and set some more. With your help we'll get twice as much done.'

Until now, Emily had managed to ignore the iron traps lying in the back of the cart. 'You're not going to kill them?'

'They're vermin, not fluffy white pets,' Lydia replied. 'If we don't kill them they'll strip the countryside bare.'

In the face of such a scornful response, Emily lost her enthusiasm for defending the rabbits and tried to think of something else to say.

'Anyway,' Lydia went on, 'the skins are worth money. My escape fund.'

The mention of an escape fund sounded more promising and she waited for Lydia to say more. When no more came, she prompted, 'I suppose you'll need to escape if the Japs invade. Especially if Uncle Cec is going to –'

'What are you talking about?' Lydia interrupted sharply.

To be honest, she wasn't sure, only that an idea had begun to form. 'We could go together.'

'Go together?'

'If you're going to escape. I could come too. You know, to Melbourne.'

Lydia frowned. 'Don't be ridiculous. You're here to be looked after while your mother's in the loony bin.'

Emily heard herself gasp and tried to catch her breath. She wanted to shout at Lydia and tell her that she was lying, that it was a cruel joke, like staying till Easter and Eunice being her governess. But without breath she couldn't speak and, at the same time, came the terrible realisation that it was true. That night before the train trip, her mother's mad chanting, and her father's desperate pleas. The hurried arrangements for Emily to stay at Mount Prospect. Her father's refusal to bend when she didn't want to go. All the clues were there, although the words *loony bin* had never been spoken.

She stared straight ahead. Everything was blurred because of the tears filling her eyes, but she concentrated on the way Dapple's haunches moved and the bobbing of his head. She began to count each step, determined not to look at Lydia, whom she could not forgive, even if her cruel words contained the truth.

The whip flicked over Dapple's haunches, jerking him into a clumsy canter across the paddock. She held on to the edge of the cart, her gaze focused on the horse and on the thought of Lydia begging for her forgiveness and being refused. When they arrived at the scrub, she got down from the cart in frosty silence and began to walk off.

'Where are you going?' Lydia called.

She didn't answer.

'Don't be silly, I need you. There's work to do. Emily …'

There was a plaintive note in Lydia's voice, and she felt a stab of satisfaction. Briefly she considered turning back, but the awful words *loony bin* pushed her forwards. She began to run and, when she heard Lydia call again, she urged herself to run faster.

She didn't stop until she found herself unexpectedly confronted by a dilapidated post-and-rail enclosure that she could not remember seeing on their outward journey. She looked around for the gate they'd gone through earlier. Where was the dirt lane? There was no sign of it; nothing but paddocks and trees and a mob of sheep clustered around a distant windmill. In her fury with Lydia, she must have run off in the wrong direction, and now, leaning against the fence, catching her breath, came the unnerving thought that she might be lost. The anger that had fuelled her flight drained away. She felt light-headed, confused by panicky thoughts about being lost and, worse, the humiliation of having to be found.

It was only after some minutes had passed that she was able to take in her immediate surroundings: the lopsided marble headstones of the pioneers' cemetery. Of course, the pioneers' cemetery. She'd glimpsed it once with Uncle Cec and wanted to stop and explore, but Uncle Cec had sheep to feed and they'd rattled past in the truck.

Buoyed by curiosity, her fears of being lost dwindled and she climbed over the rickety fence and jumped down inside the boundary of the graveyard. Some of the headstones had fallen over and lay like ancient relics, half hidden in the grass and thistles. She crouched down beside a capsized marble slab.

Here lieth the mortal remains of Annie / The beloved daughter of

George Bertram / Departed this life March 21st 1882 / Aged 17 years / Resurgam, she read.

Despite the warmth of the late afternoon she felt a sudden chill. Annie was only three years older than her. How had she died? Why did the gravestone only mention Annie's father? Was it because Annie's mother was already dead?

She whispered the word *Resurgam*. They were studying Latin at school, and her father had insisted she continue with it. He was a great believer in the power of the English language and had a special interest in etymology for which, he said, a knowledge of Latin was essential. He liked to set little tests for her, where the aim was to deduce the meaning of a word from its Latin root. Sometimes it turned out to be a Greek root, which was unfair. Ancient Greek was not on the school syllabus. Often they were led to consult the volumes of her father's *Oxford English Dictionary*. She enjoyed his tests and was proud of his praise when she did well.

She ran her fingers over Annie's name, feeling the indentation of the words cut into the marble. *Resurgam* probably meant something like resurgent, which meant revive. She imagined lying under the marble slab, earth pressing down. There would be no reviving Annie.

Everyone in this graveyard had died so young. *Departed this life*, the inscriptions read, as if the dead were going on a journey and would arrive at another life or, rather, as she corrected herself, *an afterlife*. Not that she believed in that. At least, she didn't think so. Dust to dust was more likely. She felt guilty for not believing – it was a betrayal of her father. Once or twice she'd thought about raising it as part of their etymology discussions but had not wanted to upset him. He was often upset these days, mainly about her mother.

Mother. The word dropped like a stone in a well, and she forgot to look where she was going. Before she knew it, her left leg had plunged through the sandy soil at the edge of a marble slab. Something crunched underfoot. The bones of a long-dead pioneer? She screamed, and a gust of wind blew dust in her face. All of a sudden, the graveyard was alive with malevolent ghosts. She heaved her leg from the hole, scrambled to her feet, vaulted over the fence with an ease that surprised even herself and kept going. Fifty yards on, her mind caught up with her body and she stopped, panting. Where exactly was she heading?

In the distance was the line of trees that marked the start of the scrub where she'd left her aunt. Other than that, she had lost all sense of direction. Her only real option was to return to Lydia. But how could she? It was too mortifying, and she set off randomly, hoping to spot something familiar, only for her resolve to peter out after a few dozen steps. Her mouth was as dry as a chip, and the thought of the waterbag hanging on the back of the cart was more than she could resist.

She began the trek towards the scrub, determined that when reunited with Lydia she would maintain a dignified yet punishing silence.

On arriving, Emily found Dapple standing quietly in the shade of a tree where Lydia had left him tied by a rope to a low branch. She stumbled to the waterbag and unhooked it from the cart, sloshing water into her mouth and down her chin until the front of her blouse was soaked. She went on gulping, not caring how much was wasted, until she could drink no more. It was only then that something on the tray of the cart attracted her eye – her mother's mink coat, crumpled in a heap. For a fleeting moment she half expected her mother to sit up, until reality took hold and the mink coat turned into a tangled pile of dead rabbits.

Dropping the waterbag, she bolted into the scrub, where Mrs Flynn's excited barking helped guide her towards her aunt. As Emily skirted a prickly clump of ti-tree, they came face to face. In one hand Lydia gripped a bundle of rabbits by their hind legs, while three more dangled from a wire contraption around her waist.

'Fat lot of good you've been,' Lydia said. 'Where the hell did you get to?' Not waiting for an answer, she kept walking.

At the cart, Lydia threw these last few rabbits onto the tray while Emily tried not to look at the growing lumpy mound. Instead she picked up the waterbag and spent the time making sure it was securely attached. She finished the task and turned to see Lydia observing her.

'Home, James?' Lydia asked, and swung up onto the folded grey blanket that served as a makeshift seat. She held out a hand to help Emily up. After the shock of trampling on pioneer bones, getting lost and nearly dying of thirst, then seeing a mink coat turn into rabbit corpses, she wanted nothing more than to accept Lydia's hand, but she couldn't betray her mother and hauled herself up onto the cart.

They travelled without speaking. Lydia's hand had been an olive branch and she was beginning to regret not accepting it. After all, her aunt had only spoken aloud what she herself had secretly known. Or almost known – and didn't that come to the same thing in the end? The silence felt oppressive, but there seemed no way to break it without losing face. Once more, her mother's words about *petards* and *hoisting oneself* came to her. Why couldn't Lydia say something conciliatory? Life was so unfair.

7

TWICE A WEEK MR BEATTY, the postman, delivered the
mail, leading to an anxious build-up of hope that there would be
a letter from home. Almost two weeks had gone by, and in that
time Emily had received only one short note from her father
hoping she'd arrived safely and was doing her bit to help out. *Your
mother is progressing well,* he'd written, *and should be back home
soon.* He did not say where she was. She'd reread the letter over
and over, searching for something more. But there was nothing
more, and all she could think of were Lydia's awful words and
that they were true. Sitting on the garden seat under the Chinese
elm, Emily had shed some secret tears.

Today, however, was not a mail day, and Grandmother had
announced at breakfast that Eunice was temporarily bedridden
with a wheezy chest, at which news Emily had felt a spark of

uncharitable joy. A day without the usual list of boring jobs. Or almost, as there was still the early morning task of feeding the chooks and collecting the eggs, a task that Della had off-loaded onto her. Not that she really minded. It didn't take long and was usually followed by an hour of free time, coinciding as it did with Eunice's daily piano practice. Sometimes she found Eunice's playing impossible to resist and, standing outside the piano room, she'd become lost in the melodies. It was infuriating that Eunice could have such an effect, and she had to console herself with the idea that really it was not Eunice, it was Chopin.

This morning, walking back to the house with a basket of freshly laid eggs, she couldn't stop thinking about the books in the workshop. Who did they belong to and why were they there? The questions were still on her mind as she entered the courtyard to see Della sitting at the men's dining table, dunking an oatmeal biscuit into her cup of tea. Strictly speaking, it wasn't morning teatime, but Della took her breaks when she felt like it. She wasn't a blinking navvy.

Emily put the egg basket on the table and sat down casually. To get information from Della, she needed to play her cards right. It was important not to seem too interested or suspicions would be aroused. Information was power, and Della never gave it up willy-nilly.

'Seven eggs this morning.'

The cook dignified this revelation with an almost imperceptible rise of one eyebrow. She drained her cup and called to Florrie to bring out the teapot and a cup for the skinny malink too. It was an encouraging sign that she was in the mood for a chat.

'I suppose nobody uses the old workshop anymore,' Emily

said, as if she couldn't care less.

'Not since William joined up.'

'Ah.'

'Reckoned a writer has to have a place to write. Calls himself a poet.' And then after a bit Della added, 'It's not normal.'

'Why not?' She had never heard poetry described as *not normal*, but her question confused Della and the conversation got stuck in a cul de sac of repeated whats and whys until eventually they sorted it out. Della hadn't been referring to poetry after all, even though it was a useless sort of thing as far as she could see. Her comment had been aimed at William's choice of workplace. There were plenty of rooms in the house for a desk.

'Why would a person choose an old shed with a dirt floor? He's a queer fish, make no mistake.'

Emily felt a tremor of excitement at this description of William and was wondering how she might get Della to say more, when the cook continued under her own steam.

'Poor bugger'll need a hobby now, 'scuse the language. Where the dickens is that blinking Florrie? Florrie, we're dying of thirst out here!' Della yelled.

'You mean while he recuperates?' she asked, persevering.

Della gave her an odd look that she could not interpret, before adding, '*Ask no questions and be told no lies.*'

The uninterpretable look changed to one that Emily was all too familiar with: the brick wall. Even so, she couldn't stop herself. 'Why will he need a hobby?'

Florrie emerged from the kitchen, carrying a tray with two teacups and a fresh pot of tea. She plonked the tray on the table.

'If you want gossip, you've come to the wrong place,' Della said. *'The words of a talebearer are as wounds.* Proverbs, chapter 26, verse 22. Isn't that right, Florrie?'

Florrie seemed pleased to have been asked for her opinion. 'We're not s'posed to gossip. Your gran said,' she added.

Emily turned from one to the other. She could see there was no use trying to pry information from them. Perhaps if she got Florrie on her own, but with Della there it was out of the question. She picked up the teapot and poured tea for them all. It was best to bide her time. At least she had discovered something about the workshop and that the books belonged to William. She could not wait to return.

And so she did, the very next morning, and the one after, while Eunice was still conveniently laid low. After collecting the eggs, she hurried down the path and into the workshop. She had discovered William's writing desk in a corner of the room and a hurricane lamp that, once lit, provided her with enough light to explore the bookshelves on the far wall. It remained a dizzying sight. There was no particular system or order that she could discern – novels by Jack London sat alongside *The Rubáiyát of Omar Khayyám*, and *Kim* by Rudyard Kipling. A row of *Encyclopaedia Britannica* stretched the length of one shelf. Poetry by Byron, Blake, Keats, Browning and Shelley was scattered throughout. Fat tomes piled one on top of the other turned out to be the novels of Dickens. Where, she'd wondered, was *Jane Eyre?* But if she had failed to find *Jane Eyre*, there was still much pleasure to be gained from flicking through books at random. Yesterday she had read the whole of *Frankenstein* by Mary Shelley. It was quite terrifying, but she'd been unable to stop until the last page was turned – it was lucky that Eunice had still been bedridden.

Today, feeling the need for something less ghoulish, she sat down at William's desk with *The Poems of John Keats*. Time disappeared as the rich ripe words sang inside her. *Seasons of mist and mellow fruitfulness, close bosom friend of the maturing sun.* How wonderful it would be to write like that. Her mother liked poetry too. Her mother. She must write immediately and tell her about Keats. She put down the book and took a sheet of writing paper from the box in the top drawer. Wielding William's black fountain pen, she began:

Dear Mother, I expect you haven't had time to write because of your convalescence, which I hope is going well. I am well.

She stopped at the repetition of the word *well*. Her mother would notice it, but crossing it out would create an ugly blot. There was no option but to screw up the page and begin again. She remembered that Mr Beatty, the postman, was due to arrive later and he could take her letter. Perhaps today would also be the day a letter arrived from home? Holding on to that hope, she wrote the word *Dear*, intending to follow it with *Mother*, but to her amazement the word that appeared on the page was not Mother, but *Dorothy*. No amount of blinking changed it, and she was about to waste yet another piece of writing paper when a strange idea occurred: she could actually write a letter to Dorothy.

Putting pen to paper soon unleashed a flow of words. Sentence followed sentence, until pausing to stretch her cramped writing fingers, she put down the pen and began to read through what she had written. It was a surprise to find how much of the letter was about Claudio. Admittedly, there were details here and there that didn't quite accord with actual events. For example, she had not mentioned to Dorothy that she'd been running away the morning she and Claudio had first met. And perhaps it wasn't exactly true that he was locked up at night in the shearer's quarters to stop him from escaping. But she wanted Dorothy to know that she was not mouldering away in the country; that, on the contrary, things were exciting, even dangerous. And when Claudio had whirled her around the kitchen in a wild Italian dance, she wanted her nemesis to feel green with envy.

She refilled William's pen with ink, keen to continue.

I suppose you are wondering what Claudio looks like. Everyone thinks that the Italians are short and swarthy, however Claudio is approximately five feet ten inches tall (a perfect height), *and not at all swarthy.* She paused, wishing she hadn't opened up the issue of swarthiness. Claudio was in fact olive-skinned and those words had quite a different feeling from being swarthy. Crossing it out was not an option as that would mean rewriting the whole page. Better to continue. *His hair is dark and curly, rather like Lord Byron's, if you have ever seen his portrait.* Another pause, as she glanced at the photograph of said portrait of Byron tacked to the wall above the desk. She was sure it had been cut out of a book – an act of vandalism she assumed William had committed and that she continued to find shocking.

After the effortless manner in which whole paragraphs about her dramatic and exciting interactions with Claudio had found their way onto the page, she was discovering that the business of describing him was much more difficult. So far, perfunctory details about height and hair were all she had managed. It was only when she had almost given up and was letting her thoughts drift that Will Ladislaw's smile came to her. *Middlemarch*. She was still labouring through the early chapters and Will Ladislaw had not yet made an appearance, but yesterday, sitting on the swinging seat, flicking over the pages in a desultory way and wondering if she'd ever get to the end, she'd found his name and read the statement: *He had never been fond of Mr Casaubon.* Anyone who disliked Mr Casaubon was worthy of her interest and she'd read on a little, to Dorothea's description of Will's smile. Something about a gush of inward light illuminating his eyes and a reference to Ariel. It made her own efforts seem quite pathetic. Perhaps she could ... No, it did not feel right to steal George Eliot's words.

He has a merry smile and beautiful white teeth.

She reread all she'd written. It was unsatisfactory, particularly the reference to his smile and teeth. The adjectives were far too commonplace. Glancing at her watch she saw that more than an hour had passed – she had no time to redo it. Eunice, who was now recovered, was sure to be on the warpath. She shoved the letter into the top-left hand drawer of the desk, pushing away the fact of her non-existent friendship with Dorothy and the question of why she was writing to her at all. Perhaps there would be time to finish it later, and if it missed today's mail it could go next week.

Mr Beatty was late. Emily was outside picking lavender, and the afternoon air was full of its scent. She placed another bundle of lavender into the basket and moved onto the next bush. Wielding her secateurs, she began to snip off the long stems. Despite being under Eunice's orders, there was something satisfying about it all – the bushes shorn to a neat curve, the thick sheaves of lavender piled in the basket and the comforting drone of the bees. Listening to the bees made her think about her parents, recalling a story from the time of their courtship.

They were already engaged when her father had invited her mother to stay at Mount Prospect. *A bush holiday*, her mother would refer to it, making it sound either desirable or dreadful, depending on her mood and how things stood between her and Emily's father. They'd gone for a picnic in the pony cart and been attacked by a swarm of bees that had chased them for miles. Her father always said it wasn't miles – a few hundred yards at most. Her mother had been stung three times, and her face blew up like a balloon. She said it was a bad omen and she should have taken note, then and there. Sometimes she said it with a laugh, as if it was a joke and she didn't mean it. But other times she made it sound as if she did. It was always like that. One could never quite be sure what Mother meant or what she really felt.

A series of short sharp blasts of the horn announced the arrival of the mail van, interrupting her thoughts. She dropped the secateurs and ran round the house, colliding with Grandmother as they tried to push through the front door together. Before she could apologise, Grandmother had elbowed her aside with unprecedented rudeness, charging towards the kitchen without a word of explanation.

Following her into the kitchen, Emily was in time to see Mr Beatty enter through the back door, carrying the leather mailbag.

With the most cursory of thank yous, Grandmother took it and set off for the dining room. Emily followed once more and watched from the doorway as the bag was upended onto the dining-room table. Letters, newspapers and a couple of parcels tumbled out. As Grandmother swept up the letters, sifting through them like a cardsharp shuffling the deck, Emily knew what she was searching for. A letter from William. He was expected home soon, but nobody knew quite when. Grandmother's sorting became more and more desperate until at last she gave up and let the whole pile drop back on the table.

Emily shrank back a little as Grandmother brushed past her on the way out of the room, her face set in a mask of disappointment.

Alone now, she approached the table and began to pick up the scattered letters, but there was scarcely time to glance at the first one before Eunice arrived, out of breath, in a rush of skinny limbs.

'I'll take those,' Eunice said sharply and, before Emily could take evasive action, the letters were plucked from her fingers. 'The mail must be sorted first, you know that.'

It was true, she did know. And she knew too that Eunice liked to sort the mail in private, for she'd been shooed out on previous occasions. But this time when the mail sorter clapped her hands and said, 'Off you go', she stood her ground. Somewhat to her amazement, Eunice capitulated with the face-saving proviso that there should be no talking. She nodded her agreement, feeling that she'd just won a minor battle in the war between them.

Eunice examined each item, slowly sorting them into piles, and Emily felt sure that, if she hadn't been there, envelope flaps would have been fiddled with and airmail letters held up to the light. She was certain that Eunice was a snoop and felt an undeniable sense of *schadenfreude* – a word she had been dying to use since Mrs Martingale had introduced it in class – in knowing that there would be no letters for the fake cousin. Everyone knew that Cousin Eunice had no friends and, beyond that at Mount Prospect, no family.

Her pleasure however was short-lived, and it was soon Eunice's turn to enjoy the suffering of the other as she finished sorting and turned to Emily with a satisfied expression.

'For heaven's sake, there's no need for such a long face. The whole world doesn't revolve around you, my dear. I'm sure your parents have plenty to do without writing letters for the sake of it.'

Having rubbed salt into the wound, Eunice picked up a parcel wrapped in strong brown paper. Something about the way she put it aside made Emily suspicious and she reached across the table for it. There it was: *Miss Emily Dean* written in her father's dignified handwriting. She couldn't help giving a little cry of delight.

In the privacy of the white room she examined the parcel, feeling sure it was a book. Perhaps it was *Jane Eyre*? Perhaps her father had listened to her after all? As she turned it over, delaying the moment of discovery, a wave of longing for her father washed over her. She imagined him making a special trip into the city to buy her book, thinking of her, missing her. Yes, she was positive. She couldn't stand the excitement any longer and tore at the brown paper in blatant disregard for Grandmother's *waste not, want not* philosophy. She ripped away the last bit of wrapping, and for a second her desire triumphed and her eyes shaped the letters on the dust jacket into the right words: *Jane Eyre* by Charlotte Brontë. Then came shock, as her brain registered the title: *Songs of Praise*. A hymn book.

She felt like crying and did not know whether it was from disappointment at such a utilitarian gift, or relief that she had not been entirely forgotten.

EMILY WOKE TO HEAR FOOTSTEPS hurrying back and forth in the passage outside her room. She was still lying in bed when Eunice knocked.

'Hurry up, slowcoach. Church.'

Church? Then it was Sunday again, the second since her arrival. Unlike the order of the school week, the days at Mount Prospect all slid into each other.

She pulled off her pyjamas and slipped on some underpants. Taking a clean singlet from the chest of drawers, she glimpsed her naked chest in the dressing-table mirror. It was undeniable. Even since she'd arrived they had grown. They. Her breasts. Breasts that three months ago had been nothing more than two little gumnut caps. She'd been desperate then for some kind of development. Everyone else – that is Dorothy and her

78

entourage – talked about cup sizes and having their bras professionally fitted at Buckley & Nunn's while she had remained as flat as a board. Nevertheless, she had longed for a bra and had told her mother so.

Seeing the swell of her breasts in the mirror should therefore have been cause for celebration, but it was quite the opposite. From having nothing to show, she now had too much. If only her mother had listened when she'd tried to explain. Instead Mother had been flippantly off-hand: 'Don't be silly, they're just little buds, no need to swaddle yourself in armour yet, my darling.'

She could not believe how her mother could get it so wrong. Everyone in her class wore a bra, even Veronica who stuffed hers with cottonwool. Veronica, though, was beside the point, as she did not actually need one, whereas with each passing day Emily had become more aware than ever of the way her nipples seemed to thrust against her thin cotton blouse. Where before everything felt firm, now things jiggled uncomfortably when she ran. How could her mother not realise that 'armour' would become essential?

Interrupted by another knock on the door she turned away from the mirror and hurriedly pulled on her singlet. By the time Eunice peered in, she was struggling into a dress that only last summer had been too big.

Eunice began tugging and plucking at the dress. 'You must have grown,' she said in an accusing tone. 'Haven't you got something else to wear?'

Last Sunday's skirt had not returned from the wash, and she knew her only other option was the pink-gingham puffy-sleeved lace disaster hanging in the wardrobe.

'No,' she said with vehemence.

Eunice flipped bony fingers against her stomach. 'Then hold it in while I do up the zip.'

She tried to hold in her stomach, even though it was not her stomach causing the problem. She held her breath as Eunice yanked at the side zip.

'Now turn around,' Eunice ordered.

Under scrutiny, Emily wondered if Eunice had noticed anything else – the bulges – but all she said was, 'Hurry up and don't forget your gloves.'

The black Packard bumped over the cattle grid at the end of the drive and turned onto the road. Emily was stuck between Eunice and Lydia in the back seat. She felt hot. Her hands were sweating inside her cotton gloves, and it wasn't long before the backs of her legs were glued to the seat. She could feel Lydia's irritation too; it was like sitting next to a prickly shrub.

'For goodness sake, stop wriggling,' Eunice said.

'I'm not,' she replied, her only crime a slight bump against Eunice in her attempt to avoid the prickles on the other side.

It wasn't just the heat, but the fact that she felt as if she were about to burst out of the dress. It was making her breathless. Almost worse than the inability to breathe had been the brief dismissive glance from Lydia as they'd gathered in the entry hall waiting for Uncle Cec to bring the car round to the front. It had seemed to contain everything Emily believed true about herself – that she was quite hideous. Thus absorbed in miserable thoughts, she missed some of the conversation until Grandmother's sharp tone penetrated.

'Really, Lydia, you do say the most ridiculous things.'

'I don't see why I should have to go,' Lydia responded. 'I'm an atheist.'

'Whether you believe or not is hardly the point,' Grandmother said in the falsely patient tone of someone who has had to repeat the same thing too many times. 'One goes because it is one's duty – especially in wartime. It is what keeps things going, as I've told you before.'

'You mean protecting the natural order of things,' Lydia said scornfully.

'There is nothing wrong with the natural order of things.'

Lydia gave a mirthless laugh, and even Emily could see that Grandmother had rather missed the irony of Lydia's point.

'Nothing wrong at all,' confirmed Eunice.

On arrival, the main street of Garnook was deserted, as it was every Sunday morning. Uncle Cec drove past the row of closed shops and turned right into Church Street, where most of the town's inhabitants and those of the surrounding district were now gathering. Just up ahead Emily could see Claudio perched on the dicky seat of the gig, facing in their direction. Della was driving with Florrie seated beside her. They'd set off early that morning as it took a lot longer to travel in the gig and Della hated to be late for Mass.

'Careful, Cecil,' Grandmother said sharply as Uncle Cec swerved past the gig before overcorrecting onto the left-hand verge, almost collecting a family who were dawdling along on foot.

Back in the centre of the road, the Packard cruised slowly past the crowd gathering outside the Catholic church.

'Papists,' Grandmother muttered with disdain.

'And dagoes,' Uncle Cec mused in an observational way.

'Certainly looks like a full house,' Eunice added, as if it were somehow undesirable to have so many parishioners.

Emily had seen the Italians last Sunday, a group of men standing apart from the main crowd, dressed in maroon-coloured army uniforms. She'd peered at them with interest as it dawned on her that these men were like Claudio. It was a shock to realise he was not the only one – their 'one'. She saw how the men were all talking and many of them were using their hands to gesticulate, as if vitally important ideas were being exchanged. It was the same now, and she twisted around as the Packard rolled past, keen to go on watching until Eunice gave her a jab in the side.

The car continued to the end of the street and came to a stop in front of the small limestone church. Presbyterian parishioners were dotted about outside, creating a tableau vivant almost as motionless as the row of stiff and gloomy cypress pines along the side of the church.

Entering the churchyard, she was still thinking about the Italians. How different they were from Australian men, who spoke in monosyllables, squeezing out stingy words between lips that scarcely moved. Nor did Australian men move their hands in that excitable manner, instead letting them hang limply on the ends of their arms like small dead animals, or else stuffed into the pockets of their trousers and visible only in lumpy outline.

Grandmother led the way across the yard and into the church, and with her customary authority took up her usual place in the front pew. Emily shuffled in last. It was already stuffy; the scent of lavender water competing with the sharp tang of male sweat. Wedged in beside Uncle Cec, she waited for the minister to arrive and the service to begin. Last Sunday, Uncle Cec had pointed out Elspeth McDonald, the church organist, who'd fallen in love with the travelling piano tuner, Herman the German.

'Turned out he wasn't a German,' he'd whispered to her. 'Hungarian called Lazlo. Still, everyone called him Herman the German. Fella vanished five years ago and she's never got over it. Poor Elspeth.'

Remembering this, she glanced across to see Elspeth drooping on the piano stool like a heat-stressed tulip. According to Uncle Cec, nobody knew where Herman had gone, but they weren't surprised. After all, travelling salesmen and tinkers came and went, and in that way they were always disappearing. When all of the town's church organs grew wheezy and out of tune, everyone hoped he'd turn up, although now with the war on, it was generally agreed he'd be better off staying out of sight. Even the Germans who'd arrived at the turn of the century, before the Great War, had been rounded up and interned. Germans who'd never been to Germany, and Germans who didn't even speak the language, as there was no telling what national sentiments might be aroused by Hitler's vision of a thousand-year Reich.

As the congregation waited, Emily wondered yet again why church pews had to be so horribly uncomfortable. All around her, arthritic old bones shifted restlessly, tortured by the hard benches and cramped conditions. From the corner of her eye she could see beads of sweat forming on Uncle Cec's bald head. They rolled down his forehead in droplets, only to catch in his wiry eyebrows, gleaming like dew. She had begun to sweat too. Not a breath of wind stirred the syrupy air and, as the minutes ticked by, she became aware of a sour tomcat smell seeping from Mrs Burns in the opposite pew. Despite the heat, the old woman was clad in an ancient woollen coat and, as the air inside the church grew ever hotter, the coat began to give up its malodorous secrets. It wasn't long before Emily was forced to breathe through her mouth.

Just when it seemed that the whole congregation was in danger of melting, the minister, Reverend McIver, entered through the side door and strode swiftly to the pulpit. Reverend McIver, as she'd discovered last Sunday, was a thin pale man with a flinty face. He began to speak, but she blocked out the sound of his Scots burr and replaced it with her father's voice. How many of his sermons had she listened to in her life? Hundreds. As a little girl she'd burst with pride because he was the one up the front talking. His sermon voice still had the power to thrill her, and it was his voice she heard now, issuing a clarion call to goodness, humility and unselfishness as it echoed around the high airy spaces of St Andrews, Eastmalvern Presbyterian Church.

When the sermon was finally over, Elspeth McDonald launched into the opening bars of 'O, Valiant Hearts'. Since the local boys and men had left for the war it was sung every Sunday and, like Lydia and her fondness for 'Those in Peril on the Sea', Emily was susceptible to the emotional power of certain hymns. Sharing her new hymn book with Uncle Cec, she sang with gusto. Her mind was filled with battlefield images of the Somme. It was the wrong war, she knew that, but the photographs came from a book of her father's. She began to imagine herself as a soldier, leaping forwards to her death across a foreign field. Or perhaps a nurse, with a red cross emblazoned on her white pinny, dashing out to rescue the fallen.

Her voice swelled with the others as they began the second verse.

'*Proudly you gathered, rank on rank, to war,*
As who had heard God's message from afar;
All you had hoped for, all you had, you gave,
To save mankind – yourselves you scorned to save.'

At the words *to save mankind – yourselves you scorned to save,* she felt an ache in her throat and tears sprang into her eyes as, all of a sudden, she thought of her unlce William.

9

WITH THE SERVICE OVER, THE congregation filtered out of the church and into the heat of the late morning. She knew from the previous Sunday that there would be at least half an hour of hanging about while the Mount Prospect older generation caught up with neighbours and the socially acceptable elements of the congregation. Most of the churchgoers – albeit Presbyterian – were not, in Grandmother's words, top drawer and Emily suspected that some, like poor Mrs Burns, were not in any drawer at all.

Small groups clustered wherever there was shade. Grandmother and Eunice positioned themselves in a prime spot on the south side of the church, while Uncle Cec and his friend Hector Macrae strolled off for a cigarette. Lydia ignored everyone, walking briskly out of the churchyard and turning onto the street.

Emily trailed after her at a distance, far enough away to

pretend that she was simply going in the same direction, and if questioned could convincingly assert that she had not been following. Last Sunday she had made the mistake of falling into step with Lydia, who had told her in no uncertain terms to go away and wait by the car.

She was surprised when Lydia turned right at the first corner, having expected that they were going to walk along Church Street and back – even if in single file – and take in the sight and sound of the town's parishioners. Traipsing down a deserted dusty side street was less appealing. Did she really want to follow? Before she could make up her mind, a sleek car, the colour of fresh cream, cruised past. The passenger door opened, and Lydia had scarcely climbed in when it drove off with a smartly executed U-turn.

As the car slid away Emily caught a glimpse in the driver's seat of batwing sunglasses and a cap of dark hair. It was all so unexpected that she continued to stare down the empty street even after the car was long gone.

She was still standing at the corner when a boy ran past shouting, 'The dagoes are fighting.' More boys raced by, all in the direction of the Catholic church, and even parishioners who'd begun to walk home were turning around and retracing their steps. There was a crackle of excitement in the air, and she soon found herself swept up by the rush of bodies on either side.

She reached the gate to the Catholic churchyard where boys were leaping the fence to avoid the bottleneck. Someone shoved her from behind and she almost fell as they jostled through the narrow gate, surging towards the growing crowd in front of the church.

By the time she got there, adult bodies blocked her way; there was nothing to see but the bony bottoms of old farmers and the well-padded rumps of the district's matrons. A tow-haired boy beside her dived through a gap in the adult ranks and she followed his lead. Squeezing and burrowing, she made it to the front of the large circle that had formed around a dozen Italian POWs.

As the crowd increased, she felt herself merging with those beside her until she was not exactly sure where her body began or ended. She glimpsed two of the Italians at the centre of the group circling each other. Dust rose as their boots scraped the hard dry ground, and the small group of their countrymen yelled and gestured, urging them on. The rest of the crowd joined in, whistling and hooting.

With a shout, one of the two Italians rushed towards the other, fists swinging. His opponent sidestepped and the fist-swinger careened into onlookers near her. She heard the dull thump of bodies colliding, the grunt of expelled breath. Hands grabbed the fighter and threw him back into the fray and for a split second she saw his face. It was Claudio, covered in dust and dirt, his shirt torn at the shoulder.

The other man saw his chance and leaped forwards, and suddenly they were locked together, staggering around like two performing bears. Shouts went up from the Italians. Emily heard something about the Madonna and other indecipherable Italian words. She felt the push of bodies behind her, certain she was going to be trampled.

Around her the Italian men urged the fighters on. 'Vincenzo, Vincenzo,' they chanted.

It was a shock to realise that they were urging on Claudio's enemy. The fighters wrestled to and fro, grunting and gasping. Vincenzo spat out a stream of words and, in the babble of language, she recognised that one was repeated: *communista*. The men broke away and circled each other, waiting for the opportunity to attack. *Communista*.

At first it was just a foreign word but, hearing Vincenzo hurl it like a curse, she remembered she'd heard a word like that before. *Communist*. Her father and his friend, the Very Reverend, going on about the Russians and Uncle Joe, which meant Stalin. The communists were the new threat and, after the Allies had defeated the fascists, it was the commies they'd need to worry about. 'Make no mistake,' she'd heard her father telling the Very Rev, 'they're godless atheists. World domination is their aim.' The Very Rev had agreed wholeheartedly. Only a fool would trust Uncle Joe. Surely Claudio would defend himself against the *communista* slur, but he was silent. Vincenzo's tirade of abuse seemed to bounce off him like a handful of gravel.

And then Claudio stopped fighting. He stepped back with a shrug as if accepting defeat. Vincenzo grinned and dropped his fists; his body relaxed and he looked across at his supporters with a cocky grin. It was the moment Claudio must have anticipated. He sprang at his opponent, shouting. Again, one word rose above the rest: '*Fascista, fascista, sporco fascista.*'

A cloud of dust rose as Vincenzo hit the ground. Claudio was on him like a madman. Italian voices rang out and, although she could not understand the words, she knew they were urging their man to get up, to fight. She watched, horrified and yet spellbound at the sight of the two men rolling on the ground, kicking and thrashing about. The crowd swelled and she was pushed even further forwards, specks of blood splattering across her dress and the toes of her shoes. Swept up in the turmoil, she experienced an excited madness that made her want to shout out along with the others, thrilled and terrified by the wild violence of it all.

Claudio and Vincenzo were still fighting when a change swept through the crowd. The cries died away and a hush fell as Father O'Gorman and a small group of his local parishioners arrived at the scene. The Australian men, no longer young but with bodies hardened by physical toil, grabbed the two fighters and pulled them apart like stringless puppets.

Vincenzo's right eye was already closing, and he pushed the men aside and staggered away. The crowd began to disperse. Italian prisoners were claimed by their farm bosses and hustled off to waiting conveyances. Regular churchgoers recovered themselves, remembering it was Sunday, which after all was meant to be a day of rest.

Claudio remained kneeling on the ground, blood streaming from his nose. She looked around at the departing crowd. Was nobody going to help him? And then someone bumped against her and took hold of her arm.

A familiar voice whispered urgently in her ear. 'If anyone asks, we've been together.'

She turned to see Lydia, her cheeks red, breathing hard as if she'd been running.

Lydia squeezed her arm. 'Emily?'

She nodded, but her thoughts were for Claudio, and she gestured towards him. 'He's ...'

That was all she managed to say before Lydia let go of her arm and crouched down beside him, taking a white handkerchief from her bag.

'Tilt your head back,' she said.

Blood squirted over Lydia's fingers and onto her dress, but she did not seem to notice. Emily was not surprised; she knew her aunt was not squeamish. What startled her was the tender way Lydia held her white linen handkerchief to Claudio's bloody nose – as if she really cared.

They were still kneeling in the dust together when Grandmother, with Eunice hot on her heels, arrived on the scene. Grandmother cleared her throat to signal her presence and watched on with frosty disapproval as Lydia and Claudio stood up.

'Della is waiting,' she said to Claudio.

He nodded and, as he was about to set off, glanced at the blood-stained handkerchief in his hand, as if wondering what to do with it. He made a vague gesture towards Lydia and then stuffed it in his pocket before hurrying away in the direction of Della and the gig.

Grandmother watched him leave before turning her attention back to Lydia. 'Just look at you.' Her voice trembled with suppressed emotion. Her gaze swept over Emily too, taking in her blood-spattered shoes. 'Both of you, covered in blood.'

'Blood,' Eunice echoed, trying and failing to contain her excitement.

'Come along then, before you disgrace yourselves even further,' Grandmother said, and taking Lydia by the arm set off towards the black Packard.

'You too,' Eunice said and, slipping a skinny chicken-bone arm through Emily's, jerked her along behind the others.

On the trip home, there was no discussion of the sermon or local news from members of the congregation. Instead, the Italians were the sole topic of conversation and, in particular, Claudio, and what should be done about him. Now that he'd displayed a violent streak, they'd have to send him back to the camp. It simply wasn't safe.

'I should have taken more notice of the Army's directions,' Grandmother said.

'*Sly and objectionable if badly handled*,' quoted Eunice.

'It's a damn shame,' Uncle Cec added. 'Losing a useful chap is a damn nuisance when we're so short-handed. The place is going to rack and ruin as it is.'

Lydia said nothing and gazed out of the window as if she wasn't even listening. Emily felt her heart beginning to beat faster. She had been sure Lydia would spring to his defence. She remembered how Claudio had looked after her that first day when she had tried to run away. If Lydia would not help, then it was up to her. She had to say something. Grandmother was speaking.

'You'll have to ring the military fellow first thing tomorrow, Cecil —'

'You can't send him back. It wasn't his fault.'

'Not his fault?' Uncle Cec glanced at her in the rear-vision mirror. 'What makes you say that?'

She had no clue how the fight had started or whose fault it was. For all she knew, Claudio could have been to blame. The way he had smashed Vincenzo to the ground after lulling him into a false sense of security was not exactly reassuring.

'Speak up, lass,' Uncle Cec said. 'Can't try a man without hearing the facts.'

Grandmother swivelled round and peered over the front seat, while Eunice gave her a sharp nudge.

'Emily?'

But having rushed to Claudio's defence, she could think of nothing more to say.

'Well, that's settled then,' Grandmother said.

'He'll have to go,' Eunice added.

'They called him a communist. He was defending himself.' It was all she could think of, and she had a suspicion she'd twisted it somehow, but Uncle Cec enthusiastically grasped the straw.

'Fellow's got to be able to defend himself from insults of that sort,' he said with feeling. 'Be a poor sort of cove otherwise. Can't send a man back to camp for protecting his honour.'

Emily thought Grandmother would surely protest but, after a look from Uncle Cec, she seemed to subside slightly in her seat and said nothing more. Lydia raised her eyebrows and appeared quietly amused. It seemed she had been listening all along.

10

SUNDAY LUNCH WAS FINISHED. EMILY dangled a leg over the side of the swinging seat until her foot touched the verandah and pushed off. The seat rocked gently back and forth. She had resumed *Middlemarch*, forcing herself to return to the page she'd actually reached and not jump ahead to Will Ladislaw and the plot possibilities offered by his presence. Despite her best efforts she had got no further than Dorothea's enthusiastic acceptance of Mr Casaubon's proposal of marriage. And in truth, her 'best efforts' with *Middlemarch* had been hijacked by the books in William's workshop. Novels by an American called F. Scott Fitzgerald, and *The Good Earth* by Pearl Buck. She was quite sure they were not in the school library. It was only by sticking to a self-imposed rule not to remove William's books from the workshop that she'd been able to continue with *Middlemarch* at all. She turned the page, and doubtless an onlooker would have assumed that she was deeply absorbed in reading. However, no information about Dorothea or Mr Casaubon had reached her brain for some time. She had begun to think about Claudio and the fight and whether he was alright. Had anyone thought that he might need a doctor?

There were other thoughts too, about Lydia and who she had driven off with after church. Why was it a secret? It did not seem to make sense. Nevertheless, it meant she had a pact with her aunt, an exciting development and a major step forwards in her fantasies of friendship. She only wished she understood what was at stake and had been deliberating whether to ask Lydia straight out. As yet there had been no opportunity for, as soon as lunch was over, Eunice had shooed her off to get changed into work clothes. 'It's high time you made a start on sweeping the verandahs,' Eunice had declared.

Making a start seemed to be her fate, for like Sisyphus with his boulder, she had discovered that the task of sweeping the verandahs was never-ending. The fact that she was now lying on the swinging seat was a reckless act of rebellion. The verandahs were still littered with summer leaves, dust, and mounds of fairy grass that had blown in from the dry parts of the swamp.

Her pretend reading of *Middlemarch* was interrupted by the crunch of the wheelbarrow over gravel. Grandmother and Eunice had moved to a nearby garden bed where she knew they would be dead-heading roses. As luck would have it, she was shielded from their sight by the back of the swinging seat. She heard the sharp snip, snip of secateurs as they began to talk about someone called Alma who was coming to stay the night, although she did not catch when the visit was to take place.

'We'll put her in the pink room,' she heard Grandmother say. 'I don't want Alma reporting that standards have slipped just because there's a war on.'

'Wouldn't the blue room be better?' Eunice enquired in a meek but determined voice.

Emily knew that the blue room was shabby and had a nasty stain on the ceiling where a possum had got into the roof cavity and peed. She wasn't surprised to hear Grandmother question how Eunice would even suggest such a thing, and she couldn't help smiling when Grandmother said snappily that, really, sometimes she did not know what went on in Eunice's head. After that the two women stopped talking and continued snipping off the dead blooms in silence. Then the plinking of the secateurs stopped and the sound of the wheelbarrow on the gravel grew fainter.

Emily went back to *Middlemarch*, telling herself that she must try to concentrate. She hoped that in the next chapter there would be less of the ghastly Mr Casaubon.

A considerable number of pages later, she heard a door bang close by, followed by the sound of footsteps. She sprang up, grabbing the straw broom abandoned earlier, and swished vigorously in case it was Eunice coming to check on her progress. She was so busy pretending to be absorbed in her work that Lydia's voice came as a surprise.

'What are you doing?'

'Sweeping.'

'Making a mess, more like it. I would have thought you have to sweep in one direction, not all over the place.'

It was true: she had been randomly swishing the broom about and the leaves and fairy grass were now more dispersed than ever.

'Anyway, I didn't come about that. What are you reading?' Lydia picked up the copy of *Middlemarch* lying on the swinging seat.

Before she could answer, Lydia had already tossed it back on the seat.

'Thrilling.'

Emily felt a powerful urge both to defend the book and at the same time denigrate it. She was still trying to untangle her thoughts and put them into words when Lydia plopped herself onto the seat, pushing off with her toes. On the forwards swing she sprang up again.

'I'm sure Ma's got the latest Agatha Christie. You should try that.' She took a few steps towards the edge of the verandah and jumped up, plucking a grape from a bunch hanging just below the eaves, and then tossing it away before twirling around the verandah post. Emily heard her mother saying, *For heaven's sake, you're like a flea in a fit*, as Lydia launched herself across the space between them and landed back on the swinging seat.

'They're such busybodies. That's all. Not you, I don't mean you. Which is why I know I can rely on you.' Lydia shot her a piercing glance. 'I can rely on you, can't I?'

'Of course.'

'Good. Because I really cannot stand people wanting to know my business.' Lydia fixed her with an intense look, and she knew that whatever happened, she had to quell her curiosity, for if Lydia did not want to confide in her, then so be it. She must never ask.

'Anyway,' Lydia jumped up yet again, 'you'd better get on with the sweeping. You wouldn't want to disappoint Eunice.' With that, she threw Emily a smile and disappeared around the corner of the verandah.

11

THE NEXT MORNING, AFTER THE chooks, Emily snuck off to the workshop where she intended to continue the letter to Dorothy and was already writing details of the fight between Claudio and Vincenzo in her head. She was sure that Dorothy would never have experienced anything as exhilarating, a thought that was giving her a great deal of gratification. She was up to the part where she'd gone to Claudio's aid and was kneeling beside him as blood poured from his wounds.

She entered the yard, closing the garden gate behind her. As she neared the stables, she saw Dapple harnessed to the cart. Lydia was checking the shafts and greeted her with a friendly wave. Emily felt a pleasurable frisson and waved back too eagerly.

'You're just in time,' Lydia said, ignoring the over-enthusiastic wave.

On reaching the cart, Emily saw the bundle of rabbit traps on the tray and the frisson turned from pleasure to anxiety.

'You can make up for your last effort,' Lydia continued, swinging up onto the driver's seat as if there was no question about it. She whistled to Mrs Flynn, who jumped onto the tray of the cart.

After the last time, which was also the first time, Emily had made a firm decision never again to go rabbiting. Anyway, she wanted to write to Dorothy. All of which made climbing onto the cart beside Lydia inexplicable. It was somewhat unnerving that her body had a mind of its own.

'Where are we going?' she asked as they set off down the drive.

'Back of the swamp,' Lydia replied. 'The rotten things are in plague proportions.'

They reached the archway and turned onto the road. Clip-clopping along, small bush flies buzzed around Dapple's head, and the scent of eucalyptus wafted through the air, mingling with Lydia's particular smell – dark and heady. It was the perfect time to bring Emily's fantasies of sisterly intimacy to life. How could she begin a conversation that was worthy of the occasion? What did she know that would interest Lydia? Nothing. She glanced across, hoping that Lydia might initiate something, but so far she showed no inclination to do so.

Sitting there dumbly, as they headed off to undertake a task she abhorred, all in the futile hope of Lydia's friendship, she felt a fool. She repeated the word *fool* twice under her breath. It was a word her mother often used. Sometimes she would say it in a light-hearted way: *Oh, what a fool I am*, when really she meant no such thing. And at other times, it was uttered with loathing:

What a fool I am, what a useless fool. Emily knew that the line between the gay remark, tossed off with a laugh, and the desperate angry curse was thin as tissue paper. It was impossible to comfort her mother when the gay fool became the stupid useless fool, and any attempt brought forth lacerating fury. Yet she preferred even this fury to the grim silence when her mother closed in on herself and became a wraith that no longer seemed to see or hear her.

Perhaps it was being on the cart with Lydia that had turned her thoughts to her mother, for Lydia was the one who had said those fateful words: *loony bin*. Sitting there now, she began to see a pattern to things. The way her visits to Mount Prospect had so often been preceded by her mother's increasingly erratic behaviour. Had there been other breakdowns? Other stays in the loony bin?

'Penny for your thoughts.' Lydia poked her on the arm with the knobbly end of the whip handle.

This was the moment she'd longed for, she had to say something – but not about her mother. Not that. She scrambled for inspiration.

'I was just thinking ...'

'Go on,' Lydia said encouragingly.

'... of Harry.'

It was the first thing that came to her, and Lydia glanced across with a quizzical look.

'What about him?'

Exactly. What about him?

'I suppose you'll have an enormous wedding when the war ends. It'll be a society event. And a honeymoon abroad ... or

Sydney. I've never been to Sydney ... actually I've never been abroad. Why do people say *abroad* anyway? Abroad what?'

If only she could stop her nonsensical chatter but, having begun, she felt compelled to continue, hoping that Lydia would say something in the pauses. Unfortunately, her aunt did not pick up the conversation's thread so she had to burble on, increasingly stricken with remorse. How could she have been so stupid, talking about weddings when Harry was away at the war and might never return. Poor Lydia, alone and lonely.

'You must miss him terribly.'

Lydia still did not respond, staring straight ahead. But, with a secret thrill, Emily saw a tear slide down her aunt's cheek. She felt a surge of empathy, followed by admiration for the way Lydia maintained her poise, and even for her refusal to seek comfort from her despite the fact that she was keen to offer it.

Lydia wiped away the errant tear. She flicked the whip lightly over Dapple's back and a cloud of bush flies rose up and shimmered in the air over his haunches.

Emily understood that she should say nothing more, and sent out sympathetic emanations, feeling that a great step forwards had been taken in her quest for friendship.

At the far side of the swamp they stopped in the shade of a wattle. Mrs Flynn jumped from the tray, yapping with excitement. Emily stood by as Lydia strapped the leather and wire contraption around her waist. It was familiar from the first excursion, and she knew that soon there would be dead rabbits dangling by their necks from the wire. A metallic taste filled her mouth, and she swallowed hard. Her resolve began to weaken when Lydia slid a skinning knife into the leather sheath on the belt, and she had to focus on how much she wanted her aunt's friendship.

They're only rabbits, pests that are destroying the countryside, she told herself, watching Lydia pick up a bundle of the iron traps from the cart tray.

'Waterbag,' Lydia barked.

Emily startled and unhooked the waterbag from the back of the cart.

'Shovel.'

She grabbed the shovel that lay on the cart tray.

Lydia nodded to her. 'Right. Off we go.'

Lydia strode ahead like a bold young brigand, with Emily stumbling along behind, carrying the waterbag and shovel. Mrs Flynn ran between them, darting off now and then, her nose to the ground, following irresistible animal scents. If Emily squinted and let things go a little blurry, it was possible to imagine Lydia as D'Artagnan – possibly her favourite fictional character.

The swamp lay to their right and on the left the land rose in a gentle slope covered in dry grasses. Many of the trees had died of waterlogging yet, inexplicably, others continued to thrive and had grown huge despite repeated flooding. Leaf litter and small dry branches crunched and cracked underfoot and here and there she saw massive branches lying where they'd been ripped from the trees. Some were old and grey and must have been lying there for decades, while others still had their leathery green leaves attached.

Lydia was setting a cracking pace, and Emily was struggling to catch up. 'Gosh, the storms must have been terrible,' she puffed, as they approached a tree where a branch had recently fallen.

'Don't be silly.' Lydia laughed. 'Sit under a redgum on a hot still day at your peril. They drop their limbs to save water.'

Emily skittered nervously around the tree, hoping she was out of range.

'How do you know if a branch is about to fall?'

'You don't,' Lydia replied in her customary matter-of-fact tone. 'Not until it hits you over the head.' She stopped and dropped the traps on the ground. 'This should do. Now watch so that you know how to do it.'

With those innocuous words striking fear into her heart, she tried to concentrate as Lydia demonstrated the business of trap setting, positioning the first one with care, scraping away leaves and bark, smoothing the sandy soil before plunging the long iron pin deep into the ground. With the trap in place, Lydia pressed the toe of her boot down on the metal plate. The iron jaws opened and she set the catch before hiding the whole thing from view with a delicately drizzled handful of sandy soil and some leaf litter.

'You need to be careful and remember where they are. You don't want to lose a foot,' Lydia said, and picking up a sturdy stick, tapped it gently on the centre of the hidden iron plate. The jaws sprang shut and the stick snapped, the top half spinning away, so that Emily was forced to duck as it whizzed past her head.

'Your turn,' Lydia said, handing over three traps.

There was nothing to be done but try to copy the steps she'd just been shown. She knew she had no hope, but luck was with her, for Lydia went on ahead. When it seemed that a suitable time had elapsed, she covered the first unset trap with a pile of leaves and then repeated the process twice more. By the time she caught up to Lydia, the rest were already set and she gave a secret sigh of relief. Too soon. There were still yesterday's traps to be checked.

'With any luck there'll be a dozen or more,' Lydia announced cheerfully. 'Not bad with the price of skins the way they are.'

She felt her stomach contract. The memory of coming face to face with Lydia in the scrub, laden with rabbit corpses, flashed through her mind and even the hope of a friendship where secrets would be shared – and her aunt's knowledge of all the important things would be revealed to her – had no effect on the vice-like grip that was twisting her innards. It was not propitious.

At the first trap, a quivering bundle of fur awaited them. Lydia grabbed the rabbit by the scruff of its neck and pressed firmly on the metal side plate with the toe of her boot. The iron teeth parted and she lifted the animal up. Emily found herself staring into the rabbit's terrified eyes. She locked her knees in an effort to remain steady as Lydia gripped the squealing rabbit around the neck and, with practised ease, twisted its head sharply. There was a dull crunching sound and it went limp.

She pressed her lips together, but it was not enough to prevent a high-pitched squeak from escaping.

'You see,' Lydia said, ignoring or oblivious to the squeak, 'it's not hard once you get the hang of it', and she pulled the skinning knife from its leather sheath on her belt. Lydia was soon peeling off the pelt, which was accompanied by an awful tearing sound as it pulled away from the flesh, leaving the rabbit pink and naked. For a split second Emily imagined Eunice's skinny flank. Then Lydia sliced off its head. It bounced onto the ground where Mrs Flynn pounced, sinking her sharp teeth into the bony skull with a crunch, before darting off with her prize. Lydia flung the pelt over a nearby log and plunged the knife into the rabbit's pale belly. Blood welled out of the slit and dark slippery coils slurped onto the ground.

Emily swayed, the guts glistened and she thought she saw them writhing as if, having escaped from the inside of the rabbit, they'd taken on new life as a tangled ball of wriggling snakes. She tightened her grip on the shovel, using it to keep herself upright. A hot clotted smell rose from the pile of viscera. Flies were already swarming. She wanted to look away but was sure that any movement, no matter how small, would be enough to make her lose her balance.

'Well done.'

She looked up to see Lydia smiling at her.

'I thought you might have been too squeamish.'

She managed a sort of shrug without letting go of the shovel, knowing if she did she'd fall over.

'Betty was completely hopeless. Fainted. As if weakness is a badge of womanly honour,' Lydia added scornfully.

Emily had no idea who Betty was but despised her instantly. She began to feel Lydia's praise stiffening her spine, returning muscle and bone to her legs.

'Onwards then.' Lydia flashed her a comradely grin as she attached the skinned rabbit to the wire part of her belt. 'Let's see how many we've caught.'

12

ON THE WAY HOME THEY took a different route and arrived at a gate to find Claudio digging holes for new fence posts. Nearby, a grey gelding was tied up under a tree, a saddle slung over a branch. Emily went to climb down from the cart to open the gate, but Lydia stopped her with a restraining hand.

'Claudio,' she called.

He put down his shovel and walked over, touching his hat in greeting. The bruise under his eye had turned purple.

'Does it still hurt?' Lydia asked.

Claudio shrugged. It could have meant yes or no.

'What were you fighting about?' Lydia enquired.

'*Politica.*'

'I hear you're a Red.'

'Red?' he queried.

'Communist.'

Emily felt guilty for having revealed this information in the car, as if she'd dobbed Claudio in and hoped that now, at least, he would clear up the misconception.

'Ah.' He nodded that he understood. 'Boss say this all belonging to you?'

Lydia smiled. 'Yes, that's right.'

'This way, there. There.' He pointed in various directions.

'As far as the eye can see,' Lydia said with a satisfied expression, sitting even straighter, and lifting her chin.

'Very rich – *molto grande*.'

'Oh, well, a little,' she demurred.

'All for one *famiglia*.'

This time Lydia heard the mocking undertone and looked taken aback. 'What's wrong with that?' Claudio shrugged, his eyes on her. 'There's nothing wrong with being well off,' she added tartly.

'Is nothing wrong,' he agreed, but Emily could see that Lydia was no longer sure whether he meant what he said, or the opposite.

'This is Australia,' Lydia added firmly. Nevertheless, her confident tone was belied by the way she shifted a little uneasily in her seat. And when it was clear that Claudio was not going to answer, she affected a haughty tone. 'You might open the gate.'

Claudio scratched his cheek. Emily wondered what Lydia would do if he refused. He hesitated then walked across, unhooked the chain and jumped on the gate, riding it as it swung open. Lydia gave Dapple a whack with the reins and the horse plunged forwards through the opening. As they passed him,

Emily thought she saw a look travel between Claudio and her aunt. Or did she imagine it? Something so fleeting that she couldn't be sure.

The cart continued on, rattling and bouncing over the rough ground.

'He should be grateful,' Lydia burst out. 'He could be locked up with nothing to eat but potato peelings.'

'I don't think we're allowed to lock them up,' she replied, surprised by Lydia's vehemence, and she launched helpfully into the little she knew about the rules governing POW employees, and the fact that Italy, since its surrender, was now on the same side as the Allies, something she knew from discussions with her father.

'For heaven's sake, Emily. Shut up!' Lydia interjected, giving Dapple a sharp whack with the whip.

There was no time to feel offended for immediately they were flying over the bumpy paddock, the dead rabbits leaping up and down and Mrs Flynn barking non-stop.

'Home, James, and don't spare the horses,' Lydia yelled, laughing and whooping.

Emily clung onto the edge of the cart – she was quite sure they were going to die.

When they reached the yard, she climbed down from the cart on wobbly legs. She was determined not to reveal her fragile state given Lydia's view of feminine weakness, and somehow managed to help unhitch Dapple and put away the harness. But there were still two dozen rabbits to skin. She had tried to ignore the implications of Lydia's earlier demonstration of how it should be done. No matter how strong her desire for friendship, skinning rabbits was an impossibility and it seemed as if the progress she'd made in forging a bond with her aunt was in danger of being undone.

Returning to the cart from the stables where she'd hung up the harness, she was still trying to think of a reason for having to excuse herself. Would an urgent need to use the bathroom suffice?

Lydia was tying a bit of twine around the neck of a hessian bag. She held it out. 'Shearers' quarters. You don't mind, do you?'

Although phrased like a question, Emily knew it was really an order, but she did not mind at all and took the bag eagerly.

'And get my handkerchief while you're there.'

'What?'

'My handkerchief,' Lydia repeated. 'From Sunday.'

13

FLIES BUZZED AROUND THE BOTTOM of the hessian bag as she trudged up the slope towards the woolshed and the shearers' quarters where Claudio had a room. The bag was heavy, and she had to keep swapping it from hand to hand, trying not to think of the dead rabbits, pretending instead that she was carrying something else. Perhaps books, but then who carries books in an old and very smelly hessian bag? And why would she be taking books to Claudio – and could he even read English? She wondered what time he finished work and whether he might have ridden back by now. Not that it mattered of course. The sun, having dazzled its way across the sky, was now sinking in the west but she could still feel it burning the back of her neck.

She rounded the corner of the shearers' quarters and paused to catch her breath beside a sprawling woodpile.

Nearby a windmill clanked in the light breeze, pumping water into a tank on a high wooden stand. A rusty overflow pipe stuck out from the top of the tank and, as the windmill turned, water spurted from it, splashing into a muddy puddle at the bottom of the tank-stand.

She swapped the bag to her left hand. For once, the crows, magpies, cockatoos and willy-wagtails had fallen silent together. Standing in the shadow of the building she felt a peculiar sense of dislocation, as if the rest of the world had slipped away and all that remained was this place. She gave a shiver, wondering if it was the rabbiting that had turned her thoughts in such a morbid direction.

She forced herself to move. The six doors along the length of the building were closed. Her legs were stiff and heavy, and she almost stumbled on the rough wooden step that led to the first door. If her memory was correct, this was the shearers' kitchen. There was no answer to her knock, and so she turned the handle and pushed it open.

'Hello,' she called, feeling annoyed by the quavery sound of her voice. There was no reply.

In the room was a long wooden table with benches on either side where the shearers sat to eat their meals. A large open fireplace dominated one wall. A few clinkers and a small pile of soot had fallen from the chimney since the hearth had last been swept. Crossing the room, she peered through the open doorway into the adjoining kitchen where a black cast-iron stove squatted in an alcove. A cleansing astringent smell perfumed the air, puzzling her until she saw the bunch of dried sage leaves hanging upside down on a nail over the kitchen bench. She crossed the worn linoleum and placed the hessian sack on the bench beside the sink. It was a relief to be rid of it.

Outside again, she hurried along the length of the building past the row of shearers' bedrooms and had almost reached the last door in the row when it opened, and Claudio stepped out. He was dressed in a pair of dark serge pants and a white singlet, and she could not help feeling a twinge of dismay. In her world, men never wore singlets without a shirt. It was terribly déclassé. On the other hand, Claudio was Italian, and a prisoner of war. Perhaps he was exempt from the usual standards. His hair was wet, and he had slicked it down. Already black curls were springing up in an unruly way.

'Oh, there you are,' she said and, without waiting for him to respond, rushed on. 'I thought you weren't here so I left them on the kitchen bench. From Lydia. Rabbits. Dead.'

She could hear the disjointed way she was revealing the information, and the bit about the rabbits being dead was unnecessary. 'I'll be going then.' She waved as if to indicate the direction of her going, but her feet did not respond. The only thing that had moved was her arm. 'Good-o,' she said cheerily, as if she were turning into Uncle Cec who was fond of the expression. What was the matter with her?

'You like *te*?'

'*Te*?' The word was unfamiliar.

'*Te*,' he repeated with an affirming nod. He pointed back towards the shearers' dining quarters. 'For drinking.'

'Oh, you mean tea?'

She knew that Grandmother would not approve and understood that having tea with Claudio was not the same as delivering the rabbits. She swallowed uncomfortably, making an unpleasant squishing sound that she hoped he had not heard. On the other hand, people drank tea together every day. And her throat was terribly dry.

Claudio stepped around her. She turned and watched him walk towards the dining quarters. At the door, he called to her.

'Emilia, how you liking? Sugar?'

This time her feet began to move of their own accord.

They sat at the shearers' dining table opposite each other. Claudio poured the tea. He stirred a heaped teaspoon of sugar into her tin pannikin and pushed it across the table. She took a sip of the hot sweet liquid, knowing Grandmother would not have approved of this either. A drop of milk or a slice of lemon was acceptable; sugar, on the other hand, was the choice of the hoi polloi. It was a revelation to discover how delicious it was. She took another sip, her head lowered over the mug. If only she had the courage to look at him, but it was all she could do to focus on her fingers curled around the pannikin.

'Are you really a communist?' she asked, when the silence had gone on for too long.

This time she managed to raise her eyes, but all too quickly they skittered away from his face, and she noticed something she had failed to see earlier: scraps of paper torn from a notebook, pinned to the wall, and on each, handwritten words. *Table, chair, kettle, mug,* she read, along with, she assumed, their Italian equivalents.

'Is wrong wanting same for everyone?' Her eyes flicked back to him. 'Food? House for live? Go to school?'

'Of course not.' She heard condemnation in his voice, and it made her want to contest the point. She remembered her father using the term *godless atheists*.

'But communists don't believe in God.'

'What god, why he's letting this war?'

'Because of free will.'

'Free will?'

'Yes.'

'Who is free?'

'No, not who. Free will.'

Claudio was frowning in frustration. How could she make him understand? They were getting tangled in language.

'You know, making a choice. You can do a good thing or something bad.' She paused. 'We must choose what is right: that is our duty and our responsibility.'

The words had no sooner left her mouth than she was cringing at their pompous certainty. And why on earth had she introduced God when she wasn't even sure she believed in him?

'No! We are small people, not choosing. In *Italia* the strong choosing. Church and *fascisti*.'

'But we must fight. We have to stop them.'

'Who you are stopping?' He raised his voice. 'You think in Australia you all free? You have the king. All the bosses same, by jingo. Send small people out, shooting, get shot. Die. That is all.'

He leaped up from the table and she jerked away, thinking he was going to grab her. But he rushed off into the kitchen where she heard him moving around. Her eyes darted towards the exit. Had she made a mistake? Grandmother's words about Claudio's violent streak returned to her. But thoughts of sneaking away were quickly dashed when he stepped back into the room with a plate of Della's ginger biscuits. He put them on the table and abruptly sat down again.

'What about Hitler?' she managed to squeak, determined, for reasons she couldn't fathom, to continue. 'And the Japs. And Mussolini too.' She had read how Mussolini was still at large in the north of Italy where the Germans were in control. Officially Italy was now an ally but what did Claudio really think? She had to know. The question of his political beliefs had receded before the even more crucial question of whose side he was on.

'We have to stop them, don't we?' She waited for his answer. Everything depended on it, but it seemed he would not speak.

'Yes, we must stop them.' His answer came softly, and it gave her the courage to look at him. 'Sorry, Emilia, very sorry. Not mean to frighten you.'

'That's alright, I wasn't frightened,' she replied. It was only a white lie. But her voice betrayed her, and she was mortified to realise that she was on the verge of tears. She had to leave before he noticed. She made a show of looking at her watch. 'Gosh, is that the time? Della needs me,' She ran for the door as if it was some kind of emergency, which, in a way, it was.

Just as she reached the end of the building and was turning the corner, Claudio shouted, 'Emilia.'

She turned to see him standing outside the shearers' dining room.

'You will teaching me English,' he called. Before she could think of an answer, he stepped back inside.

She crossed the paddock and took the short cut under Lydia's snake fence, hurrying through the orchard as if on an urgent mission. Her route, however, was random, the only objective being the release of inner turmoil while avoiding the others – Grandmother, Eunice and especially Lydia. It had something to do with Claudio, but she wasn't quite sure what.

She changed direction once more and began to count her footsteps in an effort to calm down.

She had just reached thirty-two when a gunshot rang out. She screamed and suddenly Lydia emerged from behind the lavender hedge carrying her gun.

'You ought to watch where you're going – I could have shot you.'

Emily knew that she was not the one at fault and that Lydia was responsible for taking proper precautions, but asserting her innocence while in such a rattled state was impossible. She could not even speak.

'Did you give Claudio the rabbits?'

She nodded.

'And my handkerchief? Did you get it?'

Damn. She'd forgotten all about that. Not wanting to admit her failure, she found herself saying, 'He lost it. On the way back from church. It must have fallen out of his pocket. At least that's what he said.'

Why hadn't she just told the truth? But it was too late to undo it now: the hole was dug and she was in it.

'Is something wrong?' Lydia asked.

'Of course not.'

The words came out with uncharacteristic force, and she saw how Lydia noticed. But such interest, which she had so often tried to elicit from her aunt, now felt intolerable. She avoided

Lydia's eye and made her face go blank. It seemed to work. Lydia shrugged and walked off in the direction of the olive tree. At the foot of the tree was a shallow stone trough where snakes sometimes came to drink on warm evenings.

The garden no longer felt like a sanctuary, and so Emily made her way to the kitchen, seeking the comforting rhythms of Della and Florrie at work – the sound of their voices rising and falling as they shared out the tasks to be done, interspersed with Della's Bible recitations and spiritual exhortations.

Once there, Della put her to work rolling out pastry for the apricot tart. It was all hands on deck. Mrs Emerson was coming to stay and due to arrive at any minute. They'd had to fly into action and prepare a special dinner.

'Who's Mrs Emerson?' she asked.

'Alma,' Della said.

'Oh.' So this was the Alma she'd overheard Grandmother and Eunice talking about when they were deadheading the roses.

Della looked across at Florrie, who was stringing beans at the other end of the kitchen table, and added with a grin, 'The Belle.'

'The bell?' Emily repeated, feeling puzzled.

'The belle of the ball,' Florrie said and giggled.

'It's too bad no-one gave us more warning,' Della complained.

'Given as we're doing all the work,' Florrie added.

'If you ask me, she's getting snappy as an old foxy,' Della said.

'Alma?' She was trying to keep up.

'Don't be daft. Your gran.' Della abandoned her vegetable preparations and moved across to check Emily's progress, only to find her attempting to conceal the hole that had opened up in the middle of the pastry. The cook took the rolling pin and shoved her aside with a deft hip movement. 'Blinking hopeless,' she said with a shake of her head.

Emily knew that on this occasion, she, not her grandmother, was the focus of Della's criticism. She stood aside and watched as the cook skilfully repaired the ravaged pastry before pressing it into a fluted tart tin. When that was done, she poured in a cup of split peas for the blind bake.

'Let's just hope it's only the Belle who turns up,' Della said, sliding the tin into the bottom right-hand oven.

'Who else would turn up?' she asked, feeling left behind yet again. Della's conversations often had this effect.

'Roy saw a swaggie on the road this afternoon. Might be heading our way.'

'With the Belle?' Emily was even more confused.

Della gave her a withering stare. 'What would the Belle be doing with a blinking swaggie? All I'm saying is he might turn up for some tucker. Wild-looking fella, so Roy reckons.'

Emily knew that swaggies came knocking from time to time, offering to do odd jobs in exchange for a meal and a place to camp for the night. Sometimes they only wanted to fill their tucker bags and be on their way. 'They're just men like any others,' Della had told her on a previous visit, when a whiskery old fellow had turned up at the kitchen door. But hadn't Della also warned her never to trust a swaggie. 'They'll cut your throat for five bob,' she'd said.

'He better not come here,' Florrie squeaked nervously.

'*Blessed are the meek for they shall inherit the earth,*' Della intoned.

'He doesn't sound awfully meek,' Emily protested, but it did not go down well, and Della declared that too many cooks spoiled the broth.

'Out you go,' she said, shooing her from the kitchen.

14

BEFORE MRS EMERSON ARRIVED, GRANDMOTHER warned everyone to make sure they were presentable at dinner. 'I don't want Alma reporting that standards have dropped,' she said, not for the first time.

Uncle Cec was ordered to put on a tie and his better sports coat, the one without patches on the elbows, and the women were to wear dresses.

'You too, Emily,' Eunice added.

Now, with a sinking heart, she opened her wardrobe to see the meagre offerings that hung there. The cotton church dress was impossible – she was sure to faint from lack of breath and she'd never be able to eat wearing it. That left the puffy-sleeved, lace-collar horror. She tugged it from its hanger, feeling resentful towards the as-yet unmet guest.

She squinted sideways in the mirror. Was it really that bad? It was worse: ridiculous and ugly, like a stupid doll from the toy department of the Myer Emporium. Why couldn't she be struck down with rheumatic fever or measles – something, anything that meant she could stay in bed? Of course. That was it, she would pretend to be ill. The cloud of gloom had scarcely had time to lift when the bedroom door opened and Eunice poked her head in.

'Come along, our visitor's here. Didn't you hear the Bentley?'

It was only once she'd spoken that Eunice seemed to notice Emily's outfit and her eyes widened. She looked as if she wanted to say something but could not find the right words. Emily wanted to say she felt unwell but couldn't find the words either.

By the time she and Eunice entered the sitting room everyone was gathered for a sherry before dinner. She was consumed with self-consciousness and tried not to look at anyone, staring instead at Uncle Cec's ancient brown brogues with such intensity that she almost shrieked when Grandmother gripped her by the arm.

'Emily, dear, I don't think you've met Mrs Emerson. You know she's a great friend of your Aunty Fran and Uncle Robert.'

Emily had only the vaguest recollection of Aunty Fran and Uncle Robert, who were not real relatives anyway. She had no idea what the connection was between them all – her parents, the unrelated relatives, Grandmother and Mrs Emerson – and, what's more, she didn't care.

Up close, Mrs Emerson's eyes were large and blue. Her skin, of which quite a lot was on show, was pale as alabaster. Florrie and Della's description – *belle of the ball* – came back to her.

'How lovely to meet May's granddaughter. I've heard all about you,' the Belle said with a low chuckle.

'How do you do,' she responded stiffly. She could not imagine what Mrs Emerson had heard about her and was sure the chuckle bore a direct relationship to the hated dress. Her fears were soon confirmed.

'What a fascinating dress,' the Belle added. 'So ... unusual.'

Just then Eunice announced that dinner was being served in the dining room, and Emily was able to scuttle through the door ahead of the others.

Grace had been said when Mrs Emerson focused her large blue eyes on Emily again and wanted to know if she had ever been to Hong Kong. Of course she hadn't, and it soon became clear that the question was a flimsy excuse for the Belle to recount the details of her six-month cruise to the Far East in 1933, a cruise she had undertaken on doctor's orders, after her husband's tragic death.

It was obvious from the lacklustre nods and smiles around the table, and Lydia's expression of excruciating boredom, that Alma had entertained those present with tales of her travels on previous occasions. Emily was not the least bit interested in the cruise, being much keener to find out about the husband's tragic death, but the Belle was in full flight.

'I was,' Alma paused for effect, 'the favourite of the ship's captain.'

'And the belle of the ball,' Grandmother added, drawing a winning smile from the guest who seemed oblivious to

Grandmother's ironic tone. It was exactly how Florrie and Della had spoken those words, and Emily allowed herself a smile too.

As the six-month cruise was relived in intricate detail, she was relieved that Alma's focus shifted to Uncle Cec, who began to clear his throat nervously, tugging the end of his nose between thumb and forefinger.

With Uncle Cec the object of the Belle's attentions, Emily allowed her thoughts to drift. Every now and then she nodded, pretending to take an interest in the conversation. The year of the cruise, 1933, was so long ago. The Belle must have been thirty-five then, a calculation she was able to make because Alma had managed to weave into the conversation the fact that she was fifteen years younger than Grandmother, who was sixty. A thirty-five-year-old belle seemed indecent somehow. Lydia was twenty-two. The perfect age, and the perfect time to get married.

She found herself thinking about Lydia and Harry's engagement, and then, without really noticing it, her thoughts drifted on to Claudio and the last thing he'd said. *You will teaching me English*. He hadn't said it as a question, or a request, but as a statement of fact. But teaching Claudio would be impossible without Grandmother's permission, and she needed a plan of how to approach her, of the arguments to use. So far she had come up with nothing more compelling than that it was a good idea, which was not an argument at all but simply an assertion, and one that Grandmother would very likely quash with a counter assertion such as its being 'quite impossible'.

At the end of dessert Alma lit a cigarette at the table. Emily was still distracted with her own thoughts, but she noticed Eunice's look of outrage. She saw too the warning stare from

Grandmother that stopped Eunice from taking action. For once she felt herself to be on Eunice's side and imagined plucking the offending item from the fingers of the fading enchantress and plunging it into the cream jug. If only she were the sort of person who could dare do such a thing – like Lydia – and she glanced across at her aunt. Lydia, however, seemed to be as lost in thought as Emily herself had so recently been, and it was doubtful that she'd even noticed Alma's transgression.

Della began to clear away the dessert plates as the talk turned to the usual topic of the war. Emily let it flow over her, catching the occasional words.

'New Guinea ... damn Japs ... Hitler on the run.'

'And poor William?'

It was the Belle who had spoken and the room fell silent. Even Della stopped in the middle of removing Lydia's plate. All eyes turned to Grandmother.

'He is not poor William,' she said in a voice vibrating with suppressed emotion, giving Alma a look of such ferocious intensity that Emily felt it zap past like an arrow on its way to the bulls-eye.

For the first time that evening, the Belle's composure cracked. She opened and closed her mouth like a hooked trout, as if searching for something innocuous to say. 'And Harry?' she finally managed, turning to Lydia.

But her new enquiry was equally disastrous for, at the mention of Harry, Lydia rose abruptly from the table with a garbled excuse and hurried from the room. Emily recalled the tear that had rolled down Lydia's cheek as they'd made their way to the back of the swamp and felt an inner glow of satisfaction at being Lydia's confidante, forgetting that her aunt hadn't actually confided anything.

After Lydia's departure, Grandmother steered the conversation into safer waters, encouraging Alma to entertain them once again with anecdotes from her travels. The social crisis passed and even Eunice joined in the laughter, albeit in a somewhat forced manner, as the Belle regaled them with her exotic tales. When a final coffee had been drunk and the meal was over, Eunice announced that it was time for cards.

Uncle Cec looked alarmed and departed, mumbling something about 'bookwork'.

The Belle placed her plump hand on Emily's wrist, leaning towards her. 'What luck you're here,' she cooed. 'You can make up a four.'

Emily was almost certain she didn't want to play cards, and felt lightheaded from the sudden proximity of the Belle's Je Reviens perfume and the closeness of her generous, though somewhat crepey cleavage. But the matter was quickly settled when Grandmother decreed that it was a splendid idea.

15

A CARD TABLE WAS SET up in the sitting room, and Eunice fetched two packs of cards from the bottom drawer of the roll-top desk. They were going to play Solo, and each of the women had a small beaded purse filled with sixpences to be used as the stakes. Grandmother counted out a pile of coins for Emily as she had none of her own.

Once they sat down and were ready to play, Eunice assumed control. She shuffled the cards, snapping them briskly, and did not wait to take her lead from Grandmother. She was not the same person at all and radiated authority.

'No table talk except for Emily's instruction,' she announced, glaring at the Belle, who had not said a word. 'Now, Emily. *If I am of sense bereft, place the cards upon my left. If I'm not demented quite, place the cards upon my right.*'

It was a rhyme she had heard before, having occasionally made up the numbers with her parents and the Very Reverend on his Sunday evening visits. At Eunice's request, she repeated it aloud, and because it was so satisfying, went on chanting it silently to herself. By the time it was her turn to deal she had managed to reverse affirmative and negative, thus placing the second pack of cards on the wrong side.

'Surely it's simple enough,' Eunice snapped.

The Belle was more forgiving and whispered some words of encouragement in her ear.

The rounds of Solo proceeded in silence except for the necessary bidding and Eunice's regular instructions.

'Never lead an ace to a solo player unless you have the king, Emily. And how many times must I tell you to breast your cards.'

Murmuring *breast your cards* under her breath, she tried not to look at the Belle's capacious bosom, but the more she told herself not to, the harder it was to keep her eyes averted. Like a compass returning to true north, her gaze was forever finding its way back to the sight of the visitor's ample cleavage. It was more than a little distracting.

Despite the ban on table talk, Eunice allowed conversation during the time it took to shuffle and deal between each round, and the Belle was always keen to take advantage of the opportunity.

'I suppose you've heard?' she said, once Grandmother had played her final card and lost an ambitious solo bid.

Emily watched as the pink tip of Alma's tongue flicked over her lips and her large blue eyes darted around each of the card players, ensuring their undivided attention.

'Ruth caught one of her Italians spying.'

Grandmother frowned as she gathered up the cards and began to shuffle. 'Spying? Surely there's nothing of importance to the war at the McDougalls'?'

'Don't be silly, May. He was up on the roof peering through the skylight while she was in the bath. Lucky Orm was away or he'd have been shot.'

'Disgusting,' Eunice burst out. 'What a primitive lot they are.'

Emily wanted to disagree but before she could summon the courage to speak, Alma continued, revealing that Ruth's Italian had been sent back to the camp.

'Quite right,' Grandmother said. 'There's no room for leniency with such an unstable race.' A quick, almost guilty expression flickered across her grandmother's face, and Emily was sure that Grandmother was thinking about Claudio and the fight outside the Catholic church.

'Apparently in the south, blood feuds and murder are rife,' Alma went on in an excited, almost breathless way. 'The whole place is quite lawless.'

Emily felt the heat rising up her neck and knew she was turning blotchy and red. She had to speak. 'Italy is the birthplace of modern civilisation.' She was quoting Miss Falugi, the history teacher, whose name, it now occurred to her, sounded Italian. It was a surprising revelation, but she could not allow herself to be distracted.

'The British were just primitive tribes when the Romans conquered them.' Her words tumbled out, and she had the sense of them splaying across the card table.

'What rot!' Eunice managed a warning shot across the bows

but having already endured an hour of Eunice's instructions, she plunged on.

'It's true. Without the Romans we'd still be living in caves and painting our faces blue. We wouldn't even have toilets.' She wasn't sure of the accuracy of her last remark, but her feelings of outrage made her reckless.

Alma gave a half-suppressed laugh and looked at her with what could have been admiration. 'That's all very well, dear,' she said, 'but the modern Italian has proved himself to be a terrible coward.'

'What do you mean?'

'It took our boys in the Middle East no time at all to round up almost the entire Italian army. A sea of white towels before they'd fired a shot.'

'White towels?'

Alma gave a sarcastic laugh. 'Oh yes, their mothers sent them off well prepared to surrender.'

'I think that's rather overstating it.' Grandmother was shuffling the cards with an unnecessary intensity.

'No more table talk,' Eunice snapped. 'It's ruining the game. And for heaven's sake, May, you've shuffled the spots off those cards.'

After that, there was no more discussion of the Italians, with Eunice vigilantly policing the rule of silence. As the Belle's pile of coins grew smaller, Eunice began to make bolder bids.

'Misère,' she announced and won for the third time in a row.

Alma was down to her last few sixpences and sighed. 'May, dear, I think we need a little something to keep our spirits up now that Eunice has almost cleaned us out.'

Grandmother agreed and told Emily to get three sherry glasses and the decanter from the credenza.

Alma drank her sherry in a single gulp. 'Just a drop more, May dear,' she said.

Grandmother poured in a little more.

'A smidgen more,' the Belle pleaded and kept her glass extended until Grandmother had filled it to the brim.

On resumption, Alma's playing went rapidly downhill – she couldn't remember her discards and reneged twice in the same game.

'Sorry,' she giggled, but Eunice was not amused and emanated an air of icy disapproval.

Soon the Belle had no sixpences left and Eunice declared the game over. She swept her winnings from the table and into her beaded purse, which was so full she could no longer close it.

Emily took the opportunity to say goodnight and carried the sherry glasses into the kitchen. After she had washed and dried them, she returned them to the credenza in the sitting room before making her way to bed. Passing the half-open door of the pink room where, despite Eunice's views on the matter, the Belle had been accommodated for the night, she heard voices. There was something irresistible about eavesdropping, but she did not want to be caught in the act. She kneeled down and fiddled with the strap on her shoe.

'Lovely evening, May. Heavens, that granddaughter. What an odd little creature. Can you imagine: *without the Romans we'd still be living in caves*. And that ridiculous dress. Have you ever seen such a thing?'

The Belle's tinkling laughter reverberated inside of Emily as if she was a hollow tube. Crouched outside the door, she felt unable to move, her heart pounding as she waited for her grandmother to come to the rescue and defend her. But, to her horror, Grandmother laughed too.

'Sybil's choice, no doubt,' she said. 'Hopeless, I'm afraid.'

From the pink room came the sound of a floorboard creaking.

'I've put out a towel and there's extra in the linen room if you need it.'

The door was opening, and she was still there, frozen. It was too late.

'May, dear, just before you go,' she heard the Belle say. It released her from the paralysis that had taken hold and she shot forwards, down the hallway, around the corner and into the white room.

She yanked the 'ridiculous' dress off over her head and threw it on the floor. How could she survive Grandmother's mocking laughter? It was too awful. The dress was to blame and, pulling on the clothes she had worn earlier that day, she picked it up, scrunched it into a lumpy ball, and stepped out through the French doors.

It was impossible to see anything; the night, inky and impenetrable, impeded her. She moved one hesitant step at a time and, with her free hand waving in front of her to ward off spider webs, groped her way across the verandah and down onto the gravel path. She stopped, waiting for her eyes to adjust, and soon the inky blackness thinned and the shapes of trees and bushes emerged. Clutching her bundle, she hurried towards the orchard.

But having reached the orchard, she stopped again. Where was she going? The whole purpose was to get rid of the dress once and for all. She couldn't just toss it away in the orchard; Lydia was sure to find it on her snake patrol. A proper hiding place was needed where it could rot away to nothing.

A gust of wind ruffled her hair and stirred the leaves of nearby trees, making a sound like the murmuring of a distant crowd. She imagined the crowd moving towards her across the paddocks, invisible in the darkness. She shivered although she wasn't cold. The breeze came from the north and still carried the heat of the continent's interior.

She heard the generator go off and glanced back towards the house. It was in darkness except for a single spot of light, a faint glow from a lamp, although she couldn't tell quite where or whose room it was. She turned away and, still without a clear plan, began to hurry through the orchard in the general direction of the yard. She entered at the opposite end to William's workshop and the stables, near the open-sided shed where all the things that had been discarded and were of no use anymore came to rest. The perfect place for the dress. She had only to find a nook or cranny in which to stuff the wretched thing where it would not be found. As she got closer, she could make out the shape of the wicker wheelchair perched on top of the cart. Who would ever think of looking under the side-saddle?

Just as she was heading towards the chair, something moved at the edge of her vision. She stopped mid-step and held her breath, listening, peering across the yard towards the workshop, all her senses alert. Had she imagined it? The clouds that earlier had made the night so black were scattering, revealing a starry sky. Her eyes flicked around the yard, searching for a sign of movement. Her ears strained to hear the slightest noise. A dog?

A fox? She tried not to think about the wild-looking swaggie that Della had said Roy had seen on the road.

Minutes ticked by and everything was quiet. She began to think that it was just her imagination, and tried to shrug in a nonchalant way, hoping it would make her feel more confident. But her body felt as stiff as a tin soldier. Still holding the bunched-up dress, she rolled her head back, in an effort to release the tension. Splashed across the now-cloudless vault was the Milky Way's pale, hazy luminescence. She gazed up at the immense starry-ness.

Something banged, bringing her back to earth. She scurried to safety under the shed roof. From there, her eyes surveyed the yard once more. Someone was near the workshop door. Was it – could it be – the swaggie? She began to edge further into the junk-filled shed until her heel hit an unseen obstacle. She lost her balance and fell onto the dusty ground. Her heart was pounding, and the sound of blood whooshed in her ears along with Della's words *they'll cut your throat for five bob*. If only she could get up and run, but fear held her captive, and for interminable seconds the two urges battled for supremacy until she could stand it no longer. She scrambled to her feet as an airy peal of laughter echoed across the yard, and a figure emerged from the background of the workshop, hurrying away towards the garden gate.

Even in the darkness Emily recognised her. The shape of the figure and the way that she moved left no doubt: it was Lydia. She felt her body unclench and all thoughts of the swaggie were swept away as she watched Lydia reach the gate. Once she was out of sight, the significance of the peal of laughter struck home.

Who was with her? Who had made Lydia laugh? Where had he gone? As soon as she'd asked herself the last question, and the *he* had registered in her mind, she found herself running across the yard. She had barely touched the doorknob when the blue door creaked open. It had not been properly shut.

'Hello?' she whispered. And then louder: 'Is anyone there?' She waited in the black of the workshop, but no answer came.

Sneaking back along the south verandah, Emily reached Lydia's window, where the blind was drawn. She stopped and listened, but all was quiet. On entering the white room, she made a surprising discovery: in her right hand she was still clutching the dress. Or was it the dress, limpet-like, that was refusing to let her go? It was an inanimate object, she knew that, but she couldn't stop the feeling that it possessed a will of its own, and instead of throwing it in a corner of the room or under the bed, she hung it carefully in the wardrobe.

She undressed in the dark and slipped into bed, lying on her back with her eyes open. Sleep evaded her as she replayed the sight of Lydia hurrying away from the workshop. What had she been doing there? Was it Claudio ...? Were they ...? Somehow the questions remained unfinished. After all, she had not actually seen Claudio. And, in any case, Lydia was in love with Harry; she was engaged to be married. Hadn't she seen with her own eyes the tears rolling down Lydia's cheeks at his mention? The reality of the single tear was insufficient for her purposes and had to be replaced with something more dramatic: tears plural, welling, brimming, overflowing. The more she thought about it, the clearer it became. Lydia had been alone at the stables; she had gone down to check on something. What that might be was still unclear and, if Emily hadn't been so exhausted, she might have worked it out. As it was, tiredness came to her rescue and she fell into a deep sleep.

Eastern Regional Libraries
Croydon Library
ph: 9800 6448

Customer name: **TILLEY, CLARE**
Customer ID: ************3912**

Items that you have checked out

Title:
 The unexpected education of Emily
 Dean
ID: 11957545
Due: 24/10/2019

Total items: 1
3/10/2019
Checked out: 1

Thank you for using your library

16

DAWN WAS BREAKING AS EMILY woke to the rattle and screech of sash windows being lifted somewhere in the house. Grandmother and Eunice were letting in the cool morning air before another day of heat. It wasn't long before her bedroom door opened. She watched her grandmother in bare feet and nightgown draw back the curtains and open the French doors, remembering her and Alma's discussion from the night before. Instead of hurt outrage, she felt a rather sickening sense that she'd overreacted. Thank goodness her attempt to hide the hated dress had failed, for the thought of someone discovering it was almost worse than the memory of what she'd overheard. Nevertheless, she closed her eyes as Grandmother turned: the treacherous words about her mother could not be easily erased.

'It's going to be a scorcher,' Grandmother said as she padded from the room.

There was no point trying to go back to sleep. Too many thoughts were crowding in, not just of the eavesdropped conversation, but also of Lydia and her laughter. People laugh on their own all the time, she told herself sternly.

Once dressed, and having checked the chooks, she found Della in the kitchen knocking freshly baked bread from a tin. Now that the baking was over they could let the stove go out.

'Or we'll be cooked too,' Della said.

Everything had to be done early before the heat really set in. Florrie had milked the cow and was still down at the dairy, turning the separator. Lydia, Uncle Cec and Roy had ridden off at dawn to check the water troughs and shift sheep. By midmorning, the sheep would go on strike, refusing to move in the heat.

The Belle had to get moving too. She needed to be home before the mercury soared and boiled the water in the radiator of her old Bentley. Grandmother, Eunice and Emily waved goodbye from the front verandah as the Bentley set off around the circular drive.

Grandmother waved the longest. 'What a tonic! We really should invite Alma more often,' she said, still waving as the Bentley motored from view.

Eunice looked less than enthused, and Emily felt a spark of fellow feeling that was quickly snuffed out when Eunice told her to go and water the hydrangeas in the long bed. 'And once that's done, the verandahs need to be swept,' she added before Emily had even had time to move.

The last hydrangea was watered and, thoroughly sick of the job, she made a feeble effort to coil up the hose and place it near the tank, knowing that on Eunice's inspection it would not pass muster. She knew that Eunice derived a special satisfaction from putting her to work; she'd noticed the barely disguised pleasure on her face. It was just as Della had said: there was a pecking order, and Eunice was on a higher rung.

It was terribly unfair, and to maintain her feelings of resentment she tried to block out the weekly wash-day sight of Florrie dragging heavy sheets from the copper, her beet-red face running with sweat. But Florrie was a servant – it was her job. Whereas she was a guest, and would never, for example, be asked to remove a rotting possum from one of the water tanks, nor a swarm of bees from the sitting-room chimney. Nor would anyone demand that she black the stove or polish the mountain of silver, set out on the men's dining table each week. The list of unpleasant jobs began to grow. She had to think about something else before the examples completely undermined her righteous indignation.

And, anyway, the verandahs were still to be swept, for which she needed the straw broom that was kept in a tall cupboard next to the laundry. Rather than go the direct route, which would have taken no more than a minute, she decided to walk the other way, thereby delaying the start of the job. She anticipated her time-wasting journey: there were ten verandahs, all of differing lengths. A few were simply empty spaces, while others were cluttered with benches and old wooden tables covered with pumpkins and onions from the kitchen garden. On the north-east corner of the house was a summer sleep-out, while wicker tables and chairs and the striped canvas swinging seat made the front verandah into a north-facing outdoor sitting room. In contrast, Uncle Cec's office verandah was dark and gloomy, enclosed by a tangle of evergreen creeper.

She began her circumnavigation by heading east. At the corner, she turned left. Red geraniums grew along the edge of this verandah, giving it a cheerful air. Ahead of her, a squatter's chair with long timber arms sat outside the billiard room door. She had almost reached it when the door opened and Grandmother stepped out.

'Just the person I was hoping to see,' Grandmother said with a smile. Emily smiled back distractedly, expecting Eunice to appear. 'Claudio's been to see me. I must say it's an excellent idea.'

'What?' She had heard the words, but their meaning eluded her.

'How many times must I repeat myself?,' Grandmother said sternly. 'And for goodness sake, don't stand there with your mouth open, catching flies. You look like a simpleton. As I was about to say: the English language can't fail to have a beneficial effect on him.'

Emily shut her mouth, scarcely able to believe what she was hearing.

'It's the language of Western civilisation, after all.'

The words 'ancient Greek' were on the tip of her tongue, but she forced herself to say nothing and listened in growing amazement to Grandmother's plan. The lessons were to take place in the courtyard at the men's outdoor summer dining table. With the war on and a skeleton workforce, it was under-used.

Of course, they would have to fit in with work requirements, and Uncle Cec would need to give the go-ahead. But when the working day was over, she and Claudio were free to meet.

Now that Grandmother had agreed to the lessons, the question of what and how to teach Claudio became pressing. Madame Dubois often read aloud to the class from famous French children's books like *Patapoufs et Filifers* by André Maurois. She made the class take dictation. Writing down the words of a great author like Maurois allowed them – *mes poulettes*, as she called the girls – to imbibe the true flavour of French culture, and the essence of the French people.

It was an inspired idea, but Emily was at a loss as to what could reveal the culture and essence of the Australian people. Most of the books she knew were not by Australian writers, nor were they about Australia. She tried to think of the books she'd read as a child and remembered *The Magic Pudding* by Norman Lindsay. But then she recalled Uncle Cec quoting Albert. *Eat away, chew away, munch and bolt and guzzle. Never leave the table till you're full up to the muzzle.* How could she ever explain the language to Claudio, or make sense of the story of Albert, the eponymous pudding, and the assorted koalas, possums, bandicoots and penguins who were trying to kidnap and eat him? Perhaps the solution lay in William's library.

The next afternoon, she sat down at the men's dining table. Claudio took a chair and sat opposite her. On the table in front of him, he put a black notebook, a stub of pencil and a small, well-thumbed Italian–English dictionary. He looked at her, waiting for a sign to begin. She cleared her throat, feeling nervous and, in imitation of Madame Dubois, announced that the first lesson would be comprehension.

'*Comprensione*,' Claudio said, nodding.

'A story by a famous Australian author.'

He nodded again. She was pleased that he was taking the lesson as seriously as she was. It gave her some confidence.

'"The Drover's Wife" by Henry Lawson.'

'The driver wife,' Claudio repeated.

'Drover,' she corrected, trying to think of how to explain it. 'Like Roy. Someone who rides along with the sheep or cattle, moving them from one place to another.'

'*Un pastore*? Is with the sheep. Keep them safe.'

Feeling that it was important to get the lesson underway, she agreed that a drover was probably *un pastore*. She began to read in a shaky voice. After a few sentences her nerves abated and her voice became stronger. Claudio listened intently, his eyes never leaving her face. She had decided to read a page and then stop for questions to make sure he understood, and was looking forwards to playing the part of the teacher, instructing him on meanings and pronunciation and the foibles of the English language. She was particularly keen to say 'foibles' to him. It was a favourite. She had already written down some words in the exercise book Grandmother had found for her, along with their meanings; words like *squatter*, *urchin* and *swagman*. Grammar would have to be explained too, and the way the mother and children spoke, for it was not proper English and she didn't want Claudio to learn the wrong way to say things. She wanted him to speak the King's English.

But when she stopped at the end of the first page, he urged her on. How could she stop now when the snake had gone under the house and was bound to come up through the cracks in the floor and bite one of the *bambini*? She had to read on. She worried that a real teacher like Madame Dubois would have insisted on sticking with her lesson plan, but in the face of his desire she gave in and continued.

She read slowly, hoping that he could follow, for there were many words that she was sure he would not know. Here and there she skipped a few lines and even a paragraph where she felt the story got side-tracked and Claudio began to fidget. It was the snake that held them in suspense.

Of course she had read the story in preparation for the lesson but reading it aloud to him, the harshness of the woman's life and her terrible loneliness became so real that she felt it as her own and there were moments where tears blurred the words. She reached the last few lines and her voice grew husky. '*Mother, I won't never go drovin'; blarst me if I do!*'

She spoke the words of the eldest boy as if they were her own. And then the last line, where the mother hugged the boy to her worn-out breast and the sickly daylight broke over the bush. With her head still bowed over the book, she quickly wiped her eyes, erasing the evidence of her unprofessional behaviour.

Taking in a breath, she looked up to see Della and Florrie standing at the end of the table. How long had they been there?

She could not remember hearing the squeak of the kitchen flywire door, nor had she registered the crunch of footsteps on gravel. Della was holding a wooden spoon as if she'd been in the middle of stirring something, and Emily noticed that Florrie's eyes and the tip of her nose were red.

Della nodded a wordless thank you, before touching Florrie on the arm and, with a movement of her head, indicating the kitchen. They retreated inside, leaving Emily and Claudio sitting opposite each other.

She fiddled with the book, closing and straightening it, but it was not enough to quell the awkwardness she felt. The protective shield of her teacher-self shrivelled like an insect wing against the glass of the kero lamp.

'*Brava*, Emilia. Was beautiful. Sad, her life.' Claudio's face was lit up. 'She got him, chop up. Like Lydia, she kill him. Very good story, Emilia.'

Claudio's praise was for the story, but it did not stop her from feeling that she had achieved something too. It buoyed her up and helped her recover momentum, for it was important not to rest on her laurels – the real teaching was yet to begin. Words had to be written down and explained, pronunciation corrected and the rules of grammar applied. Claudio threw himself into it with gusto, and she soon had to go in search of a new pencil for him.

17

LIFE AT MOUNT PROSPECT CONTINUED to follow its usual pattern, which for Emily included her furtive morning visits to William's workshop during the time that Eunice was absorbed in her piano practice. Now there was a new addition: by late afternoon she and Claudio were often to be found at the outdoor dining table, working their way through Henry Lawson's short stories. Sometimes they abandoned formal lessons, moving to the kitchen garden instead, where Claudio had taken over from Old Stan, the one who had retired because of his rheumatism.

Della was pleased to have him tending the vegetables, and Emily had heard her tell Florrie, 'Mussolini's got a real green thumb.'

When together in the kitchen garden they practised conversation. Claudio's English had improved already under her tutelage. Sometimes Emily tried out her Italian too, for he had taught her some words and phrases. *Il mio nome è Emilia. Oggi il cielo è blu.*

The Italian words thrilled her with their extravagant and sensual sounds, and it was exciting to speak to him in a language that nobody else knew, even if she was only commenting on the weather or introducing herself. Once he even sang a nursery rhyme to her from his childhood. It began *trotta, trotta, bimbalotta.* The rhythm of the words made them easy to remember.

'From my *nonna*. Is not proper Italian,' he told her. 'Is *dialetto*.' But it had made him sad, and he did not repeat it.

Today Claudio was staking the tomatoes as she weeded nearby, working along a row of beans. He wore a white singlet and a pair of baggy khaki shorts. In spite of the army's rules, he no longer wore the magenta-dyed uniform, and not even Eunice seemed inclined to make an issue of it.

From beneath the brim of her straw hat, Emily cast furtive glances in his direction. His arms and shoulders were the colour of burnished copper, a description she couldn't wait to include in her still-unfinished letter to Dorothy. She poked the weeding fork into the soil at random. The white singlet and baggy khaki shorts would need to be replaced by something more distinguished. He had moved a little way ahead, and she watched a bead of sweat form at the base of his neck, in the hollow just below the edge of his black curls. She felt it burst, salty, on the tip of her tongue, and swallowed hard. The drop of sweat rolled down his spine and sank into the cotton singlet.

Claudio hammered in another stake with the wooden mallet then sat back on his heels. He turned to her, lifting the front of his singlet to wipe the sweat from his face, and she glimpsed his strong pale belly, which made her thrust the weeding fork deep into the ground. She twisted it, pulling out the mallow weed with clods of dark soil still clinging to its roots.

'What did you do before the war?' she asked.

'Ah, before the war. Eat, drink vino, sing.' He grinned. 'You?'

She would not be put off. 'I'm serious, Claudio.'

'I am going to study. Engineer.' He saw the look of surprise that she quickly tried to mask. 'You don't believe?'

'No, I mean yes, of course I believe you.' She felt caught out with all her secret prejudices – the ones she did not believe she had. She was not like Grandmother and Eunice. 'Did you study?'

Claudio shook his head. 'No. War come and I am *conscritto*.' He frowned, searching for the English word.

'Called up?'

'Yes. Not free, you understand. We must fight. Both of us.'

'Both of us?'

Claudio slipped a hand into the side pocket of his trousers. He took out his little notebook and, from between the pages, produced two worn black-and-white photographs. She rose as he handed her one of the photographs. Two young men dressed in Italian army uniforms stood stiffly side by side, their expressions serious. One, she recognised, was Claudio. He put his finger on the image of the young man beside him.

'Umberto,' he said in a husky voice. 'Dead in Libya. *Era gentile, mio bel fratello*. He is only twenty.'

She knew *fratello* meant brother – he had taught her all the family words. She wanted to say that she was sorry but the phrase remained lodged in her throat. He handed her the second photograph. A family portrait of mother, father, the two soldier sons and two girls stared back at her.

'Mama and Papa.' He pointed to the older girl. 'Regina. Gone.'

She glanced at him. Did he mean that she was gone forever, that she had died, or that she had gone somewhere else? Again she wanted to speak, and again the words would not come.

He touched the face of the younger girl. 'Milena. Fourteen now.'

They stared at the photographs together.

'What will you do when it's over? The war, I mean.'

Claudio looked at her and she could not read his expression. 'I will go home.'

He took the photographs from her almost roughly and put them back in the notebook.

'Free man again.'

He walked across to the waterbag hanging on a branch of the nearby apple tree. She watched him lift the bag and pour water into his mouth without touching the spout. Some of the water splashed over his face and down his chest. She was thirsty too, but it was impossible to cross the few yards that separated them. All she could hear were the words *free man again*. He did not want to be here: his life was elsewhere and this was a prison even if there were no bars or chains.

Having drunk his fill, Claudio hung the waterbag back on the tree. He returned to the tomatoes and picked up the mallet. She watched him move away down the row, feeling the gulf between them – and something else too. Guilt, for she knew she wanted him to stay here, she wanted him to remain a prisoner. She sank down and poked her fork into the ground beside a clump of weeds.

'Emily?'

She turned to see Lydia, dressed in jodphurs and riding boots, a stockwhip looped over her shoulder. How long had Lydia been standing there? What had she seen? There was nothing to see. Nothing.

'Be careful.' Her aunt's eyes sought hers and would not let go.

'About what?' She could not look away, although she wanted to more than anything.

With a motion of her head Lydia indicated the weeds next to the fork. 'Nettles,' she said. 'You need gloves or they'll sting like mad.' And with that, she adjusted the coiled stockwhip firmly onto her shoulder and walked off towards the yard.

18

THE NEXT MORNING, AS EMILY dragged a hose along the verandah, she found herself thinking of Lydia's warning about the nettles. She knew it was really about staying away from Claudio, and there could only be one reason why: Lydia wanted Claudio for herself. It was an unwelcome thought, and with it came equally unwelcome memories such as Lydia tending to Claudio's bloody nose, and the night she'd heard her laughing by the stables. The more she thought about that night, the more she was sure Lydia hadn't been alone.

She reached the end of the verandah and poked the hose under the first hydrangea. One more job on Eunice's list, and in this hot weather the wretched things had to be watered every morning. 'Ten minutes on each,' Eunice had instructed her. She walked across to the water tank and turned on the tap, adjusting the pressure to a gentle flow, so that the water soaked into the soil and did not run off onto the gravel pathway. It was going to take two hours, enough time to read some chapters of *Middlemarch*, which, ever since beginning the lessons with Claudio, had been neglected. With the hose drizzling on the hydrangea, she sat on the windowsill outside Lydia's bedroom, next to the flyscreen that was propped against the wall. Lydia had taken it off so that she could throw her cigarette butts into the garden bed, something that infuriated both Grandmother and Eunice, who were forever complaining about picking the filthy things up.

She opened *Middlemarch* at the place she'd last reached to discover that Dorothea and Casaubon had arrived in Rome on their wedding journey. It seemed that her morning was destined to involve Italy and Italians, and she wondered if Claudio had ever visited Rome. She would have to ask him.

As she read on with growing interest, her left hand strayed to her chest. It had become a constant worry – had they grown even bigger? If only she did not feel so naked in her light summer blouses. They were not tight-fitting in the way of the church dress, but even so, her need for a bra was becoming ever more urgent.

Her mind drifted from the page, and she began to think about whether there was a haberdashery shop in the main street of Garnook and, if so, whether it sold bras. There was a baker and a butcher, a bank and a general store that sold all kinds of goods, possibly even women's underwear. But how could she get there without asking someone to take her? Which also meant explaining why she wanted to go. No, it was impossible.

Putting the book down, she went to move the hose. On her return, she sat on the sill again. Without the flyscreen, all she had to do was open the window and swing her legs around, and she would be inside Lydia's room in a flash. And in Lydia's chest of drawers, there would be bras to spare. Nothing could be simpler.

Lydia, however, had made it clear that she considered her bedroom to be sacrosanct and, without her permission, entry was forbidden. The invitation of the first evening had never been repeated, despite Emily lingering in the hall outside the door, hoping to be invited in. The ban on entry extended to everyone in the household, which meant there could be no dusting, cleaning or putting away of clean clothes unless Lydia chose to do it herself, which she didn't, a fact ascertained by the most cursory glance through her bedroom window. It was apparent to Emily that even Grandmother was powerless to enforce the normal rules.

With *Middlemarch* once more forgotten, she walked up and down the verandah, wrestling with temptation and her conscience, while waiting for the obligatory ten minutes to pass before moving the hose to the next hydrangea. Supposing she could overcome her moral scruples, there was still the matter of whether she had the gumption to act. Her mother had told her more than once that gumption was of vital importance and a person lacking in it was not worth very much at all. She feared that she was exactly that person, and wondered, not for the first time, how her mother failed to see this.

She paced the verandah, feeling obsessed by the growing pile of bras in Lydia's chest of drawers. Why not simply ask if she could borrow one? It was the logical thing to do. And yet ... and yet. To ask meant exposing her need and the risk of rejection. Worse still was the thought of Lydia's piercing gaze and the possibility that she might have to undress in front of her. Something more was at stake too, although it remained murky and half thought, relating to secrets, no matter how innocent.

But if she wasn't going to ask Lydia directly, she had to face the reality that entering the bedroom uninvited was risky. If Lydia found out, she would be merciless. Yet the window had begun to exert a magnetic force, so that with each turn along the verandah, she found herself moving ever closer, her footsteps slowing and her eyes darting towards the forbidden territory.

For the watering of three hydrangeas she continued to wrestle with herself. Then, after placing the drizzling hose carefully at the base of the fourth shrub, she gazed around, taking in the sweep of lawn and the orchard beyond. Crimson rosellas squabbled noisily in the pear tree. A pair of magpies carolled on the lawn, and a chirping flurry of sparrows flew in and out of the sprawling grey-leafed bush beside the water tank. Bird and animal life abounded, but she was in luck: there was neither sight nor sound of a human being.

Just as she had imagined, the window slid up easily, and she was quickly inside the room. She pressed herself against the wall, waiting for her eyes to adjust to the dim light and her heart to stop pounding, when something fluttered on the edge of her vision. Someone was emerging from the wardrobe. Lydia! Her legs gave way unexpectedly and she slid to the floor like a ragdoll. Escape was impossible. Better to remain huddled on the floor and hope against hope for mercy. She closed her eyes and waited for the furious assault.

Seconds ticked by and nothing happened. What was Lydia doing inside the wardrobe anyway? She squinted across the room – she was still there! And then a snort of laughter burst from her as she recognised her own reflection in the wardrobe mirror.

The room was as messy as it had been on that first night, when Lydia had invited her in. The bed was unmade and blankets trailed onto the floor where a pillow also lay. She reached out and picked up the pillow, holding it to her face, breathing in the lingering trace of Lydia's particular smell. The shock of seeing Lydia, even though it had turned out to be an illusion, continued to reverberate through her body. The soft feel of the linen pillowcase, and the faint-yet-pungent scent trapped in its weave, helped to calm here. After a bit she got up and lay down on the bed to recover more fully. A few minutes was all she needed.

She let her body sink into the mattress and found herself staring at the framed photograph of Harry on the bedside table – the one she'd been unable to absorb due to the shock of Lydia's nudity. She saw now that Harry was leaning against the side of a car in his army uniform. In the background was the orchard, and she wondered if Lydia had taken the photograph. The sleeves of his shirt were rolled up, and his bare forearms were folded across his chest. The creases in his pants were crisp, and his slouch hat looked brand-new.

She rolled over and picked it up. Harry's face was in shadow, but she could just make out a wispy moustache and the shape of his mouth, a shy half-smile on his lips. What would it be like to kiss that mouth? She closed her eyes, concentrating on the imagined sensation of his lips against hers. It was something of a failure; she couldn't feel anything.

'Where on earth has she gone? There's water all down the path.'

At the sound of Grandmother's voice, her eyes sprang open.

She popped up like a jack-in-a-box and slid off the bed away from the window, dropping the photograph of Harry onto the floorboards beside her with a clatter. Irritated footsteps clicked past on the verandah, followed by the sound of the hose scraping along as it was dragged to a new position.

'Really, Lydia is the end. Leaving the window open like that. The house will be filled with flies.'

A second set of footsteps approached the window. She froze.

'Typical. No thought for others,' added Eunice as she pulled down the window with a bang.

Resting against the side of the bed, Emily waited until Eunice's footsteps retreated. She reached over and picked up Harry's photograph and, with fumbling fingers, returned it to its place on the bedside table. Halfway to the door, the awareness of what she'd seen caught up with her, and she turned back hoping she was mistaken. A single glance was enough to dash her hopes. The glass had split in two and, though it was held in place by the frame, the crack line was all too visible.

Her heart skipped a beat and her thoughts tumbled over each other: *Hide it. No, leave it, deny everything. Just go. No-one knows.*

She reached the door and opened it a sliver, peering out into the hallway. It was empty, and she darted through, pulling the door shut behind her before sidling along the passage to the white room where she collapsed on the bed.

Barely a second had passed before there was a sharp tap on the glass of the French doors. She looked up to see Grandmother and Eunice staring in. It seemed there was to be no respite. She had to finish the job and, with Eunice chivvying her along, she returned to the watering.

The hose was on the last hydrangea when she saw Lydia, Uncle Cec and Roy riding across the paddock towards the house. The knot in her stomach tightened like a fist. An image came to her of Della holding a chook upside down by its feet; on the chopping block – a stump blackened with the blood from previous beheadings – lay an axe. The chook had accepted its fate and was already limp. There was no point flapping and squawking; it was all over.

She glanced across at Lydia's window and briefly considered the possibility of re-entering the bedroom and stealing the photograph. But the window, which earlier had exerted such a magnetic attraction, now repelled her with equal force. There was nothing to be done except to confess. Yes, that was it.

She would go and confess and that way it would be over or, if not over, at least it would have begun. Oddly enough, with this recognition, calm descended and the knot in her stomach dissolved.

She wound up the hose and left it beside the tank before returning to the white room to wait. She knew that, after a long morning shifting sheep, Lydia would want to change out of her jodhpurs. With the door to the white room open, and Lydia's room just down the hall, she was sure to hear her aunt arrive.

On registering the click of Lydia's door, she began to count and when she reached a hundred – enough time for Lydia to have changed clothes – she left the room. Standing in the passage outside her aunt's closed bedroom door, her feeling of calm began to give way to panic, but she forced herself to knock. She took a step back and waited, but nothing happened. The door did not fly open. Lydia did not call out: 'Who's there?' or 'Go away.'

She knocked again, and again there was no response. Perhaps there was a chance to avoid the confrontation after all. A chance to take the photograph and hide it, leaving its disappearance as an unsolved mystery. Her fingers closed over the wooden doorknob and twisted. With a push, the door opened and she stepped into the room. Too late she saw Lydia lying on the bed.

Worse still, she was holding Harry's photograph on her chest.

'He's going to die.' Lydia spoke in a small flat voice.

It was not what she expected to hear. She moved towards the bed. 'Who?'

Lydia sat up and thrust the photograph at her. Still discombobulated by the mention of death, Emily found herself staring once again at the cracked glass across Harry's face.

'It's –' she began, but before she could form the next two words, Lydia said them first.

'My fault.'

'Your fault?'

'He's going to die, in fact I'm sure he's dead already, and it's all my fault.' Lydia put her hands to her face and began to sob.

Emily stood by the bed holding Harry's photograph, watching her weep. Intermingled with shock and confusion at Lydia's claims was a growing sense of relief that her confession might no longer be necessary.

In her fantasies she had sometimes imagined scenarios such as this where Lydia came to her for comfort and advice. However, she was never able to bring the details of these occasions to mind – could not envisage what her aunt came to her about, or what advice she gave. Even though she tried hard to give life to their exchanges, the specifics simply never came. Now she seemed to be in a real-life version.

She placed the photograph of Harry back on the bedside table and, with some trepidation, sat down on the bed. She thought about putting her arm around Lydia's shoulders, but that would have required some awkward manoeuvring. Instead she rested a sympathetic hand on Lydia's leg and waited.

After a bit, a muffled voice spoke from behind a screen of hair and hands, 'Handkerchief. Dressing table, top right-hand drawer.'

She slid off the bed and shot across the room, removed a handkerchief from the drawer and returned to her position. Lydia took it and blew her nose.

Curiosity had overtaken her initial shock, and her responsibility for the broken glass seemed irrelevant now; nothing compared to Lydia's claims that she had caused Harry's death. How could she get her aunt to speak?

'I'm sure he's not –'

'How would you know?' Lydia cried. 'Look at it', and she waved towards the cracked photograph.

'But –'

'Don't you understand? It's a sign. I don't love him – I never have – and I'm responsible for his death.'

She waited but Lydia said nothing more, staring at her in desperate sort of way. Exactly how the cracked photograph was linked to Harry's imminent or actual death was confusing, but Emily instinctively understood that a lack of love could be deadly. Even so, she wanted to reassure Lydia and tell her she was wrong and that she was not to blame, and anyway, Harry was most probably alive, in fact he was sure to be alive, and even if he were dead, which he wasn't, it wasn't her fault. But the consoling words refused to be spoken.

Just as she was wondering what to do next, Lydia suddenly leaned in and, despite the awkward angle, wrapped her arms tightly around her. It was over in an instant and, before she had time to reciprocate the hug, Lydia pushed her away and hopped off the bed. 'Breathe a word and I'll kill you.'

The next thing Emily knew, she was standing outside the bedroom door, her head spinning. She stepped back and, stumbling somewhat, hurried along the passage, not stopping until she reached the kitchen, where she poured herself a glass of water and sat down at the table. She needed to think about what had happened, about Lydia's confession. About her causing Harry's death. It was mad, she knew it was, and she laughed uneasily.

'What's so funny?' Della emerged from the pantry carrying two large jars of bottled peaches.

Emily wished she could tell Della. But it was impossible. She jumped up from the table.

'I can't tell you, otherwise I'll be killed.' She laughed again, not knowing what else to do, and ran from the kitchen leaving Della with a puzzled frown.

By midday the thermometer on the front verandah had tipped ninety-five degrees. Uncle Cec predicted it would reach a hundred and ten by late afternoon. He was anticipating a record. For the last forty years he'd kept a daily log of the weather, including temperature minimums and maximums, wind direction, rainfall and other climatic conditions such as fog, hail and frost. There was nothing to be gained from a heatwave – stock and pasture suffered – but Emily could see by the glint in his eye that he was nevertheless hoping for a record, as if it were a personal achievement and something to be proud of.

Nobody had much appetite for lunch. It was too hot to eat, and they sat in desultory fashion around the dining-room table, picking at salad leaves and thick slices of cold mutton. A couple of times she glanced at Lydia, hoping to catch her eye, but Lydia did not respond; in fact she did not speak at all except to ask to be excused before Della brought in the teapot.

19

THAT AFTERNOON, WITH THE HEATWAVE still in full swing, Emily was excused further chores and had the freedom to escape to William's workshop. Once there she sat at his desk and opened the top left-hand drawer of the desk, took out the unfinished letter to Dorothy and read over the last few pages describing the fight between Claudio and Vincenzo and her courageous intervention. She imagined an envious Dorothy reading it, and had to give herself a severe reminder that pride cometh before a fall.

She filled William's fountain pen with ink and leaned back in the chair. What else to write? The question of Claudio's political views still troubled her, but it felt risky to put such things on paper, although imagining the look of horror on Dorothy's face made it tempting. Then there was the fresh herbal sort of smell he had, and the way the bead of sweat had rolled down the little hollow at the back of his neck when they had been working in the kitchen garden. But, no, she couldn't write about the bead of sweat. It was a secret.

She closed her eyes and let her mind drift. Not that it really drifted: it was more like a limpet that had latched onto a rock. The rock of Claudio. She opened her eyes and sat up straight. She really ought to try to give Dorothy a more rounded picture of her visit. She couldn't just write about Claudio. But her enthusiasm for such a task waned immediately, and she put the letter away in the desk drawer. It could wait.

Since discovering William's library she'd been devouring books like a glutton at a banquet. This morning, however, she'd made a promise not to begin anything new until the last page of George Eliot's masterpiece was turned. Reading willy-nilly, and without regard to whether the books chosen were really classics of English literature, she would never reach the goal she'd set for herself. For example, she had not been able to put down *The Count of Monte Cristo* but, from the point of view of her mission, reading a French novel was time wasted. Yet defining the category was also tricky. Was *The Call of the Wild*, for example, a classic of English literature? She suspected that it was not and that she had lost yet more valuable time when she should have been reading Shakespeare.

William's hefty *The Complete Works of William Shakespeare* had done nothing to inspire confidence. She'd tried to make a start on the plays last year without success and hoped that in the not-too-distant future she would discover a passion for them, for without Shakespeare she could hardly claim to have read the classics.

Her father was fond of quoting the Bard (as he called him). Her mother too, although it was always the same line: *How sharper than a serpent's tooth it is to have a thankless child.* Sometimes she said it as a joke, but not always.

Would she really need to read all of Shakespeare's plays? And what about the sonnets? A representative sampling was surely acceptable. It was the same with Dickens. Otherwise there was just too much. It struck her that so far she had approached the task in a haphazard way and that she really ought to make a proper list in alphabetical order. To avoid beginning such a burdensome task, she left the writing desk and walked across the room to William's library, having decided that it would be useful preparation to peruse the bookshelves first. Reading the titles, she assured herself, was not the same thing as reading the book itself.

As she shuffled along, absorbing titles, still hoping that she might come across *Jane Eyre*, her foot bumped something. She looked down to see a book on the ground, surprised not to have noticed it there before. Perhaps a mouse running along the shelf had dislodged it, as the books were all piled up at random, and it was possible that this one had been balancing precariously for some time. She picked it up, glancing at the title and fully intending to shove it back on the shelf.

Fanny Hill or Memoirs of a Woman of Pleasure. The words *woman of pleasure* held an immediate attraction. But the title did not announce itself as a classic and, anyway, she had to honour her promise. On the other hand, there was no harm in simply flicking through a few pages. Allowing herself this slight relaxation of the rules, she read on the inside cover that the author, John Cleland, was born in 1710, a fact that seemed to elevate the book's status. Surely any novel written that long ago and still read by people today had to be considered a classic? It was a slippery slope and she knew it. But knowing was not the same as being able to stop herself from acting. It would not hurt to at least discover what the term *woman of pleasure* meant. It was her duty, in the name of education.

She curled up in the big leather armchair and began to read. The first sentence went on for more than the length of a normal paragraph, and she had decided to abandon it when her father's voice, admonishing her to *try, try and try again*, intervened and kept her going. In the first dozen pages, the eponymous heroine, Fanny, set out for London to seek her fortune after the death of her parents. Once she arrived in the city, she was 'rescued' from wandering the capital's streets by a kindly older woman. At her new lodgings Fanny retired for the night with a certain Phoebe.

Emily had begun to skim over the text, still unsure whether she could really be bothered reading on, when Phoebe began to caress Fanny with, as the author put it, *lascivious touches*. All of a sudden, Dorothy's words popped into her mind. *She's just an old lesbian. She* was Miss Maunder, the headmistress, whom Emily was rather in awe of. She had never heard the word *lesbian* before and, looking it up in the dictionary later, she'd felt quite shocked. Now, to her amazement, simply by reading about Phoebe's caresses, she began to experience the lascivious touches as if they were happening to her and, exactly like Fanny, she found herself *transported, confused* and *out of herself*. Pleasure was engulfing her whole body, reaching such a pitch of intensity that she heard herself moan. There was nothing she could do to stop it.

Emily returned to her senses, lying in the armchair, staring up at the workshop roof. It was like looking at the night sky, for it was dotted with pinpricks of light where roofing nails had fallen out or rusted away. She felt confused. What time was it? Had she been lying there for hours? Her thoughts were sluggish, and her body floppy, as if her bones had dissolved. She gathered her strength and sat up in the chair, pulling down her skirt from where it had become twisted around her waist. Guilty feelings were making themselves felt and, in order to assuage them, she immediately made herself a promise: she would not read another word of *Fanny Hill*.

In the days that followed, it turned out that not even her increasingly squeamish feelings of guilt were enough to stop her. She discovered that Fanny soon moved on from Phoebe, and the descriptions that ensued, of Fanny's sexual adventures with the many young gentlemen who made her acquaintance, were terrifying for their violence and, yet, at the same time, tremendously exciting. Each time she picked up the book, she oscillated between wanting nothing more to do with the sensations that reading of Fanny's exploits aroused in her body, and an overwhelming desire for that very arousal. It didn't matter how much she reprimanded herself, she seemed to have lost all willpower. She kept promising herself that she would stop reading, but it was only when she had turned the last page that she was able to do so.

20

ON THE FOURTH DAY OF the record-breaking heatwave, everyone was resting, lying on couches and daybeds throughout the house, garments unbuttoned and silk hand fans fluttering, while outside the sun throbbed with relentless intensity. The house was silent except for the creak and groan of the roof expanding in the afternoon heat.

Emily lay on the leather daybed in the billiard room, looking out across the paddocks at the shimmering heat haze. She could see a mob of sheep, like rounded grey boulders, huddled under the shade of two pine trees. She imagined them panting, their mouths ajar and flanks quivering. A small flock of galahs flew past and she saw one fall, spiralling down in an awkward flap of wings. It hit the ground and did not move. It was the heat, Uncle Cec had explained. Sometimes birds just dropped out of the sky.

Her mind wandered. Where was Claudio sheltering? The shearers' quarters would be unbearable. Even protected by thick walls and wide verandahs, the homestead was becoming uncomfortable. She closed her eyes, intending to think about Claudio, but strangely it was thoughts of Harry that came to her. It was all terribly sad and she couldn't help feeling sorry for him, fighting on the frontline, in love with Lydia and longing to be with her, reading her letters over and over until they fell apart and wondering why no more had arrived.

The letter part of the fantasy proved distracting when she remembered that there was still no further word from home. It surprised her to realise that she had not thought about home for some days. It felt like a sort of betrayal — of herself and of her mother — and she was relieved when her thoughts returned to Harry in the muddy trenches of the Western Front. It was the wrong war, but she simply could not shift the action to the jungles of New Guinea. Her mind would not cooperate.

From the devastation of the Somme, she drifted onto the problem of her need for a bra, which had still not been solved, wondering what to do about it. Although Lydia had ignored her since the startling revelations about Harry, there remained the fact of that brief and exhilarating hug. And there was the confession itself, divulged to her, as one would to a trusted friend. It gave her hope that she might approach Lydia more directly and she began to think about getting up and going in search of her aunt. In a minute. But a minute passed, and she did not move. The heat had sapped all her energy.

The sun had gone down hours ago, but night had brought no relief. To add to it all, the air was filled with the shrill drumming of a cicada outside the French doors of the white room. In an effort to escape the demented drilling she buried her head under the pillow, but it made little difference.

She kicked at the sheet, which had become twisted around her legs. The more she struggled, the more entangled she became, as if the sheet had a will of its own and was determined to hold her prisoner. When at last she managed to free herself, she swung her legs over the side of the bed and stood up. The cicada continued boring a hole in her head.

She stepped onto the verandah and the cicada, alerted to the presence of something foreign, stopped its infernal din, leaving the echo-y silence of an empty cave. A breeze, still carrying the heat from sun-blasted paddocks, blew strands of hair across her face. Just to her right was the dark shape of William's old punching bag. She pushed it with her fingertips and set it swinging.

At the edge of the verandah, she hesitated, surprised to find herself there at all. But then the hot night drew her on, and in a few strides she felt the sharp scratch of buffalo grass on the soles of her bare feet. She looked up at the starry sky, feeling the flutter of air against her face. An unexpected sense of elation rushed through her body and, throwing back her head, she twirled on the spot until, overcome by dizziness, she lost her balance and collapsed on the lawn.

The grass pricked her skin, uncomfortable but not unpleasant. The black sky was filled with diamond-bright stars. In Melbourne the stars were paler, and fewer in number. The sky was smaller too, bumping against the tops of city buildings, unlike the vast, unreachable expanse into which she was now gazing. Drifting.

Then something rustled in the bushes and she sat up with a start. A night bird shrieked, and the flap of a moth's wing brushed her face. Dry leaves crunched under the weight of a passing creature. The sense she'd had of being protected by the warm night air deserted her, and she felt invisible animal presences all around, observing her movements, taking in her scent, listening to her every breath. The night belonged to them and she was an intruder. She sprang to her feet and ran back across the lawn.

In bed again, with the sheet pulled up to her chin, something odd happened. She began to notice the pressure of the sheet against her nipples. By moving a little one way and then the other, a pleasant tingling sensation was created. Without thinking of what she was doing, she pushed up her cotton pyjama top and gently squeezed one breast. A rush of pleasure fizzed in the place between her legs. It was the same kind of feeling she'd experienced while reading *Fanny Hill*, only more so, and perhaps she should have expected it. But she had not and she gave a shocked gasp. Since finishing the book, she'd tried to avoid even thinking of Fanny's exploits. Now those exploits came rushing back, to be followed, once again, by an image of the regal Miss Maunder and a memory of the headmistress's special presentation to the class on 'Self-Reverence and True Modesty'. In her mind, she heard Miss Maunder's words with new force. According to the headmistress, there were only two types of girls: 'good-time gels' and 'gels who respected their bodies'. Good-time gels were doomed to a miserable life, cast out from decent society and destined for penury. Miss Maunder had made it clear that enjoyment of bodily pleasure was the indelible signature of the good-time gels.

Practising the self-restraint that she'd shown with *Fanny Hill* – that is, once she'd finished the book she had resisted rereading certain passages despite the temptation to do so – proved to be impossible in relation to her own body. Each night, before falling asleep, her fingers found their way between her legs and, with the memory of Fanny's adventures to aid her, she discovered how to arouse herself. There was no need to read *Fanny Hill*, or even to think of Fanny's adventures at all. If only she could stop doing it, and she promised herself that tomorrow – yes, tomorrow – would be the very last time.

21

AFTER A NUMBER OF TOMORROWS, Sunday came around once more and, standing in the church with hands clasped together and head bowed in prayer, she'd begged God to give her the strength to resist the temptation of her body. It was the first real prayer she had uttered in a long time, mentally addressing God with a capital G out of a hopeful respect, having earlier downgraded him to a lower case g because of his probable non-existence.

Whether it was the power of prayer, or the fact that Eunice had added to her workload, she could not tell but, over the next few days and nights, she remained pure and did not think of Fanny at all. Nor did she visit the workshop. The letter to Dorothy, which had grown to more than ten pages, was still unfinished. There were many more things she wished to tell Dorothy, but they would have to wait. In the meantime, at least, the torments of the flesh had receded.

Sitting now at the men's dining table as the afternoon was drifting into evening, she waited for Claudio where they had arranged to meet for a lesson. Only minutes earlier Grandmother had released her from polishing the brass firescreen in the billiard room. In fact, Grandmother had seemed quite annoyed to discover Eunice's hand in it and had muttered something about 'slave labour' before telling Emily to run along.

Claudio was late. Perhaps he was not coming at all. She went to the kitchen flywire and called out to Della. 'Have you seen Claudio?'

Della came to the door. 'Wagging school, is he?' she said with a laugh.

Della always called it *school*. Since the first lesson, she and Florrie often came to listen. They were especially keen on the stories. Verbs, nouns and adverbs were of less interest.

'He was here for arvo tea,' Della said. 'Haven't seen him since.'

She waited for another ten minutes before setting off in search of him, although she was halfway up the rise towards the shearers' quarters before admitting to herself that this was her goal. It was only to check in case something had happened; she didn't bother to think what could have happened or what use she would be in the event that it had.

At the shearers' quarters, the door to Claudio's room was wide open. Otherwise she would never have peered in. The room was small and square. A cupboard took up part of one wall. Under the louvred window was a narrow shearer's stretcher bed made up with a grey blanket. Beside the bed was a small table with a piece of lino glued to the top. A hurricane lamp sat on the table. At the foot of the bed was a large tin trunk and, next to it, a pair of boots, the heels worn down and tongues hanging out as if exhausted.

Having failed to find Claudio, there was no reason to linger, but seeing his boots brought an unexpected lump to her throat. They spoke of his presence and his absence all at once. How lonely he must be. She hovered in the doorway, reluctant to leave. It was all so modest – there had to be more. She wanted to know something more about him, and it was this desire that drew her eye back to the trunk at the end of the bed. What harm could there be in taking a look?

She moved into the room. Kneeling down, she flicked open the latches and pushed up the lid of the trunk to find herself staring at a thick white towel. Until now, she'd completely forgotten the Belle's story about the cowardly Italians and their snowy white towels, packed by their mothers and which they had waved in surrender. She had dismissed it as just another fiction, made up by an unreliable storyteller. But here one was, exactly as the Belle had described.

It didn't prove anything. Claudio would never have surrendered without a fight. Hadn't she seen him in the churchyard? For the first time it occurred to her that Claudio might have fought Australians. Perhaps he'd even killed some. Obviously he'd fought on the wrong side, but it all seemed a long time ago and so far away. Kneeling at the open trunk, she wondered what was worse: that he was a coward who'd waved the white towel at the first sign of fighting? Or a brave warrior who had killed Australian soldiers? She couldn't help it – she hoped he hadn't been a coward.

She was about to close the trunk when something attracted her eye. She leaned forwards to get a closer look and realised, with a shock, that it was Lydia's white handkerchief lying, neatly folded, in the centre of the towel. It was almost invisible, white on white, except for a faded brownish stain that must have been Claudio's blood. There was no doubt about it. This was the handkerchief Lydia had asked her to collect the day she'd taken him the rabbits. And now here it was, freshly laundered and carefully stowed away. Why hadn't he returned it to Lydia? She could hear Della saying: *Curiosity killed the blinking cat.* Then her mother's voice joined in: *What you don't know can't hurt you.* But it was too late now, she did know, even if she was still unsure what, exactly. She let the lid of the trunk fall shut and left the room, hurrying away around the corner of the building with her mother's words echoing inside her head.

Back at the house, Florrie was now sitting at the men's dining table with a large enamel bowl of hot water, plucking a headless chicken. Her dress was covered in feathers, and fluffy bits of down were stuck in her stiff black hair.

'You won't find him,' Florrie announced. 'He was looking for you. They've gone off to fix a mill.'

'Oh.' She made a disappointed grimace while experiencing a secret rush of relief. The combined discovery of Claudio's white towel and Lydia's handkerchief had left her feeling rattled. She collected her books and lesson notepad from the table. The clotted reek of hot wet feathers and the sight of pimpled chicken flesh were making her nauseous. No wonder there were vegetarians in the world. It was something her mother had embraced during a short infatuation with Percy Grainger and his music, but her father had put a stop to it. He had the patience of Job, he'd told Emily, but even so, there were limits.

Intending to leave her books and papers in the white room, she took the verandah route around the house. When she got to the billiard-room door it was open, letting in the hot air. Grandmother and Eunice would be irritated. She entered the room and pulled the door closed behind her. What did it matter if Claudio had surrendered without a fight? It was better than being killed in action. But why had he kept Lydia's handkerchief? Why hide it away like a treasure? She wished the word *treasure* had not occurred to her. As she passed the billiard table, the equally unwelcome word *keepsake* popped into her head. And then something on the edge of her vision made her glance towards the mantelpiece. Books slipped from her fingers, banging onto the floorboards, and her breath burst from her in a shocked exhalation.

'Roy?'

He was standing beside the mantelpiece. But he wasn't allowed in the house. She looked around for Grandmother. Had she given her permission? There was nobody else in the room and Roy was moving towards her. Her heart was banging against her ribs.

'It's alright,' he said quietly. 'No need to be scared.'

'I'm not.' And then in an attempt to prove she was in control of things, she said, 'You shouldn't be in here.'

He stopped in front of her, and she saw that he was holding the greenstone axe head. He did not try to hide it.

She pointed at the stone. 'That belongs on the mantelpiece.'

Roy looked down at the axe head, turning it over in his hand.

The verandah door opened, and Grandmother stepped inside. She was halfway across the room before she saw them.

'Roy?' she said in a startled voice. 'Emily?'

Roy nodded to Grandmother. 'Missus.' Then he nodded to Emily too and, without hurrying, walked past them both and out through the door.

'What is going on? What was Roy doing in here?'

There was no time to think. The safest answer was always ignorance. 'Nothing. I don't know.'

Picking up her dropped books, she departed the room via the internal door. Grandmother called her name, but she ignored it and hurried along the hallway until she reached the white room. She threw the books on the bed, closed the door and left. She did not want to be questioned and was sure that her grandmother would not pursue her into the orchard.

At the cherry plum tree, she stopped. Where had Roy gone? There was no sign of him.

It was ten past seven and Uncle Cec had not arrived for dinner. Grandmother said grace and gave the go-ahead for those present to begin without him. There was no point letting the meal get any colder.

Uncle Cec finally arrived at half-past seven. He pulled out his chair and sat down unceremoniously. 'Roy's gone.'

Grandmother's fork paused in mid-air. 'Gone? He was in the billiard room this afternoon.'

Eunice startled as if she'd been shot. 'Billiard room? What was he doing in the billiard room?'

Grandmother turned to Emily, which made Eunice do so too.

'Emily?' Grandmother enquired.

'I don't know. He didn't say anything to me.' She had not made a conscious decision to lie; it was as if the words spoke themselves while she watched on.

'Well, he's not there now,' Uncle Cec said. 'Best damn stockman and he's up sticks and gone. Damn and blast the man.'

'Language, Cecil,' Grandmother said.

'He must have had a reason to leave.' Lydia spoke for the first time.

'Family business, I expect.' Uncle Cec speared a piece of meat with an aggressive thrust of his fork.

'If he has family business he should ask for permission to leave,' Grandmother responded.

'Oh, for heaven's sake,' Lydia broke in. 'He's not at school. Anyway, he's sure to come back when he can.'

But Uncle Cec was not to be appeased. 'The place is going to rack and ruin. If this damn war doesn't end soon we might as well walk off the joint too.'

'That's quite enough,' Grandmother said. 'Let us at least enjoy our dinner without having to listen to your prophecies of doom and gloom.'

In the days following Roy's departure, Emily waited for someone to notice that the greenstone axe head had disappeared from the billiard-room mantelpiece. But no-one did. She'd thought of confiding in Della and asking her advice as to whether she should tell Grandmother that Roy had stolen it. She felt sure Della would know what to do, and yet, each time there was an opportunity to ask her, she had prevaricated. It was the memory of how Roy had kept the knowledge of her presence behind the pine tree to himself that first day. Didn't she owe him the same silence? And then there was the other half-formed question: who did the axe head really belong to? The more she thought about it, the less certain she was that Roy had stolen anything.

22

EMILY WAS DRYING THE LAST of the washing up, silently lamenting the fact that what had begun as a choice the first night of her stay had become a chore. Now she was expected to help in the kitchen after dinner whether she wanted to or not. She picked up the gravy boat, feeling the injustice of it all.

Beside her at the sink, Florrie was scouring a pot when she cocked her head like a startled chook. 'Someone's coming,' she said, anxiously. Florrie did not like surprises.

Emily listened. From outside came the sound of an approaching vehicle.

'Who the devil could that be?' Della said. She too was listening intently.

'Lydia?' Emily suggested, knowing that Lydia was staying the night at the McDougalls' to keep Ruth company while her husband, Orm, had gone to see his banker in Melbourne.

'Thought she was coming back with you lot tomorrow after church,' Della said.

The sound of the vehicle's engine grew louder and then stopped. A door banged, and they heard footsteps hurrying along the verandah.

'What are you waiting for?' Della took the tea towel from her and gave her a push.

It was her job to go and investigate but, like Florrie, she felt a little anxious, for nobody ever called at Mount Prospect after dark. On the other hand, if it were Lydia, then Ruth might be the driver and she was keen to meet her. When Ruth had come to pick up Lydia, she'd been in the workshop, writing to Dorothy.

With Della urging her on, she left the kitchen, only to hear the car engine revving and the crunch of wheels over gravel, signalling that whoever had arrived had already departed. She entered the sitting room to find everyone clustered just inside the French doors. In the centre of the group was a figure in army uniform, leaning on a pair of crutches. Grandmother, Eunice and Uncle Cec were ushering the man forwards and, when they moved apart, Emily found herself staring into a familiar pair of deep-set eyes and a pale unshaven face. She felt the force of his gaze and looked away. It was then she realised what her eyes had been refusing to register: from below the knee of his left leg, there was nothing, just a flap of limp empty trouser leg.

'It's William. William's home,' Grandmother said in a tremulous voice.

'Where's Lydia?' Eunice piped up, looking around in bewilderment, for the shock of William's arrival seemed to have temporarily erased her memory.

Uncle Cec broke away from the group, and took hold of the whisky decanter from the marble-topped credenza. Emily thought he was going drink straight from the decanter, but instead he fumbled for two glasses and splashed whisky into each, before lifting one to his lips and gulping down the contents.

William swung his crutches forwards, followed by his good leg. He reached an armchair and sank into it just as Uncle Cec arrived and thrust a glass of whisky into his hand. Like Uncle Cec, he drank it down in a single gulp.

After that, everyone waited, as if time itself had stopped and they were holding out for a word from William to release them. But he remained silent. He stared straight ahead again to where Emily was standing in the doorway, for the general paralysis had affected her too. She could tell by his unblinking eyes that he was not seeing her. His vision was inward. Her own gaze was drawn to the empty trouser leg where some part of her mind kept attempting to see an ankle and boot to match the other one.

Suddenly Grandmother clapped her hands, breaking the spell that had come over them. What were they thinking? William must be starving. She rushed to the door, shooing Emily out in front of her. Eunice followed, a step behind.

In the kitchen Della and Florrie were hovering, keen to discover who had arrived so unexpectedly, but neither Grandmother nor Eunice said a word, their faces blank. Now that she had been released from shocked immobility, it was as if movement itself were saving Grandmother from collapse. Together, she and Eunice rushed to and fro, from pantry to kitchen table and back, ferrying Della's egg and bacon pie and cold meat from the safe, and slices of homemade bread, a jar of chutney and some rhubarb and apple tart.

Della drew Emily aside and gave her a look that needed no interpretation. 'Well?'

Florrie hurried to join them.

'It's William,' she whispered.

'Never!' Florrie clapped a hand over her mouth. She hadn't meant to shout. It did not matter, for Grandmother and Eunice were utterly focused on loading the tray and seemed not to hear.

Della's powerful fingers were squeezing her arm. 'What about his leg?'

'You knew? You knew about his leg?'

'Blasted bloody war,' Della fumed, leaving the question unanswered.

'Why didn't you tell me?' She couldn't help feeling that the cook had betrayed her and turned to Florrie. 'Florrie? Did you know?'

'Your gran said we weren't to say. *We must protect the child,*' Florrie added in an uncanny imitation of her grandmother's voice.

Emily tried to pull away from Della. 'I'm not a child.'

'Tell me,' Della insisted, still gripping her arm. 'How is he in himself?'

'I don't know. He hasn't spoken.'

Della let her go then, which was a relief as her arm had begun to throb. Seeing Grandmother pick up the tray with Eunice in close pursuit, she hurried across to open the door and followed the two women out of the kitchen.

Uncle Cec was alone in the sitting room. 'Gone to bed,' he said, in answer to the expression on Grandmother's face.

'But he must be hungry, he has to eat ...' Grandmother set the tray down on the credenza. Her face was crumpling as if she was about to cry, and it struck Emily for the first time that her grandmother had emotions in the same way that she herself did. How could she have imagined otherwise? And yet it was true that she'd never given it a thought. Grandmother was a pillar of strength who held everything together, the rock on whom they all depended. She was the one who enforced the rules and laid down the law, harrying them all to do better and not to let standards slip. The idea that she might feel sorrow, fear and uncertainty was so alarming that Emily felt light-headed and had to put a hand on the back of the nearest chair for support. She wished she could say something comforting but no words came. She was not ready to accept what she'd seen. She did not want Grandmother to be a mere mortal.

It was not yet nine o'clock, but the safety of the white room beckoned, and she slipped out of the sitting room without even saying goodnight and was soon in bed. She turned out the light and lay down. The curtains were open and she could see the shape of William's punching bag outlined against a faint glow of moonlight. If only she could stop thinking about William's leg. The missing bit. There was an old man in a wheelchair whom she'd often seen outside the Eastmalvern train station. He had no legs, just stumps that in winter were wrapped in a tartan rug. He smoked skinny rolled-up cigarettes, and the ends of his fingers on his smoking hand were dark brown, and his face was grey and all sunken valleys. Her father said the old fellow had been a soldier in the Great War and that he deserved better. She always tried not to notice him and had even wished he would die, for that way she'd never have to see him again.

At least William had one leg, and a bit of the other one, although having half a leg did not seem to be much better than no leg. To distract herself she began to sing softly, the first thing that came into her mind. '*Ten green bottles, hanging on the wall and if one green bottle should accidentally fall ...*'

But that was as far as she got before being startled to a stop by the jangly sound of the telephone extension bell in the hall outside the billiard room. Someone was making a telephone call. Were they ringing the McDougalls' in order to tell Lydia?

23

THE SUN HAD ONLY JUST breached the horizon when she woke, but light suffused the room, for she no longer bothered to close the curtains at night. Something was different, but what was it? As soon as she saw the punching bag outside she remembered. William was home.

After breakfast they set off for church without him. She'd heard Grandmother calling and knocking on his bedroom door, but when they gathered on the front verandah waiting for Uncle Cec to bring the car round there was no sign of him.

Now the black Packard was turning out of the homestead drive and onto the road, and a mausoleum-like atmosphere had settled over them all. Emily watched the landscape whizzing past. She began to count the fence posts.

Uncle Cec let them out opposite the church before driving the car further down the street to park under a tree. Emily fell into step with Grandmother and Eunice as they hurried across to Lydia, waiting near the church gate; she had never seen Lydia so pale.

'Where is he?'

'He wouldn't come.' Grandmother reached out and took Lydia's hands.

'Is he ... how is he?' Lydia asked, her voice cracking.

Grandmother shook her head, her mouth set tight. Emily felt sure it was to stop herself from crying.

A matronly woman approached on her way into the church yard. 'We're all praying for him, you know,' she said, rather too enthusiastically.

Grandmother flicked her a disparaging glance. 'That wretched party line,' she said, when the woman was out of earshot.

'Gossips, the lot of them,' Eunice added.

'What does it matter,' Lydia said. 'It doesn't change anything', and she pulled away from Grandmother. Emily watched her move past the familiar groupings of parishioners and saw how their heads turned, their eyes following Lydia as she entered the church. The news of William's return had spread like a grassfire.

The service was over and, as they made their way outside, Reverend McIver took Grandmother's hand and patted it.

'You must be strong,' he said in a firm voice. 'God's will –'

But before he could go on Grandmother withdrew her hand and, straightening her spine, drew herself up to her full five feet. She looked him in the eye, which meant craning her head back.

'God's will be damned.' She turned away and, linking arms with Eunice, moved towards the church gate.

On the drive home Emily glanced at Lydia and wondered what she was thinking. If only she could make some kind of connection, something to break through the isolation that seemed to be afflicting everyone since William's arrival. His homecoming had changed everything. Poor Lydia. William was her brother. He was Father's brother too. A vision of her father with one leg caught her by surprise, and she had to stifle a sob.

The car bumped over a pothole, knocking her sideways. She quickly tried to right herself, knowing how Lydia hated being jostled or even touched by accident. But instead of recoiling or snapping at her, Lydia grasped her hand and squeezed it briefly. They had both taken off their church gloves, and the feel of Lydia's warm dry hand scarcely had time to register before she let go. Tears sprang again into Emily's eyes. She blinked them back, knowing that it was not her right to cry.

They had not been home long, and Emily was setting the table for the Sunday roast, when Grandmother appeared in the doorway.

'Go and see if Lydia has found William, would you, my dear? Tell them to come to lunch.' There was a look of despair in Grandmother's eyes that she wished she had not seen.

She knocked on Lydia's bedroom door, but there was no answer. Nor was there an answer from William's room and, after searching the house and then the garden, she was about to give up when she remembered the workshop. They were sure to be there, and with that knowledge came the unwelcome memory of her visits and the traces of her presence that she'd not had a chance to remove. The never-ending letter to Dorothy in the desk drawer. The books she'd read and left in a pile by the desk. *Fanny Hill.* What had she done with it? A prickly wave of heat enveloped her, and she sensed sweat beading on her forehead and under her arms.

On her way to the workshop, every footstep felt heavier and harder to take than the last. She was still thinking about *Fanny Hill* and the awful shame and embarrassment that accompanied it, when Dorothy drifted into her mind. What would Dorothy do? Emily remembered how Dorothy had been seen smoking in the street in her school uniform by a pillar of society. Naturally, the Pillar had reported her, but Dorothy had denied it point blank. It must have been someone who looked like her.

Everyone knew it was Dorothy, but not even Miss Maunder was able to force a confession from her, so magnificent and vehement were her denials. Even the Pillar of Society grew uncertain and declared that perhaps he'd been mistaken after all. Denial at all costs. Was she up for that?

She stopped in front of the blue door. It was ajar, and she could hear voices. It was not eavesdropping because she was about to knock, and she'd been sent to call them for lunch.

'You can't. You mustn't.' Lydia's voice dropped, and Emily could not make out the next words, despite shuffling closer, her ear to the gap. There had been something urgent and desperate in Lydia's tone, and she felt the hairs on the back of her neck prickle. If only she could hear what was being said, but the dialogue remained indistinct.

Then came the sound of scuffling, and a sharp cry from Lydia. Footsteps. Emily jumped away from the door and arranged herself as if she were only now arriving. She was just in time for, a second later, Lydia burst from the workshop and ran straight past her towards the house in a turbulent rush. She wanted to follow but, remembering Grandmother's instructions, she moved back to the doorway and called through, 'Lunch is ready.' There was no reply but it was enough. She had done her duty.

The atmosphere in the dining room was subdued. William had not yet appeared. Uncle Cec stood at the sideboard carving the leg of mutton as Della moved around the table in her usual stately manner, her lips moving, no doubt with holy phrases. Emily thought she heard the words *to everything there is a season*, but she couldn't be sure. She remembered the words that followed – *a time to every purpose under heaven* – and felt a surge of annoyance at Della. What purpose?

Apart from Della's whispered biblical quotations, the room was quiet. When Della finished serving and had retreated to the kitchen, Emily waited for someone to mention William's absence, but nobody did. She expected Grandmother to say grace, but she held her peace, her gaze fixed on some indefinable spot across the room. How long were they were going to sit there, not eating? What if he did not come? She thought about saying grace herself but did not have the nerve. She was wondering who would break first when the door swung open, banging against the edge of the sideboard.

William hopped across the room, swinging his crutches. He reached the chair between her and Grandmother, opposite Lydia. As he manoeuvred himself into his seat, his eyes were on his sister, but Lydia stared fixedly at the meal in front of her.

He leaned his crutches on the table next to his chair. Still nobody spoke, and the air vibrated with tension. Emily had a wild urge to once again hide under the sideboard as she'd done after biting Eunice.

'I shall say grace,' Grandmother finally announced. *'For what we are about to receive may the Lord make us truly grateful. Amen.'*

Emily murmured 'amen' with everyone else, one eye on William. He did not say amen, his gaze still focused on Lydia. Knives and forks clinked against plates as they began the meal. She could hear the click of Uncle Cec's teeth as he chewed and an unpleasant squishy sound of food being swallowed. Without conversation, the whole business of eating together felt too intimate. She sawed at a slice of mutton, attempting to detach the rind of greyish fat. Her stomach heaved and she abandoned the meat, focusing instead on a roast potato, wondering if William was going to eat, for he had not yet taken a single bite.

Uncle Cec cleared his throat. 'Better to end up without a leg than be blown to bits.'

Grandmother's knife rattled against the edge of her plate as Uncle Cec persevered.

'Remember that Wilson fella from Gootmaroot? Came back from Gallipoli with one arm. Damn good stockman. And he could still shear a sheep quicker than most men.'

William was taking no notice of Uncle Cec. His sole focus was Lydia, willing her to look at him, and Emily found herself willing it too, but Lydia did not waver. And then, to her astonishment, William lifted a crutch and placed it across the table. Perhaps because it was so utterly unexpected, Uncle Cec pretended not to see it and continued to talk about the one-armed Gallipoli veteran who was not only a 'ringer' but could roll a cigarette one-handed while at a canter.

Everyone else watched in frozen disbelief as William slowly and deliberately pushed the tip of his crutch against Lydia's plate. Nobody moved, not even Lydia, who must have known what was going to happen. Her plate teetered on the edge of the table and then toppled into her lap, meat and vegetables splattering over her and onto the floor.

William swung his crutch down and pushed himself up out of his chair. He grabbed the second crutch and left the dining room.

In his absence, a new and altogether more eerie silence overtook them all. Grandmother went to Lydia's aid, helping her up and taking her off to change out of the soiled clothes, while Eunice, on hands and knees, picked up the food that lay scattered under the table and carried it out to the kitchen. Florrie came in with a basin of hot water and a cloth to clean the Persian rug then left again. Emily and Uncle Cec remained in their seats.

She could see that Uncle Cec had decided to ignore the entire incident. He ate his meal as if nothing had happened, as if everyone else were doing the same thing, even though nobody was there except for her. She picked up her knife and fork and, imitating Uncle Cec, forced herself to take a mouthful of food. She chewed for a long time; her throat was too tight and she thought she might choke.

Grandmother returned alone and reported that Lydia was too upset to eat. She sat down, put her serviette on her lap and lifted her cutlery in an effort to maintain some semblance of normality. Eunice came back from the kitchen and followed suit. What had happened was still too fresh, and the implications of it too strange and unknown for it to be spoken of.

But civilised conversation on neutral topics was beyond them all, and it was not long before Grandmother gave up her pretence and excused herself. Eunice was next to leave, and then Emily asked to be excused also – a formality she addressed to Uncle Cec, the only remaining diner. He nodded in an absent-minded way and she left the room, not knowing where to go or what to do with herself.

In that frame of mind she returned to the white room, sat on her bed and picked up *Middlemarch* – she still wasn't even halfway through. But, as was so often the case, she could not concentrate. All she could think of was the incident. What had happened between Lydia and William to provoke him in that way? The scrap of conversation she'd overheard held the clue, but what did it mean? Lydia saying: *You can't. You mustn't.* Perhaps he had not been provoked. Perhaps he was …

She searched for a word that might describe him, remembering something she'd read about soldiers in the First World War who had suffered from shell shock. It was a better word than *mad*. Mad – like her mother. Why did that have to come into her mind? She tossed *Middlemarch* onto the bed and stood up. The house felt empty and desolate, as if everyone had gone to ground. She was gripped by an overpowering sense of restlessness. There had to be something to do, somewhere to go.

Once through the French doors, she gave William's old punching bag a passing push. At the end of the verandah she stepped down onto the gravel path. She had not made up her mind where she was going or what she was intending to do, but the path led her on towards the yard and she did not resist.

She heard the sound of male voices and instinctively slipped behind an oleander bush. Peeping through the leaves she saw Claudio and Uncle Cec at the gate. Claudio was carrying a collapsible shearer's stretcher, and Uncle Cec a rolled-up mattress. Claudio opened the gate, and she watched them reach the blue door and head inside the workshop.

24

WILLIAM DID NOT COME TO dinner. It was a dismal affair with everyone avoiding eye contact as if even a look could lead to something disastrous. They tried to keep up appearances and make conversation, but their words got lost and muffled in the heavy atmosphere. There was only one thing to speak of, but it was impossible.

When the meal was over Emily went as usual to the kitchen to help with the washing up. She took a tea towel from the stove rail and began to dry the dishes. Florrie and Della were in the middle of a conversation.

'But what's wrong with him?' Florrie said.

'War is what's wrong with him,' Della replied. 'You're too young to remember the last one. Half came back mad as hatters. And he's lost his leg, poor bugger. How would you like it, with only one leg?'

Florrie lifted one foot off the ground, trying to balance as she scrubbed the meat pan. She wobbled and had to put her foot down again.

'You shouldn't swear, Della,' she said not for the first time. 'Specially with her', and she gave a prim nod in Emily's direction, indicating that she was looking after her even if Della had temporarily lowered her standards.

She smiled back at Florrie. The truth was that she did not mind Della saying *bugger*. At first it had been thrilling to hear swear words; now, with everything the way it was, they were the only words that felt appropriate.

Della opened the warming oven and removed a covered plate, putting it on a tray along with some cutlery, a serviette, a little jug of gravy and a set of silver salt and pepper shakers.

'Come on, Florrie,' she said. 'You'll have to take it down.'

Florrie dropped the pan in the sink and swivelled around, her work-reddened hands dripping water onto the floor and a look of alarm on her pudding face.

'Why do I have to go?'

Della spooned a dollop of thick cream onto a slice of lemon meringue pie and put that on the tray too. 'Because there's no-one else and it's not my job to go traipsing down there.'

'Traipsing down where?'

Della and Florrie both turned to her. She could see Della's mind working and wished she'd kept quiet. She wasn't at all sure she wanted to be involved. But it was too late.

Della picked up the tray. 'Workshop, and don't dilly-dally.' The cook thrust the tray into her hands before she could protest, while Florrie rushed across and opened the flywire door.

With Della prodding her from behind she soon found herself out on the kitchen verandah, holding the tray. Florrie banged the flywire shut and then the door, cutting off all means of retreat. She heard Della call out, 'Good luck.'

Dusk was falling as she walked down the path to the workshop, passing the rose hedge, heavy with fragrant pink blooms. A few tardy bees, laden with pollen, were still buzzing around them. A lone white cockatoo, flying towards the home swamp, gave its harsh squawking cry and she flinched. *What a nervous nelly*, she imagined her mother saying.

The closer she got to the blue door the more anxious she felt. She had used the workshop as if it was her own and, after the events of lunch, who knew what William was capable of? Her hands trembled and the plate slid to one side of the tray. Reaching the door, she put it down on the ground and knocked.

Before she could make a run for it, she heard William call out 'Enter' in a commanding voice.

Once inside the workshop she hesitated. It no longer felt like her domain.

'What are you waiting for? You're late.'

She startled, and the cutlery jangled against the plate. One foot in front of the other. She moved towards the light – a small yellow flame flickering inside the glass of the hurricane lamp – trying to hold the tray steady.

Cigarette smoke hung in the air around the big armchair. Everything looked smudged, including William's face. An ashtray on a stand that she had not seen before was beside the armchair, filled with cigarette butts. On the other side, the lamp sat in its usual spot on a low stool. There was no space for the tray. She waited, expecting some instruction, but William took no notice of her and drew deeply on his cigarette, before blowing out another plume of smoke.

'Where should I put it?' She tried to sound matter of fact and not reveal her nerves.

A hand emerged from the miasmic cloud and yanked the lamp off the stool. Kerosene sloshed and a blue and yellow flame flared up. She yelped, expecting the lamp to explode and, when it didn't, she had to cough a few times, as if the first yelp had been a cough too. She placed the tray on the stool and straightened up. William held out the hurricane lamp for her to take. Her anxiety was beginning to transform into something else. Did he expect her to stand there holding the lamp while he ate?

'Hook,' he said, in answer to her unspoken question, and waved towards a hook on the beam behind him. 'So they sent you?'

She hung the lamp on the hook and avoided his non-question.

'If there's nothing else –' she began, before he interrupted.

'Try the desk, bottom drawer.'

Her stomach twisted, like one of Florrie's dishrags. What had he discovered? Her letter to Dorothy? But it was in the top drawer. Or was it? Now she couldn't remember. And *Fanny Hill?* Where had she left it? She had a vision of herself in the armchair, limbs splayed.

His crutch jabbed her in the thigh. 'Get a move on.'

She shifted back to avoid being jabbed again. A flash of anger flared, and the sympathy she'd felt because of his leg burned up in the heat of it. At the desk, her eyes flicked over the desktop, searching for incriminating evidence of her recent presence, but the light was so dim she couldn't see and she didn't dare to waste a second. The bottom drawer was stiff, and it took all her strength to pull it open, where she found a bottle and a small glass. On her return, she handed them to William, glimpsing the label: *The Famous Grouse*. She had seen a similar bottle on the marble-topped credenza and knew it was Scotch whisky.

His hands shook as he took it, and he had trouble removing the cork, but she did not offer to help. He splashed the whisky into the glass, right to the top and, as he went to gulp it down, she saw her chance and set off for the door.

'Hey, you, wait a minute.'

She turned around, trying to remain calm. 'I do have a name.' She felt furious and also that she might burst into tears. Whatever happened, she would not cry.

'Good for you, Emily,' he replied with a mocking laugh.

'Why do you have to be so rude? Everyone's just trying to help.'

'Is that so? Well, I don't want everyone's help. I can do without your rotten pity.'

He said it with such venom that she felt assaulted. She had to get away, and this time made for the door without stopping.

'That's right, Persephone, run back to the light,' he called behind her.

She let the door swing shut with a bang and raced towards the house, shrieking when a leafy branch flicked her in the face in the dark. It was on reaching the kitchen door that his parting taunt caught up with her and she heard the word *Persephone*. Wasn't she the wife of Ulysses? No, that was Penelope. Despite her anger, she found herself wondering about it, and why William had called her by that name. Not that she cared. Whatever happened, she was never taking his dinner down again. It would have to be Florrie's job, and she would have to go whether she liked it or not.

25

THE FOLLOWING EVENING EMILY WAS determined to avoid the kitchen after dinner. But nor could she face the sitting room, where Grandmother and Eunice were busy at their needlework, and Uncle Cec with studying the *Australian Turf Guide*. At least her role as Della and Florrie's assistant had enabled her to avoid this dreary fate despite Grandmother's desire for her to learn crocheting or embroidery. 'Something to do with your hands,' she'd said, a phrase that made Emily feel queasy, reminding her of other things her hands had been doing. There was no chance of spending the evening with Lydia either, as she had hurried away as soon as the meal was over. In the end, there was only one place left to go.

'Been wondering where you'd got to, haven't we, Florrie?' Della said.

Florrie turned from the sink, her face pink and damp from the heat of the water. She smiled and nodded.

'Still, you're here now,' Della added, taking William's plate from the warming oven.

Emily watched Della load the tray. She would not deliver it; they couldn't make her. They were servants and she didn't have to obey them. But defying Della was easier said than done and, when the cook held out the tray, she found herself accepting it without a word of protest.

This time the blue door was slightly ajar and with a prod from her foot it swung open. She entered, pausing to let her eyes adjust to the dim yellow light. She cleared her throat in order to announce her presence but there was no response and her fragile confidence began to evaporate. She was determined not to be a coward. 'Gumption,' she whispered and tried to assume a confident expression as she set off.

To her surprise, the armchair was empty. She put the tray down on the stool and immediately began the trek back across the room, feeling relieved at William's absence. Halfway to the door she stopped. It was the perfect opportunity to retrieve the letter to Dorothy, and return *Fanny Hill* to the bookshelf.

She was about to open the top drawer of the desk when something moved in the shadowy part of the workshop where the lamplight did not penetrate. William emerged, swinging his crutches. Once he'd sunk into the armchair, he spoke. 'Come.'

It was just how he'd spoken last time – single-word orders that reminded her of Lydia, and she felt the return of the same feelings of resistance and anger towards him. But then he continued in a friendlier tone. 'So, Miss P, you came back after all.'

'My name is not Miss P.'

He ignored her rebuttal.

'Sit down.' He waved at the footstool. 'If you have time,' he added. 'I don't want to keep you from more important things.'

She couldn't decide whether he was making fun of her and was preparing to refuse his offer, even as her bottom was sinking down on the footstool. It was odd the way her mind and body could have such different ideas. She was quite sure that she did not like him at all.

In a minute, she would get up and leave. There was nothing to stop her. He couldn't treat her like a ... the word *servant*, recently used with some condescension in regards to Della and Florrie, popped into her head, and she wished she'd put her foot down there too. It was Florrie's job.

'You'd better have this.' William was waving a book at her. 'Unless you've finished it? It's rather a compelling read, don't you think? *Fanny Hill, Memoirs of a Woman of Pleasure.*' The title rolled off his tongue with relish as he tossed it to her.

She caught the book, feeling shame suffuse her body. Meanwhile, William pulled the tray onto his lap. It was her opportunity to leave, but she found herself unable to move and continued to sit, an inert lump, watching him eat.

'It's a classic,' she croaked.

He looked up from the rabbit fricassee.

'Otherwise I wouldn't have.'

He waited for more.

'I'm reading them all ...' She faltered. 'Before I get married.'

'Them all?'

'The classics ... of English literature.' Saying it aloud, she was beginning to have doubts.

He nodded, as if giving the matter serious thought. 'And then you're planning to marry?'

She gave a weak sort of nod.

'I suppose when you're *very* old.'

She couldn't help a look of surprise.

'People have died before finishing the classics.'

'Oh.'

'Still, it's probably better to die trying than just get married. Anyone can get married. Not everyone can read the entire canon of English literature.'

Was he mocking her again? She felt a wave of mortification.

'So you've become a reader,' he went on. 'Are you a writer too?'

She was still wallowing in humiliation and it took some time before she even understood what he had asked her. Was she a writer too? As if it was a normal thing. A question that nobody had ever asked her before; she had not even asked herself, except that the letter to Dorothy had become more and more like a story, like something a writer might write. A small flame flickered inside her. She wanted to answer, but did she dare? And then before she'd made up her mind, there was no chance to say anything.

'Shit!'

The tray went flying, everything scattered onto the floor, and a plate broke as William gripped his stump.

'Shit, damn and blast to bloody hell.'

She had leaped up as the tray crashed to the floor. 'I'll go –' she began, meaning, go and get help.

'No!' he shouted between the flow of curses. 'Whisky.' He waved towards the desk.

She returned with the bottle, and he grabbed it from her, gulping it straight down. His face was wet with sweat, and he was breathing as if he'd been running. She felt scared and wanted to leave, but was afraid of provoking a further outburst and kneeled down instead to pick up the dinner things. She put pieces of the broken plate on the tray, along with the cutlery and salt and pepper shakers. She scooped up bits of sauce-covered rabbit and Della's rhubarb fool as best she could while the sound of William's laboured breathing and half-stifled groans continued.

'No good for anything. I'm a dot and carry one, a bloody peg leg. A cripple.' He spat out the ugly words.

Crouched on the floor, she watched him. Sweat still ran down his face. He gritted his teeth, eyes closed and face screwed up against the pain.

'Tell Della I'm sorry about the plate.'

It was the signal for her to leave, and she got to her feet.

William opened his eyes and looked up at her. 'Are you really different, Miss P, or just like all the rest?'

Before she could reply, he closed his eyes again. She hovered, uncertain as to whether she'd been dismissed or not, and trying to decide on an answer to his question. He didn't open his eyes and still unsure of the right answer – or whether there even was one – she departed carrying the tray and its debris.

Back at the kitchen, Della took the tray from her. 'What happened?'

'It was an accident.'

It was odd, but she found herself wanting to protect William.

'You should be more blinking careful,' Della said, dumping the remains of the rhubarb fool in the chook bucket. 'And you can put that bit of stew on a tin plate for the foxy.'

She did as she was told. When she'd finished, she turned to see Della holding up a book.

'What's this?' The cook waved *Fanny Hill*.

How on earth had it ended up on the tray? That Della should discover its contents was too awful to contemplate and, with a supreme effort of facial contortion, she forced her mouth into a wonky smile.

'Oh, William's, I suppose. I'll take it back tomorrow.' And with that she plucked the book from Della's hand.

26

THE NEXT DAY, AS SOON as breakfast was over, she took the chook bucket and egg basket and departed for the chook yard. Stuffed into the waistband of her skirt and disguised by her untucked blouse was *Fanny Hill*. She'd made up her mind to throw it into a waterhole in the swamp where it would never be found. Having made the decision, she couldn't wait to be rid of it and sped through her chores.

The resident clucky hen made the usual protests, squawking and flapping in her daily refusal to move off the eggs. She was an aggressive pecker with a malevolent glint in her beady eye, and the war between them had been escalating. Della had shown her how to grab the chook by the tail and fling her off the nest, but it required nerves of steel. Sometimes she just couldn't face it. She gathered the eggs from the other nesting boxes, and cleaned the water trough with the straw broom before refilling it with fresh water. Rather than return to the kitchen and the possibility of delay, she left basket and bucket in a corner of the yard. She would collect them later, once *Fanny Hill* was no more.

She scrambled under the bottom wire of the fence and entered the swamp. Along the dry fringe, river redgums spread their branches with lavish abandon, leaves sweeping the ground as willy wagtails hopped from branch to branch, noisily asserting their territorial claims. Overhead, cockatoos swirled in screeching gangs, and a pair of spur-winged plovers swooped past just above her head. She set off, weaving her way around clumps of rattly reeds, fallen logs and dead waterlogged trees. There was no sign of water; it had to be further in.

She picked up a stick and twirled it. Her mind wandered, and she found herself thinking of the last disturbing encounter with William. *Are you really different, Miss P, or just like all the rest?* What had he meant? Different how? And from whom? And anyway, did she want to be different?

Of course she was different from Grandmother – she was old. Eunice was old too, and yet sometimes she'd felt a dreaded sense of them being alike. And what about Lydia? Wasn't Lydia different? And didn't she want to be like Lydia? To wear clothes in that effortless way; to be beautiful and strong and not care two hoots about what anyone thought? But if she wanted to be like her, then they would be the same. It was all rather confusing. Didn't it come down to the fact that being different meant being odd, or wrong? Like Mother? She swiped her stick at a thistle and watched the silky threads explode into the air ahead of her.

It was strange how her longing for her mother had gradually receded, and how she no longer yearned for a letter from her. The occasional short note from her father was enough. As her mother faded into the background, it had been Dorothy who'd remained, kept alive as the addressee of that unsent letter. Which brought her straight back to William's other question. Was she a writer?

Before she could give further consideration to this crucial question, the ground began to slant upwards in a gentle rise and she soon found herself standing on a shallow bank before a pond of murky water. Without further ado, she pulled *Fanny Hill* from her waistband and hurled it away. For an excruciating moment the book floated on the milky grey surface. She held her breath as the pages absorbed water. Slowly, slowly, it sank, and she gave a great sigh of relief as the book was at last consigned to the deep.

With *Fanny* gone, she was a reformed character, and to prove it to herself she decided to undertake some housework without any prompting from Eunice. She began in the dining room, dusting and polishing the dining table and sideboard, before moving to the sitting room. Kneeling at the sitting-room hearth, she was reminded of Cinderella and was overcome with self-pity, forgetting that it was, in fact, her own choice. She took the hearth brush and began to sweep up the sooty ash that had fallen from the chimney.

'You could just say no.'

She twitched at the sound of Lydia's voice.

'I find it works.' Her aunt approached.

'What do you mean?'

'All this housework. You don't have to do it.'

She could feel the familiar prickling and knew her neck was turning a blotchy red. 'Father said to pull my weight.'

'That sounds like him. I suppose he said *don't be a burden.*'

He had, more than once.

'Anyway, I don't mind.' She was hoping to impress Lydia with her stoicism, but even to her ears it sounded pitiful, and the expression on Lydia's face confirmed it.

When her aunt opened the credenza cupboard and took out a bottle of whisky, she looked away, not wanting to be accused of being a stickybeak. But Lydia held up the bottle.

'For William.'

'Oh, I thought you ...'

'... had taken up drinking whisky during the day?'

'No, I didn't mean that.'

Lydia cocked her head, waiting.

'I thought you and William ... after what happened at lunch. I thought you'd fallen out.'

Lydia's face tightened, as if reacting to a sudden pain. 'We had an argument. I suppose it's because you're a singleton, you don't understand what it's like to have brothers. We fall out, and then we fall in again.'

She wanted to ask what the argument was about but feared being rebuffed. She was already a little stunned by how many words Lydia had addressed to her.

'Anyway,' Lydia went on, 'given the choice, I'd rather take him a bottle of whisky and let him get drunk, than help him ...' But instead of finishing the sentence, she waved her hand as if waving away whatever it was that remained unsaid. She frowned, as if realising she'd said more than she wanted to. 'Well, don't let me stop you from pulling your weight.'

'You're not,' Emily tried to assure her, but her aunt was leaving. When the door had closed, she abandoned the hearth and sat down on one of the replica Queen Anne chairs. Her enthusiasm for housework had completely evaporated. The revelation that William and Lydia had *fallen in* again had taken the wind from her sails. It meant she was not the only one to visit him. She was not as special as she'd thought, even though she had only now discovered that she wanted to be special. Which did not even make sense, as so far her experiences with William had been mainly unnerving and unpleasant. She wasn't even sure that she wanted to go back. But was that really true? He had asked questions that she hadn't stopped thinking about. How else would she find out the answers if she didn't return? And what had Lydia meant? Given the choice between taking William whisky and helping him to do ... what? If only she'd been able to hear what they'd been arguing about that day, but all she had was Lydia's enigmatic fragment. *You can't. You mustn't.*

Empty pea pods lay in a pile on the outdoor dining table. She split open a fat pod, popped two peas in her mouth and dropped the rest into a tin bowl. It was early evening, time for Claudio's lesson, but she had given up hoping that he would come. She'd scarcely seen him since Roy's departure and, in that time, Uncle Cec's forehead had developed permanent corrugations.

'The place is going to the dogs,' he'd said at lunch that day. 'Claudio does his best, but he's not a stockman's bootlace and he couldn't crutch a hogget to save his life. Just as well I've got Lydia. Good as any man.' He'd given Lydia an approving nod before ruining the compliment by adding, 'But you can't run the show with a couple of ring-ins.'

A familiar litany of complaints followed about the lack of rain and the plague of rabbits, and the hand-feeding of stock, which cost a fortune. 'If things don't improve soon, I'll have to start selling the ewes,' he'd declared.

It was the same at every mealtime, and Emily was sick of hearing about it all. After she'd been called a ring-in, Lydia seemed to be sick of it too, and as soon as Uncle Cec began to complain she tried to drown him out by reciting 'Said Hanrahan' in an exaggeratedly tragic tone.

'We'll all be rooned, said Hanrahan, in accents most forlorn. Outside the church 'ere Mass began, one frosty Sunday morn.'

Now, sitting outside at the table, the chorus to the poem was going round and round in Emily's head in an infuriating way, and it was only when Claudio suddenly appeared with his notebook and pencils that it stopped. He sat down opposite and began to shell the peas with her.

'Quicker this way,' he said, 'and then we have school.' Like Della, he had begun to call it school.

When all the peas were podded and delivered to the kitchen, she told Claudio that she would go and get her books.

'Is a beautiful evening – we can walk instead and make conversation lesson?' he suggested.

They walked through the garden and into the orchard. Claudio

211

was right: it was a beautiful evening, warm and still. She asked him the usual questions to make sure his grammar was improving.

As they circled around the south side of the house, they saw William on his crutches, moving slowly down the path from the kitchen towards the gate leading into the yard. After he'd gone through the gate, they lost sight of him.

'Where he was fighting?' Claudio wanted to know.

'Where was he fighting,' she corrected him. 'New Guinea.'

'The Japs?'

She nodded.

'Very sad for Lydia. Her brother.'

'Yes.' It was sad for her, but she couldn't help wishing that he had not brought Lydia into the conversation.

'She is a beautiful woman. *Molto bella*,' he added with an admiring half-whistle.

They had been walking in step but, on hearing these words and, worse still, the whistle at the end of them, she faltered, her arms and legs losing their rhythm.

'Indeed,' she managed to say, almost tripping over her own feet.

Claudio didn't seem to notice anything odd and kept moving.

'But she's terribly untidy. Her room is an awful mess.' She heard herself speaking and wanted to stop and, at the same time, she wanted to say something much worse, although she couldn't think what. Something that would obliterate Lydia's beauty. They kept walking and the conversation moved on to other things, but she could no longer concentrate. The spectre of Lydia's beauty, and Claudio's enthusiastic appreciation of it, had ruined her mood.

27

EMILY SAT DOWN IN THE wing chair that she had just dragged across from a dusty corner of the workshop. She was sick of sitting on the footstool. William was smoking and took no notice, his meal untouched on the side table.

Almost a week had passed since she'd first taken down his dinner and she knew what to expect now. There was an order to things. William liked to eat his dinner in silence. Food was fuel, needed to keep him alive and not something pleasurable, an idea that she found disturbing. She wondered whether he'd always been like that or whether it was the war but, so far, had not dared to ask. She was still trying to work out a way to ask him about his question: whether she was different from all the rest. The hope of discovering an answer had continued to draw her back to the workshop. An answer that would reveal something about her to herself, although she had not quite admitted to being the object of her own interest. It was not the done thing to be interested in oneself. One had a duty to think of others, as her father often said.

In that light at least, she had done Florrie a favour, for delivering William's dinner should really have been her job. Florrie had developed a phobia. The sight of William swinging his crutches and hopping across the courtyard as she stacked the firewood for the stove was enough to send her fleeing into the kitchen, emitting little cries of fear. She couldn't cope with his missing limb, and Della was fed up with the whole palaver. 'You're getting on my quince, Florrie,' she'd say. 'It's just William, same as ever, 'cept for missing a bit of leg.'

Although he'd still not begun to eat, Emily knew from previous visits that when he had finished his meal, it would be time for talking and a glass of whisky. This was the moment she looked forwards to, although not without trepidation as it was impossible to second-guess his mood or what he would talk about. She was grateful, however, that he'd never again mentioned *Fanny Hill*. He swore quite a lot and had even once said 'fuck', which shocked her more than she cared to admit. She'd tried to cover it up, to no avail. 'Off you go, Miss P, back to the nursery,' he'd said sarcastically.

William was not like an uncle and sometimes, when she thought about it, she could scarcely believe that he was her father's brother. He was more than a decade younger. But it wasn't just that. For instance, she had never heard her father swear. But perhaps the war had changed William. Perhaps before the war he hadn't sworn either. He'd told her that he was a different man now, one-legged and busted up to buggery. 'Twenty-five going on a hundred,' he'd said morosely.

Apart from that he did not talk about the war, and she did not ask him, even though she had questions. She wanted to know what exactly had happened to his leg. She knew he had been wounded in New Guinea and wondered if Harry had been with him then and where Harry was now? Sometimes she could feel herself wanting to tell him about Lydia – how she didn't love Harry. Something always stopped her. The vision of a furious Lydia.

Sitting in the wing chair, waiting, she broke the silence. 'Aren't you hungry?'

Since she'd put the tray on the side table, he had made no effort to slide it onto his lap. He had barely seemed to notice that she was there at all. He leaned down and picked up the bottle of whisky from beside the armchair. He took his glass and began to pour. His hands were steady, and he filled it to the top without spilling a drop.

She knew what this meant – he had been drinking. She had seen how the first glass was always the hardest to fill; his hands shook so much that the whisky spilled. The second glass was a little better, but it wasn't until the third that his tremors stopped. And yet he did not seem to get drunk. Or at least, he didn't slur his words or laugh too much, or even turn red in the face the way she had seen Uncle Cec do once or twice. It wasn't like that. Instead he became darker and more concentrated, as if inside him everything was black as pitch.

She watched as he tossed back the contents of the glass in a single action.

'No woman's ever going to want me now. That's it for me.'

She waited, but he said nothing more and filled his glass again. How could she console him when, in truth, she could not really imagine what sort of woman would want a man who spent most of his time in a semi-dark workshop, smoking cigarettes and drinking whisky, whether he was one-legged or not. Admittedly she did not know a lot of women, apart from family members. There was her mother's best friend, Pearl, but she was married. And Miss Maunder, who was a lesbian and ancient. And her teachers – Mrs Martingale and Madame Dubois and Miss Falugi. Perhaps Miss Falugi, being unmarried, was a possibility. She wore her hair in an attractive French roll, but her earlobes were pierced, which was a black mark against her, pierced ears being considered déclassé. Now that she thought about it, Emily wondered why that was the case and whether it was an immutable rule. And if Miss Falugi were Italian as she suspected, and quite probably a Catholic, was that also to be counted against her?

Claudio was Italian and a Catholic, although if he was also a communist, which he had not denied, then he didn't believe in God and so couldn't really be called a Catholic. However, on any scale, a communist was worse than being a Catholic. At the heart of her rambling train of thought was the dawning recognition that, so far in her life, she had accepted a great deal as truth that might, in reality, be simply prejudice.

Would William object to pierced ears? she wondered, the question returning her to the present where William was saying something.

'Not that you'd know about that.'

'About what?' she asked.

'The feel of a woman's breast in the palm of your hand.'

She felt the telltale tickle of heat rising up her neck and was relieved that he was unlikely to notice in the dim light.

'I'm a useless cripple,' he continued in a bitter voice. 'Have a look around. There's no three-legged animals here. They're knocked on the head because they're no damn use.'

She could think of nothing to counter the brutal finality of his statement, and William too seemed to have run out of words, turning his empty glass around and around, staring into it as if it were a crystal ball and the answer to some important question could be found there.

And then it came to her. 'Like Lord Byron.'

William glanced up with a frown.

'You know,' she said, 'his foot. He was a cripple too, but famous … and handsome.' She felt herself blushing and hurried on. 'And he swam the Hellespont.'

She stopped, wishing she hadn't mentioned the Hellespont as William had never expressed a desire to swim, let alone strike out across a major stretch of water. Why had she mentioned Byron at all? He had a club foot, but it was hardly the same thing as missing half a leg. If only she could take back her words, and she stared down at her lap to avoid the scornful – or possibly angry – look that William was sure to be directing towards her.

'So you know Bryon,' he said. 'I'm impressed.'

She knew she should reveal the truth: that she did not know Byron at all and had never read a single one of his poems. Her knowledge was limited to what Mrs Martingale had told them in class in one of her increasingly common *divertissements*. He had sounded wonderfully romantic. They were studying Wordsworth at the time, but Mrs Martingale, for some reason known only to

217

herself, had abandoned Wordsworth for a biographical sketch of Lord Byron, who wasn't even on the syllabus. But William's praise was too precious and she could not bring herself to give it up.

'*Childe Harold's Pilgrimage* is a work of genius,' he added.

She smiled and nodded – the prospect of a literary discussion on some child called Harold was making her feel sweaty. But at least William was no longer talking about being a useless peg leg.

The armchair creaked as he levered himself up. He leaned over and felt around at the back of the seat.

'Here,' he said, and tossed her a small torch.

She turned it on and together they made their way across the room to the book wall. William knew what he was searching for and it did not take him long to find it. He pulled out a slim volume from high up on the shelves. They returned to their chairs and, once settled, he opened the book and flicked over the pages, searching for something.

'"Darkness",' he announced, 'by Lord Byron.'

'*I had a dream, which was not all a dream.*
The bright sun was extinguish'd, and the stars
Did wander darkling in the eternal space,
Rayless, and pathless, and the icy earth
Swung blind and blackening in the moonless air –'

The words wove a powerful spell, and a terrifying death-filled vision of the end of the world unfolded. Cities were burned to the ground and forests extinguished in crackling blazes, men turned into ghouls and fiends, birds shrieked in fear as the natural world devoured itself, and no love was left.

'*The winds were wither'd in the stagnant air,*
And the clouds perish'd; Darkness had no need

218

Of aid from them – She was the Universe.'

Upon reading the final lines William closed the book. Neither of them spoke, still under the devastating spell of Byron's apocalyptic vision. She could not imagine a gloomier poem – the earth reduced to a *lump of death, a chaos of hard clay* and the last two surviving men dying in horror at the sight of each other. Her attempt to cheer William up was a dismal failure, and when he picked up the bottle of whisky and poured them both a glass, she felt so miserable and distracted that she gulped hers down without thinking. An explosion of fiery heat hit the back of her throat, sucking the air from her lungs, and making her cough and gasp as tears poured from her eyes. When the coughing had stopped, she made the miraculous discovery that the burning sensation had become a pool of warmth in her stomach.

After the second drink she began to feel hot, her limbs loose. The outside world was turning into a distant memory and time was slowing down; everything was happening in a stretched-out way. William's face was stretching out too – and blurring. Or was that her?

'If I could just forget, but I can't. And no use plucking out my eyes – it's on the inside, in my head,' he was saying.

She tried to concentrate, unsure whether he was reciting another poem. His face was moving in unexpected ways. She hoped he would not ask for her opinion. He filled her glass for the third time, and the whisky slid down her throat even though she had made up her mind not to drink it. Thoughts and actions had become uncoupled. William was still speaking but she could not hear properly – it was as if she was underwater.

She got up and began to walk towards the door. The room

was the deck of a ship in rough seas, and everything was rocking and sliding. If only she could make it to the door – she had to breathe fresh air.

The journey back to the house seemed to take forever. Her feet would not cooperate and, instead of travelling in a straight line up the path, she listed to the left and found herself stumbling through the orchard in the dark.

When at last she found her way to the south verandah and entered the white room through the French doors, she lay down on her bed without undressing. Instead of feeling better, as she had hoped, the slightest movement brought a wave of nausea. All she could do was to remain as still as a corpse. Even closing her eyes was out of the question, for it made the room spin.

She could not tell how much time passed in this way before a summer storm swept in from the west. Thunder rumbled, and through the French doors she saw the flash and flicker of sheet lightning. Water rushed along the gutters, sweeping up leaves and sticks and gurgling into downpipes, filling the rainwater tanks and pooling outside the billiard room where the ground sloped the wrong way and the verandah had subsided. The wind strengthened, and she heard the crack of a tree branch as it split and fell, and the relentless banging of a loose sheet of iron on the garden shed. Frogs emerged from their hiding places to rejoice noisily. She wondered how long she was going to suffer and if she was ever going to feel normal again.

28

'*AND ROUND ABOUT THE THRONE were four and twenty seats: and upon the seats I saw four and twenty elders sitting, clothed in white raiment; and they had on their heads crowns of gold.*'

Della was mincing meat for rissoles and had been reciting nonstop ever since Emily had crept into the kitchen, her head in a vice with an invisible sadist tightening the screws. She sat down at the kitchen table, hoping that a cup of weak tea might make her feel better. Della's voice, usually so comforting, even when the topic was biblical violence and revenge, was definitely not helping.

'*And out of the throne proceeded lightnings and thunderings and voices.*'

On the matter of lightnings and thunderings, the cook's tone rose accordingly. Emily winced as each word struck her head like a hammer blow. She wanted to ask Della to stop but couldn't summon the energy. Florrie bustled across and put down a plate of kidneys and bacon. It was the final trigger. Her stomach heaved and a rush of heat flared up from within, sweat beads popped on her forehead, and the room began to tilt. As she got up from the table, Florrie's alarmed face hove into view. She tried to say that she felt sick but it was too late. She closed her eyes and vomited.

Grandmother put a little bell, a jug of lemon barley water and a glass on the bedside table.

'Tummy wog. Best thing is rest and you'll be up and about in no time.'

On the other side of the room, Eunice closed the window. 'No time at all,' she echoed, before moving back to stand beside Grandmother.

'If you need anything, just ring the bell.' Grandmother rested the back of her hand on Emily's forehead. 'Normal,' she said. 'It can't be too serious.'

Emily attempted a weak smile from her sickbed, grateful for their ministrations, and relieved that tummy wogs needed no causal explanation. She had caught sight of Della in that awful moment after her stomach had rebelled and delivered its contents onto Florrie's recently polished kitchen floor. She was sure that Della had smelt a rat – a whisky-soaked one. It was seeing the cook's expression that had made her feign a sort of semi-faint, knowing that she would not be able to hold out in the face of an interrogation. Thank goodness Grandmother and

Eunice had not the slightest suspicion. Nevertheless, she wished the two nurses would hurry up and leave her in peace. Even their unusually benign presence felt too demanding. All she wanted to do was sleep.

When she woke, her headache had receded, and the nausea was gone. She poured a glass of lemon barley water and gulped it down, wondering what time it was. It felt like afternoon, and the thought of something to eat was quite appealing. But so too was lying in bed. She propped herself up with pillows and gazed out at the garden. It was a cool cloudy day and every now and then raindrops splattered on the roof before the wind whisked them away. The lawn was strewn with branches and leaves ripped from the trees by the brief but violent storm of the night before. In the pear tree, parrots began to squabble and squawk. A family of blue fairy wrens hopped about on the verandah, catching insects.

Hunger was beginning to get a grip, and she wondered whether to go down to the kitchen for a slice of cinnamon teacake and a cup of tea when Claudio walked across the lawn pushing a wheelbarrow. Sinking back against the pillows, she watched him come to a stop. He began to rake up the leaves and pile branches into the barrow. He worked with an easy rhythm, and she remembered working alongside him in the kitchen garden and wished she were beside him now. But watching him was also enjoyable. There was no need for sly glances; she could stare as much as she liked, grateful that the wide verandah sheltered the room from the sunlight, so that looking in from outside all one could see were shadows.

When the barrow was full, and just as the clouds had dispersed and the sun came out, he leaned against the trunk of the pear tree and took out his tobacco pouch. She watched, her thoughts drifting like the smoke from his cigarette, murmuring lines from Keats's ode 'To Autumn'. She wanted to introduce Claudio to Keats, sure that he would respond like her, and secretly hoping that he would be impressed by her feat of memory. Committing 'To Autumn' to memory made her feel like the person she wanted to be, admired for her intelligence and grace, rather than the guilty sexual degenerate she feared she was becoming.

Remembering Mrs Martingale's instructions to the class, that poetry had to be felt and not read out like a laundry list, she stopped murmuring and recited aloud with expression.

'... *to swell the gourd, and plump the hazel shells*
With a sweet kernel; to set budding more,
And still more, later flowers for the bees,
Until they think warm days will never cease,
For Summer has o'er-brimm'd their clammy cells —'

She paused, feeling unnerved by the *o'er-brimm'd* and *clammy cells*, which felt far too close to her experiences in the big armchair. It was the word *clammy* in particular, and she was trying to think of a more tepid sort of poem when Claudio straightened up. He threw his cigarette on the ground, grinding it under his boot. She followed his gaze and saw Lydia walking through the orchard in his direction.

Her spine stiffened, every part of her coming to attention. Was Lydia just passing by, or was she heading directly to Claudio?

What could she want with him? Perhaps she had come to give him instructions about a job, in which case it would not take long as Lydia never wasted words. She said do this, do that and, on the whole, one did it.

She was still hoping that Lydia would veer away, but she did not. She reached Claudio and began to speak to him, running her hand through her hair, pushing it off her face in a characteristic gesture that made Emily's throat feel tight. She watched as Claudio said something in reply. She heard Lydia laugh and sensed it ripple through her body. That same laugh, just like the night she'd tried to get rid of the dress and seen Lydia outside the workshop. Then Claudio stepped back, behind the pear tree. To Emily's consternation, Lydia followed him.

She threw off the bedclothes and moved across to the window, but her view was still obscured by the tree. Her heart was racing, and she felt her stomach lurch and knew it was not the whisky. How long would it take her to put clothes on? She felt conflicted between staying at her post or going in search of them. But she couldn't tear herself away in case there was something more to see, although she dreaded seeing it, whatever the 'it' was. And then Lydia reappeared, pushing a hand through her hair again as she walked off towards the yard.

She waited, glued to the window. Where was Claudio? What had happened? Had they ...? She tried to stop the word *kissed* from being thought, but it was too late. Claudio stepped into view and she saw him glance after Lydia before he turned in her direction. She bounded across to the bed and pulled the bedclothes up to her chin, as he ambled across to the wheelbarrow. He lifted it up and wheeled it away towards the compost heap at the far corner of the orchard. She heard him whistling and allowed herself a malicious thought about whistlers but couldn't sustain it.

Everything that she had managed to forget or not to think, or justify and distort, surged into her consciousness. The truth could no longer be denied. Lydia and Claudio were in love. Why else would Lydia have sworn her to secrecy? And that night in the yard beside the stables, when Lydia had laughed: he must have been there. She'd been lying to herself, pretending that it wasn't true. What's more, the handkerchief proved it. He'd kept it as a love token.

Eunice's head popped around the edge of the door. 'Oh good, you're awake,' she said. 'Feeling better?'

There was no time to hide her misery, before Eunice had reached her bedside.

'Dear, oh dear,' she clucked, and Emily burst into tears despite herself. Crying in front of Eunice was the last thing she wanted to do. 'It was like this for me too,' Eunice soothed. 'We just have to make the best of it. Waifs and strays, both of us', and she sat down on the end of the bed, patting the bedclothes in the region of Emily's legs.

As Eunice's words penetrated, she pulled her legs up, out of reach. That Eunice should think they were alike was too awful to contemplate. She had a mother and a father. She was going home in two weeks. She would never be a waif or a stray. The urge to put Eunice in her place and make their differences abundantly clear was almost overwhelming, but the habits of her short lifetime held her back. She couldn't be so rude. Meanwhile Eunice was scrabbling about under her dress from where she produced a handkerchief.

'Here you are,' she said. 'Wipe your tears.'

Knowing that it must have been tucked into the elastic of Eunice's bloomers, she took it, barely suppressing a look of appalled disgust; just as she feared, it was horribly warm to the touch. She tried unsuccessfully to hold her breath, but the sickly intimate scent of Lily of the Valley talcum powder insinuated itself into her nostrils. A vision of baggy bloomers and skinny old shanks rose up. She gagged, and was forced to disguise it with a coughing fit, at the end of which she saw that Eunice was holding something else that must have been in her hand since she'd entered the room: a folded-up piece of yellowing material.

'Second-hand, I'm afraid, but beggars can't be choosers. I've been meaning to give it to you. It's well overdue – I can't imagine what your mother was thinking.' Eunice put the material on the bed and stood up. 'If I were you, I'd get up. Lying in bed in the daytime is a recipe for melancholy.'

Eunice's sympathetic tone had gone, replaced with something more familiar and censorious, for which she could only feel relieved. This version of Eunice was so much easier to dislike.

Once the door had closed and she was alone again, she picked up the thing on the bed, holding it gingerly with the tips of forefinger and thumb. To her enormous surprise it was a bra. She held it up, remembering how much she had been prepared to risk to acquire such an object. The cotton was thin and yellow from repeated laundering. She knew she ought to feel grateful to Eunice for coming to the rescue, but the thought of putting on a bra that had once encased those ancient breasts made her feel queasy. More than that, it seemed to confirm the link that her fake cousin had made: that they were both 'waifs and strays'. They were alike. She remembered William's words about whether she was different and tossed it to the floor.

She lay down and pulled up the bedclothes again. But as soon as she closed her eyes, Claudio and Lydia rose up, arms around each other in a passionate embrace. She squeezed her eyes shut more tightly. Colours flashed and stars sparkled in the darkness, but her internal vision of the lovers refused to budge. She opened her eyes. It was no use – Eunice was right. Lying in bed had become a recipe for melancholy. A tear rolled down her cheek and she abandoned herself to the paradoxical pleasure of her misery. Before long, however, although she did not want to admit it, she began to feel bored.

It was inevitable she would return to the bra. She leaned over and picked it up. Could she stand to put it on? Giving it a cautious sniff she was relieved to discover that it smelled only of freshly washed cotton. Perhaps it was not Eunice's after all? Might it have once belonged to Lydia? The more she thought about it, the more she convinced herself that this was the case. It was true that Lydia's breasts were as round and plump as peaches, but that was now. She'd been fourteen once too.

It took a great deal of fumbling about before she managed to put it on. At the dressing-table mirror she turned side-on before facing it again. She pushed out her chest and felt a surge of excitement at the curve of her breasts, an excitement that not even the knowledge of Claudio and Lydia's liaison could destroy. She hoped it was not evidence of something trivial in her nature that she was able to feel this way and thought of her mother, whose mood sometimes improved with trivial distractions.

With the bra on, there was no point in going back to bed. What's more, she was quite ravenous and it was almost time for afternoon tea. With any luck, Della might have made drop scones.

29

WITH *MIDDLEMARCH* TUCKED IN THE crook of her arm, Emily set off around the house, destined for the swinging seat on the front verandah. Grandmother and Eunice had departed in the Packard on their monthly do-gooding pilgrimage to deliver fresh vegetables to the needy of Garnook. Eunice was the driver, a fact that Emily found secretly impressive. Not even her mother had a driving licence. More importantly, however, the absence of Eunice meant she had time on her hands. She was looking forwards to lolling on the swinging seat without fear of being harassed. With any luck she might even manage another chapter of *Middlemarch*.

Flea was snoozing on the seat, and she shooed him off before sitting down. She opened the book, flicking over the pages, trying to find her place and thinking, for the hundredth time at least, about Lydia and Claudio's kiss behind the pear tree. That she had not seen the kiss was true, but she was in no doubt that it had occurred. Why else had Claudio been avoiding her these last few days? *Work*, an inner voice responded, but she brushed it aside. If he'd wanted to come, he would have, even with Uncle Cec cracking the whip. She stared at the page: *It was in that way that Dorothea came to be sobbing as soon as she was securely alone.* She felt a rush of fellow feeling for Dorothea and a pressure at the back of her eyes that hinted at forthcoming tears.

The seat rocked, and Lydia plonked down beside her.

'Good god, still reading that dull book.' She did not wait for an answer. 'You've been avoiding me these last three days.'

'No, I haven't,' Emily lied.

Lydia jumped up from the seat and grabbed her by the arm. 'Doesn't matter. Come on. I need you.'

Resisting was not an option and, despite everything, once in Lydia's orbit, she lost the will to do so. Pulled along in her aunt's wake, she followed her to her bedroom. Once inside, Lydia kicked the door closed. Emily took in the unmade bed, and the clothes heaped on the corner chair. As always it was a mess: magazines were scattered on the floor. Some roses in a vase on the dressing table had dropped all their petals, and she caught the whiff of rank flower water. Harry's photograph lay face down on the bedside table. She moved across and perched on the end of the bed.

Lydia opened the door of her wardrobe, took something out and tossed it at her. 'This should fit.'

A white tennis dress landed in her lap. Her heart sank. 'But I'm hopeless.'

'Never mind. It's only doubles and we need a fourth.'

Doubles? With whom? And where? Not that it mattered – the ignominy would be the same, whatever the time and place.

'I don't have a racquet, or any shoes.'

Lydia dived back into the cupboard and extracted a pair of sandshoes. 'If they're too big, you can stuff some cottonwool in the toes, and there are racquets galore in the hall cupboard.'

She looked beseechingly at Lydia, but her aunt's face was not encouraging.

'Try it on.' Lydia had her hands on her hips.

'Now?'

'No, next week. Yes, of course now. We have to be at the McDougalls' by three,' she said, and walked over to the dressing table, took out her silver cigarette case and lit a cigarette. Lydia opened the window to let out the smoke before turning back. 'For heaven's sake, take off your clothes. Or shall I undress you myself?'

The thought of Lydia unbuttoning her blouse or tugging down her skirt was alarming enough to finally galvanise her into action. She unbuttoned her skirt and tried to gain time by folding it, until Lydia, alert to such delaying tactics, threw her cigarette out of the window and whisked the skirt from Emily's hands.

She tossed it on the floor. 'Blouse,' she ordered.

It was just what she had been dreading, for it meant revealing Eunice's cast-off bra, which was not only embarrassing due to its worn-out state but, after three days of constant wear, was beginning to smell. She had planned to wash it in the bathroom handbasin and hang it on a coathanger by her bedroom window to dry overnight. But she'd been afraid it would not dry and had delayed taking any action.

Under Lydia's observant eye, she unbuttoned her blouse and slid it off. She tried to fold her arms across her chest, partly to hide the bra but also because she felt naked and vulnerable. Lydia, however, was having none of it, and wrenched her arms open. At the sight of the bra, she said nothing. Instead she turned away and opened the top drawer of her chest of drawers. After rummaging for some time she returned with a creation of pale pink satin.

'Here. Get rid of that ghastly old thing.'

Emily took the pink bra. But now she did not have enough hands to undo the old one. Her brain had stopped working; she could only manage one thing at a time. Lydia grabbed her by the shoulders, spun her around and began to undo Eunice's bra. Feeling her aunt's firm warm fingers on her skin, she had a flash of Phoebe from the pages of *Fanny Hill* and could not prevent an involuntary shudder.

Lydia yanked at the bra strap. 'Stay still.'

'Sorry.'

The trick was to turn her body into a lump of wood, an object that did not feel, and could not respond. And her mind – she had to empty it of thoughts, for one thought led to another in disturbing ways. Soon the old bra was removed and the pink satin replacement expertly fitted.

'Arms up,' Lydia said, and she felt the dress slide over her head. Lydia stepped back to scrutinise the result. 'Good enough.'

The sandshoes turned out to fit quite well too – there was no need for cottonwool.

30

A SHORT TIME LATER, EMILY found herself helping Lydia harness Dapple to the gig, after which they set off for the McDougalls' with their tennis clothes in a bag. They did not want to arrive in dusty tennis whites. At least Lydia didn't; Emily did not want to arrive at all. She knew her serve was hopeless and that humiliation awaited.

The McDougalls' property, Rose Park, was four miles down the road. It was a balmy day, not too hot and, according to Lydia, 'Perfect for a game of tennis.' On their arrival, a tiny man with a wrinkled walnut of a face helped them down from the gig. Emily tried not to stare.

'Thank you, Jack,' Lydia said.

As Jack led Dapple away, Lydia met her puzzled gaze. 'Jockey. Not anymore of course. Now he looks after the horses.'

Emily nodded.

'Racehorses,' Lydia added.

The house was two-storied and grand, built from great blocks of pale stone. A young woman in a pinafore greeted them at the front door.

'Good afternoon, Iris,' Lydia said, as they stepped into the entry hall.

Emily felt her eyes widen at the sight of the expanse of tiled mosaic floor and the magnificent cedar staircase, curving up to unknown realms. Halfway up there was a landing where the stairs changed direction and behind it light slanted through a tall stained-glass window.

'Shall I take your bag, Miss?'

Overawed by the opulence around her, she was scarcely aware of relinquishing the bag to Iris. Mount Prospect was suddenly reduced to a rambling farmhouse filled with shabby Persian rugs and faded upholstery. Even the billiard room with its spacious dimensions, the walls decorated with racing prints and oil paintings from the 'artistic side of the family', was nothing compared to the grandeur of the McDougalls' entry hall. She felt a squirming embarrassment remembering her boastful accounts of Mount Prospect to Dorothy, and then secret relief as she reminded herself that they had only ever taken place in her imagination. Thank goodness too that she hadn't sent the letter, for it contained further fanciful descriptions of the homestead. Why on earth had she mentioned a turret?

She was still gazing up at the stained-glass window in which the figure of a bold young woman was striding forth with a hunting bow in one hand and a great staghound by her side, when a not-quite-so-young woman in a tennis dress, carrying a racquet, bounded down the stairs. Reaching the landing, she passed in front of the window and Emily had the peculiar sensation that the huntress had stepped out of the window and was now leaping down the stairs towards them.

'Lydia, you're here at last.'

The woman gave Lydia a quick kiss on the cheek leaving behind a smudge of her dark red lipstick. 'And you must be Emily. I'm Ruth. Come on then. Let's get you both changed. Betty's here already, practising her serve.'

They hurried after Ruth as she whisked them back upstairs – with Emily wondering if Betty was the same Betty who'd failed the rabbiting test – and into an enormous guest bedroom where, magically, Iris had already laid out their tennis dresses on the bed.

Ruth lounged against the chest of drawers, twirling her tennis racquet, radiating an unnerving vitality as Emily wondered how she was going to survive the coming ordeal. She was sure Ruth would show no mercy to a weak serve. Even more pressing than the thought of her serve was the problem of undressing in front of a stranger. If only she could follow Lydia's example and shrug off her clothes without a hint of embarrassment. As she fiddled with the buttons on her blouse, she hoped that Ruth would at least look in another direction. But it was not to be.

'Are you enjoying your holiday, Emily?' Ruth asked.

'Yes, thank you.'

'What a fibber,' Lydia said with a laugh. She had already changed into her tennis dress and was pulling on her sandshoes. 'She tried to escape on her very first day.'

A whoosh of prickly heat enveloped her. How ghastly that

Lydia had known all this time and never said a word. Claudio must have told her, which made it even worse. She attempted a casual laugh that stuck in her throat.

'Come on, slowcoach. Hurry up.' Lydia picked up the tennis dress and held it out for her, while at the same time she mouthed something to Ruth.

'Ah,' Ruth said. 'I think I'll go and see how Betty's getting on. You know the way, Lydia.'

She experienced a wave of embarrassed gratitude towards both women, for she understood that a message had been given. At least undressing in front of Lydia was tolerable; it would be the second time she had done so today.

Once suitably attired for tennis, she followed Lydia into the garden and along a walkway covered by a wrought-iron rose arbour heavy with summer blooms. They passed clipped shrubs and winding paths edged with hedges of lavender, and grand beds filled with delphiniums, foxgloves and many other flowers, whose names she did not know. Further away, huge trees with capacious canopies soared skyward. The limits of the garden were not visible.

A gardener was at work trimming the edges of a green expanse of a lawn. It was all quite magnificent, and she couldn't avoid a surge of dislike for Rose Park. In the face of its splendour, the status she'd accorded Mount Prospect was collapsing. She was beginning to feel quite dejected and so it was a relief to be distracted by the sound of someone hitting tennis balls. They emerged from the rose arbour to see Ruth and Betty warming up on the reddish-brown *en tout cas* court.

It was soon decided that Ruth, as the best player, would partner Emily. The foursome gathered at the net to decide who should serve first. Ruth tossed a coin: it was Betty to serve.

'Just don't faint on me,' Lydia said to Betty with a mocking smile, confirming Emily's suspicion that Betty was indeed the Rabbiting Fainter.

The game began. Most of the time Ruth shouted 'mine', and it was Emily's job to scuttle out of the way. But there was no avoiding her service game. She trudged to the baseline and turned to face Betty, who was bouncing on her toes at the other end of the court in an annoyingly confident way, swiping her racquet through the air with swishy practice shots. Her blonde hair was pulled back into a ponytail and it too swished up and down as she bounced.

On her first attempt to serve, she missed the ball altogether and had to pretend that the sun had got in her eyes. On the second go the ball plopped over the net with all the power of a half-deflated balloon. Caught unawares, Betty could not reach it in time, and the ball dribbled to a stop before she arrived at the net.

'Well done,' Betty said, dripping with irony, and took up her position inside the service box ready for Emily to serve to Lydia. It did not escape Emily's notice that Betty no longer bothered to bounce at all.

The game proceeded and was quickly lost fifteen-forty when Emily double-faulted on the rest of the points. Tears of rage and shame pricked her eyes as she walked to the deuce court.

Ruth jogged over and squeezed her shoulder. 'Buck up, it's only a game,' she whispered. 'And don't worry about Betty – poor thing's got thick ankles.'

Even in the depths of her despair, she couldn't help a smile.

Ruth smiled back. 'C'mon, kid,' she said in a Humphrey Bogart voice.

She decided that despite the ostentation of Rose Park, she quite liked Ruth. They lost three sets to love. Lydia and Betty were both good players, and not even Ruth could overcome the handicap of having her for a partner.

At that juncture Iris arrived with homemade lemonade and ginger biscuits, and the four tennis players retired to a rug on the lawn beside the tennis court. It wasn't long before they began to talk about the war and the men who had joined up from the district.

'Pity Orm's too old to serve,' Ruth said, lying back on the rug. 'He likes killing things.'

Lydia laughed. Betty, on the other hand, looked shocked. 'You shouldn't say things like that.'

'Why not?' Ruth blinked at Betty in a seemingly innocent way. Emily watched with interest, wondering how Betty would respond, for she thought that Ruth's question was not really innocent at all, but concealed a challenge. Betty must have thought so too, for she shrugged and refused to answer.

Ruth turned to Emily. 'I don't think you've met my husband,' she said, and went on to explain that Orm was quite a bit older than her.

'Where is he, anyway?' Betty asked, clearly trying to inveigle her way back into the conversation.

'Mucking about with the horses, I expect,' Ruth said. 'Anything to avoid tennis.'

Emily wondered how old Ruth was. She had noticed some wrinkles on her neck and felt sure she must be at least thirty.

'Has anyone got a cigarette?' Lydia asked.

Ruth reached for a packet of Craven A on the edge of the rug. She put two in her mouth and lit them both before handing one to Lydia.

The conversation rambled on in a desultory way, the afternoon sun filtering through the leaves of the trees above. They spoke about people Emily had not met, and after a while she drifted off into her own thoughts. At first it was annoying to find Dorothy intruding until she was able to picture her nemesis waiting to be invited onto the rug. Now Emily was the one with the ability to give or withhold, and she was in no hurry to beckon Dorothy forwards. No, it was Dorothy's turn to experience what it was like, loitering on the outer, waiting for the invitation that never came.

Perhaps in a minute, she might deign to look up …

'How's William getting along?' Betty's voice jolted her from the daydream.

'Alright, I suppose,' Lydia replied. 'Better off asking Emily. They're thick as thieves.'

Betty gave her a questioning look. 'Emily?'

All eyes were on her as she tried to collect her thoughts, still recovering from the secret rush of gratification at being elevated to the position of the one in the know. Lydia had handed it to her, just like that. She couldn't respond with any old thing. How *was* William? But she discovered that she did not know what to say. How was he? Bitter, furious and unhappy? Interesting and marvellously well-read? Could she say that he was probably an alcoholic? She could hardly tell them of his drunken cursing, of his despair that his life was no longer worth living. That no woman would want him. That he'd never again feel the shape of a woman's breast in the palm of his hand. She tried to blink away a sudden vision of Claudio's hand enclosing her breast, and the imagined feel of his palm against her nipple.

'Emily?' It was Lydia's voice.

'Look at her – she's away with the fairies.' Ruth reached across and grabbed the toe of her sandshoe, giving it a tug.

'He's quite well, thank you …' was all she finally managed, aware that her response was hopelessly inadequate.

'What a fund of information you are,' Ruth said in a teasing way.

She could feel her lips moving, scrambling for something impressive that would hold their attention. But it was too late; Betty had already moved on.

'Any news of Harry?' Betty said, turning back to Lydia.

'No.' Lydia's answer was sharp, but the Rabbiting Fainter was not so easily put off.

'You'd better hope the Japs don't get a hold of him. I've heard they don't take prisoners.'

Lydia scrambled to her feet and, without saying another word, rushed away towards the house.

'Talk about putting your foot in it.' Ruth glared at Betty, who had the good grace to look slightly chastened.

'Should I …?' Betty half rose, but Ruth shook her head.

'No, I'll go,' she said, and hurried away.

'I don't know why Lydia had to run off like that,' Betty said in a patently insincere tone. 'I didn't mean to upset her.'

Anyone could see that she was more than satisfied with the effect she'd had. Emily, for her part, nursed a secret feeling of superiority, for she knew things that Betty did not. She knew that Lydia had rushed away not out of love for Harry but the very absence of it. If Harry had been captured by the Japs and murdered, then it was all Lydia's fault, for her lack of love had left him vulnerable. Of course it wasn't her fault, she reminded herself; that was just Lydia's theory. And Harry hadn't been captured. Although perhaps he had. It was impossible to know for sure.

Now, with only the two of them left, she couldn't think of anything to say. Betty was silent too, and after a while her feelings of superiority were replaced by the exact opposite. She felt quite inadequate, being of so little interest that her companion couldn't be bothered making conversation. It was almost a relief when Betty suggested a return to the tennis court.

It was a one-sided affair and, after a couple of love games, Betty called a stop to it.

'I'll teach you how to serve instead,' she offered, much to Emily's disappointment, as she had begun to hope that they could adjourn to the house – the mansion – where she might have the opportunity to explore. Ruth had mentioned something about a ballroom with a chandelier that had been imported from France in the 1920s. Orm, so she had discovered from the conversation on the rug, was fabulously rich.

'You can't go through life with a serve like that. You'll be a social pariah.'

Emily wanted to point out that at least she didn't faint at the sight of a dead rabbit. Nor did she have ankles the size of a heifer. Naturally she couldn't actually say either of those things and gave in to Betty's urgings to practise her swing.

'You're doing it all wrong.'

She would have liked to swing the racquet down on the Fainter's blonde head. That she was doing it all wrong was hardly news. Betty stood behind her and together they held the racquet and swung it through the service action. They did it a few more times, and she could feel Betty's breasts against her back, which was both distracting and horrible, and at the same time sort of exciting. It did not seem all that long ago that she had never thought about her body at all and now, whatever she did or thought, it was always intruding.

She gripped the handle of the racquet more tightly and tried to concentrate on her service action and Betty's instructions.

'Your body has to remember it – like a dance step; it's there in the muscles and all you have to do is let the body do the work.'

After a few more swings with Betty holding on too and her breasts squishing against Emily's back, the movement began to feel quite fluid. It was time to put it into action. For the first time since she had stepped on the court, she thwacked the ball in the centre of her racquet and watched in amazement as it whizzed over the net and into the corner of the service box.

'Bravo, well done,' Betty shouted. Tennis was rather boring, but she couldn't help feeling a burst of pride, along with a sudden liking for her coach, whose ankles were really not that fat.

She kept practising and was soon managing to get the ball over the net and into the service box more often than not. She even won a service game, although she suspected that her opponent had not really tried.

The afternoon was giving way to early evening by the time they had finished the set and decided to stop. It was only then that Emily became conscious of Lydia and Ruth's continued absence.

'I hope Lydia's alright,' she said as they gathered up the balls.

'Of course she is,' Betty replied. 'She's just being dramatic. You know people are talking about her and the Italian.'

'What?'

'They say he was fighting over her after church.'

She could hardly believe what Betty was saying. 'No, he wasn't. He was fighting another Italian. They were fighting about politics.'

'Oh. Well, it's only what I heard. Lydia had her arm around him apparently.'

'He was bleeding. She was trying to help.'

'Ugh. Wouldn't catch me.' Betty shook her head as if touching an Italian was a repulsive thought. 'Anyway, I suppose you'd know if ...'

'If what?'

'If there was anything going on. I mean, Harry's been gone a long time. She wouldn't be the first.'

The camaraderie that she'd been feeling towards Betty evaporated. Claudio had not been fighting over Lydia that day after church. She was certain of that. But Betty was right: Harry had been gone a long time, and what she knew but others didn't was that Lydia no longer loved him. The conclusion that Emily had been resisting for so long could no longer be denied – and now everyone else was talking about it too. Claudio and Lydia. She felt a surge of violence towards the bearer of this unwanted information and wished she had the courage to say the word that was on the tip of her tongue. *Bitch*. Or something even worse. But she could not do it.

'There's nothing going on,' she said in a tight voice. 'And if it's alright with you, I'm going to find Lydia.' With those words, she stalked towards the tennis court gate.

'But what about the court? The bagging? Who's going to help me?' Betty wailed.

She didn't reply and marched off in the direction of the house. What a ghastly gossip the Fainter had turned out to be, she thought self-righteously, choosing to forget the hours she had spent in the kitchen trying to winkle information from Della about any and all goings-on.

The further away from the tennis court she got, the more her self-righteousness waned to be replaced by a flat, dull feeling, almost as if the air itself had become heavy and was weighing her down.

Back at the house, the front door was open and she slipped inside. She remembered about the ballroom and wondered whether she should go in search of it, but the thought of getting lost put her off. Anyway, she'd come to find Lydia. But did she have the right to go upstairs on her own? The house was cool, almost cold, and she gave a little shiver. The door had been open, but she couldn't shake off the feeling that she was an intruder and wished that Iris would come. Iris or one of the other servants, as Ruth had made vague reference to the staff, of whom Emily was sure there were many, unlike Mount Prospect.

She couldn't stand around in the entry hall forever and, deciding it was acceptable to go upstairs and get changed out of her tennis whites, set off across the expanse of tiled floor to the staircase.

Upstairs she found the bedroom again, but the door was shut. She knocked and, when there was no reply, she opened it and peered in. The room was just as they had left it.

She sat on the bed and thought about going to look for Lydia and Ruth, but it no longer felt important. The conversation with Betty had left her feeling so deflated it was an effort to do anything but wait for Lydia to find her, and she lay down on the bed. As it turned out, she did not have long to wait.

The door flew open and Lydia burst in. She was carrying her shoes and socks, her tennis dress half unbuttoned. She dropped her shoes on the floor and was undoing the last of the buttons on her dress when she noticed Emily and gasped.

'My god, Emily. What are you doing? You gave me a shock.'

She didn't think an answer was expected and watched dully as Lydia pulled off her dress.

'Don't just sit there watching me like the sphinx. Get changed. If we don't hurry, we'll be going home in the dark.'

They travelled in silence until Rose Park was lost from sight, and they had turned onto the road to Mount Prospect. It was not complete silence as Lydia hummed every now and then. Emily could not stop thinking about what Betty had said. She wanted to think about something else.

'Betty taught me how to serve.'

Lydia smiled. 'Really? Good on her.'

'You were gone for ages.' She hadn't meant it to sound like a reproach. Or perhaps she had.

'I was trying on clothes. Ruth has the most gorgeous dresses. From Le Louvre.'

'Ah.' She tried to make it a casual and affirming *ah*, while wondering how Ruth got her clothes from a museum in Paris. Perhaps with such wealth anything was possible.

'Not the museum in Paris,' Lydia continued as if she had read Emily's mind. 'The dress shop in Collins Street.'

'I knew that.' She was sick of not knowing things.

'Ruth's very generous,' Lydia added.

She had an urge to say something mean about Ruth. She did not know why or, rather, she did not want to examine the fact that she wished to puncture Lydia's good mood. She was about to respond that it was easy for the rich to be generous, when an image of the woman in the cream-coloured car that had whisked Lydia away that day after church popped into her head. It was Ruth. How had she not recognised her before?

'I saw you.'

'Saw me?'

'You and Ruth. After church that day. I saw you get into her car.'

'You were following me?'

'No. I mean, I thought you were just going for a walk.'

'How dare you follow me.'

She felt a nervous fluttering in her stomach. Lydia was on her high horse. 'I didn't mean to be following. Anyway, what does it matter?'

'Because what I do is my business,' Lydia shouted.

'Why are you so angry?' Emily shouted back, surprising herself.

Lydia seemed surprised too. 'What are you shouting for?'

'Because you were.'

'Well, that's because ... Oh, never mind ...' and Lydia gave the reins an angry shake, which Dapple ignored. He plodded on at the same steady pace while Lydia stared ahead, her face set. It was clearly the signal for the conversation to end. But Emily had found her voice, and she was not ready to let it go. Betty's words were still ringing in her ears.

'Betty thinks you're having an affair with Claudio.'

There, she had said it. Every muscle tightened in anticipation of another angry reply. She did not expect Lydia to admit it; in fact she expected a forceful denial. What did she hope to achieve? She wasn't sure, but perhaps in Lydia's denial she would hear an echo of the truth. She kept her eyes on the road and waited, listening to the sound of Dapple's hooves on the gravel, the *ark ark* of a crow as it flew overhead.

When nothing had been said for at least thirty seconds she glanced across. Lydia, it seemed, was ignoring her.

'Because of the fight. You had your arm around him.'

Still Lydia said nothing. It was infuriating.

'Everyone's talking.'

Lydia smiled. At last a reaction. 'Good for them.'

'But shouldn't you tell them it's not true.'

'Why would I do that?'

It was tantamount to a confession; the very thing Emily was trying to elicit from her aunt and yet had dreaded.

'So it is true.' Her voice sounded thin and too high, and she hoped that Lydia had not noticed.

In fact, Lydia laughed. 'I don't know why you listen to Betty. She's a nitwit.' And with that, she began to sing. '*Would you like to swing on a star, carry moonbeams home in a jar, and be better off than you are, or would you rather be a mule …*'

At the word mule, Lydia tapped her with the whip. 'Come on, join in.'

She did not feel like it but, with Lydia's urging, and not wanting to reveal the true state of her feelings, she managed to sing along.

31

EMILY KNOCKED ON THE BLUE DOOR.

'*Entrez,*' William called.

It was early afternoon. Recently she had begun to visit him during the day in order to help with his daily constitutional.

He was sitting in the armchair as she approached, wearing a pair of shorts that came down to the knees. She had almost become used to the empty trouser leg, but now, seeing the raw end of his stump and the way the bit of leg hung limply over the edge of the seat, she felt herself inwardly recoil. She was sure he had seen. He noticed everything, and she expected him to make her pay, for he had abandoned social niceties like the smoothing over of awkward moments.

'Think I might need a little drop before we go,' he said, surprising her by letting it pass. She hurried across to the desk, glad to have something to do, and collected his glass. By the time she returned to the armchair, William was ready with the whisky bottle. He poured himself a generous shot and downed it in a single gulp. She tried not to stare at the bit of leg. It was exerting a pull.

'It's alright,' he said drily. 'You can look at it.'

'I wasn't,' she rushed to defend herself. He had not let her off the hook after all.

He poured himself another glass of whisky, tossed it back and heaved himself out of the chair with the help of his crutches.

After circumnavigating the homestead via the orchard, William suggested that they continue for another round. She agreed. So far he had not been in a talkative mood, but she was still hoping that he might raise again the question of her being a writer. It was on her mind. Progress was slow, and each time his crutches hit the hard dry ground he had begun to grunt through clenched teeth. She could see that he was pushing himself and pretended not to hear when he began to curse under his breath.

'Fuck,' he swore, lurching against her as a crutch slipped into a hole. 'Got to get stronger if I'm going to live,' he muttered. 'Not that I've decided about that yet.'

'About what?'

'Whether I want to live.'

She almost missed her step and gave a little hop as if it was deliberate.

He glanced at her. 'And don't say it,' he ordered.

'What?'

'Life's a precious gift and other Christian rubbish.'

'I wasn't going to.' It was not a total lie – she had no intention of invoking Christianity. But more than anything she wanted to say something that would inspire him about life. The alternative was too awful to dwell on, even if her last attempt at life-giving affirmation had ended in Byron's depressing poem and a bout of drunkenness.

William was sweating profusely. She had begun to sweat too, feeling his every step and trying to think of what she could possibly say to give him hope. Each time he sucked in a breath, he made a sort of whistling sound and, by the time they reached Lydia's snake fence, his knuckles were clenched white around the handles of his crutches. She felt responsible, and that she had been negligent in her self-appointed role as nurse-companion and should not have allowed him to walk so far. But she pretended not to notice his discomfort, remembering how her mother would say, apropos of her father: *Never forget, Emily, that men have their pride.*

She and William stood beside the fence, waiting for his breathing to settle. After a while, he poked a crutch at one of the snakes hanging on the fence.

'Pooh, what a pong.' They exchanged a grin. 'Come on. Home, James,' he said, sounding like Lydia.

They began the journey back to the workshop. Halfway there, she saw Claudio walking towards them, carrying a pick and shovel over his shoulder. As they passed each other, he faltered, as if he was about to stop. All she could think of was that he had betrayed her with Lydia. But could it really be called a betrayal if he'd never been interested in her? If he had only ever loved Lydia? Still. He had betrayed her. They both had.

'To hell with you,' she thought with sudden savagery and went past with her head held high.

But William must have seen something in Claudio's face. 'What's the matter with him?' he asked. 'He's not giving you any trouble, Miss P?'

She shook her head, feeling traitorous blood rush into her cheeks.

'You're blushing.'

'I'm not.'

'You are. Face as red as a penny bunger.'

'Anyway, it's not me.'

'Not you what?'

'You know. Lydia. And Claudio.'

There, it was said. She waited for him to respond, feeling the weight of her words. Lydia hated gossips – busybodies knowing her business and blabbing it about. Thinking of Lydia made her feel guilty and at the same time self-righteous. Why shouldn't she say it? She wanted to say it, to blurt out the words that had been tormenting her. 'They're in love.'

William grinned. She couldn't help feeling offended.

'It's not funny.' Her voice sounded prim. 'It's nothing to laugh about. He's a prisoner of war.' She was beginning to sound like Grandmother or, worse, Eunice. Her mouth felt tight and disapproving.

'How do you know they're *in love*?' William asked, emphasising the words in an exaggerated way.

She had already said too much. But now that the secret was

out, she did not want to stop. They had reached the workshop, and she pushed the door open, letting William enter first. Something was compelling her to speak.

'Because I've seen them.'

In her mind's eye, Claudio and Lydia were standing under the pear tree. This time they did not step out of view. This time, they moved towards each other into an embrace and a lingering kiss.

'Kissing,' she added.

William had reached his desk and she waited for his response, daring him to contradict her. She was hoping he would say something – ask a question or offer an opinion – for without it, how could she say anything more? And yet she wanted to say more. She felt reckless and, when he did not speak, the words flew out of her mouth like moths from an opened drawer.

'They're actually lovers, you know.'

The words hung in the air like smoke signals before William, standing at the desk with his back to her, blew them away with a hoot of laughter. How dare he laugh? The situation was serious. She had to convince him. Betty had said everyone was talking, everyone knew.

'If you don't believe me, ask ...' She got no further for William turned towards her, leaning on a crutch, holding some sheets of writing paper from which he began to read aloud.

'*I suppose you are wondering what Claudio looks like. Everyone thinks that Italians are short and swarthy ...*' He paused and shuffled the pages. 'Let's skip ahead. Here.'

He began to read again with exaggerated expressiveness. '*His teeth are as white as ivory and his smile is merry and yet tinged with melancholy as he is far from home and longs for his family. His hair is* dark and curly, rather like Lord Byron's.' He laughed. 'So I'm not the only one to remind you of George Gordon.'

She could not respond, stuck in an appalled frozen silence. Then in a teasing tone that she knew would haunt her forever, he read on.

'If you could only see his proud dark eyes, and feel the warm touch of his nut-brown skin. His lips are like ripe fruit, and the scent of crushed strawberries wafts on his breath.'

The wafting scent of crushed strawberries! What insanity had possessed her? She gasped for air and tried to shout 'stop' but just like the dream she'd had the first day at Mount Prospect when she'd fallen asleep at the end of the driveway, all she could manage was a feeble squeak.

William shuffled the pages again. 'Let me see. Ah, yes …'

She leaped at him, grabbing at the letter, but he held it up, just out of reach, waving the sheaf of papers above his head, while balancing with one crutch.

'Claudio, Claudio, wherefore art thou, Claudio.' His laughter dinned in her ears and a blazing humiliation rose up from which she knew she would never recover. Something happened to her then. She grabbed the crutch, yanking it from under his arm and, before he could steady himself, shoved him with the end of it as hard as she could. He twisted, pages flew through the air as he fell to the ground with a heavy thud, his body contorted at an awkward angle. He lay still. She was still too, stuck to the spot like Lot's wife. It was only the crutch falling from her hands that released her from immobility. She turned away and ran for the door.

Outside, she did not stop and raced up the path, through the back orchard to the south verandah. She was about to pull open the French doors to the white room when something or someone moved inside the room. In her agitated state, she didn't know if it was real or imagined, but the possibility of confronting another human being was too awful. She had to be alone, and swerved away, rounding the corner to the billiard-room door. Once inside she scuttled past the billiard table and along the passage until she reached the bathroom.

She locked the door and slid down onto the floor. Her breathing was all wrong, full of gasps and exhalations and odd gulping noises that she couldn't control. She lay on the cool tiles until she was able to catch her breath, and slowly sat up. What should she do? The bathroom, with its lockable door, was her only sanctuary.

Steam hung in the air and the bathroom walls dripped with moisture. She lathered soap onto the washer and scrubbed until her skin turned red and tingled painfully. If only she could get rid of everything. She rinsed the washer out under the tap and rubbed it roughly over her face before sliding down until her head was under water and her hair floated out like Ophelia's. With her eyes closed she tried to empty her mind of all thought, but the same sequence recurred over and over, like a piece of film stuck in the projector. She saw herself striking William with the crutch; saw him fall on the floor where he lay in a dishevelled heap. And then it began again, stuck in the same loop.

'Emily?' she heard Lydia calling. 'Are you in there?'

She pushed her feet hard against the end of the bath and surged up, causing a wave of water to slosh over the edge. The water continued to ripple as she gripped the sides of the bath.

'Emily?'

The doorknob was turning.

'I'm in the bath.'

'What are you doing in the bath at this hour? I want to talk to you.'

She watched the doorknob turning.

Lydia banged on the door. 'Open up. I need you.'

'Go away.'

'It's important. Please.' There was a hint of pleading in Lydia's voice but that was soon replaced by an irritated command. 'Let me in!'

She stared at the door, willing Lydia to go away. She closed her eyes against the banging and rattling. Seconds ticked by and the water grew cool. Then the banging stopped. When the water had turned completely cold, she pulled out the plug and watched it swirl and gurgle away. There was no sound from outside the door. She was sure that Lydia had gone.

32

THE AFTERNOON SLIPPED INTO THE early evening without her noticing. After returning from the bathroom and changing into fresh clothes, she sat on the bed for ages. What was she going to do? Would William tell Lydia what she'd revealed to him? Would he – had he already – shown her the contents of the Dorothy letter? Much worse was William's revelation that her letter to Dorothy, far from exemplifying her promise as a writer, showed her to be quite without talent. The memory of his mocking laughter made her feel ill with shame. And then, the way she'd knocked him down and left him lying on the floor of the workshop. If only she could leave now, and never return. But how was that possible?

A sudden explosion of noise brought her distracted thoughts to a temporary and startled halt. Two long rings and one short one: the sounds echoed along the hallway from the extension bell outside the billiard room. Two long and one short. It was a telephone call for Mount Prospect. Of course – that's what she had to do. Telephone Father and tell him to come at once. It was an emergency.

She flew from the room, racing down the hallway. What kind of emergency? It didn't matter, she would think of something. She rounded the first corner, turning right, then left, then right again until she arrived at the entry hall, skidding to a stop beside Grandmother, just as she was replacing the receiver onto the cradle.

'Goodness,' Grandmother said. 'Whatever's the matter?'

'Oh, nothing,' she gasped. 'Was that –?'

'Harry. He's on leave and coming to visit.' Grandmother gave a delighted clap. 'Why on earth hasn't Lydia let us know? What a secretive little minx she can be. Goodness, she'll be thrilled. He's arriving a day early.'

Grandmother took her by the arm, and she wanted to pull away – she had to telephone her father, she had to tell him to come. But, instead, she found herself propelled through the house with Grandmother calling out to Lydia.

'It's just the tonic we all need. I think we should organise a little party, don't you?'

She found herself nodding as they reached Lydia's bedroom.

'Lydia,' Grandmother called, knocking somewhat tentatively on the door. 'Good news.'

There was no answer. Grandmother turned the doorknob and opened it a crack.

'Lydia, dear, are you in there?' When there was no reply, she pulled the door shut again, turning to Emily. 'Perhaps she was going rabbiting. Run down to the yard and see if you can catch her. Quick sticks.'

With Grandmother urging her on, she had no choice but to obey. Once she arrived in the yard, she could see no sign of Lydia, but she hadn't gone rabbiting for the pony cart was still in its spot in the open shed.

She stopped at the blue door and called out, 'Lydia, Lydia.' There was no answer.

Back at the house, she found Grandmother waiting in the kitchen.

'I couldn't find her,' she reported.

'Have you looked in the orchard?' Grandmother was already moving towards the door. 'Come along, she must be about somewhere.'

There was nothing to be done: the telephone call to her father would have to wait until Lydia had been found.

They roamed through the orchard, calling. Mrs Flynn appeared and trotted along with them, but of Lydia there was no sign.

'Where on earth can she be?' Grandmother was becoming irritated.

As they walked across the top lawn, Eunice joined them. Grandmother gave her the good news about Harry, before asking if she'd seen Lydia. 'She seems to have vanished,' she added.

Eunice shook her head, and together they returned to the house via the billiard room.

'Lydia,' Grandmother cried out again.

As they walked down the passage past Lydia's bedroom door, Eunice paused. 'I suppose you've checked her bedroom?' she asked.

'Of course,' Grandmother replied, but Eunice was already opening the door. She pushed it wide open and stepped into the room. Emily and Grandmother followed. The wardrobe door was open and some clothes lay on the floor in Lydia's usual messy way. But Emily saw at once that something was not right. The clutter of make-up and beauty products on the dressing table had disappeared leaving imprints in the dusty surface. And when she looked at the wardrobe, all that remained was a row of empty clothes hangers.

'They've really gone,' she said in an awestruck voice.

'Gone?' Grandmother echoed.

Eunice moved to the open wardrobe. 'Where are her clothes?' She turned to Emily. 'What have you done with them?'

Before she had an opportunity to express her outrage at Eunice's presumption, Grandmother shook her by the shoulder. 'What do you mean, *they've really gone*? What do you mean, *they*?'

She felt her lips twitch under the pressure of words that could not be spoken.

'Tell me,' Grandmother urged.

'I can't.'

'Yes, you can. You must.'

She pressed her lips together, shaking her head. From the corner of her eye she saw Eunice step towards her.

'Answer, you ungrateful little wretch.'

Before she could reply, she felt the sting of Eunice's hand on her cheek. Shocked tears sprang into her eyes and a fury rose up in her. It served them right – let it be known, she didn't care.

'Claudio and Lydia. They've run away together.' She began to laugh. It wasn't funny – it was terrible and everything was wrong – but the laughter took charge, gusting through her, and she couldn't stop until Eunice slapped her again. This time it was a relief, and she subsided into silence.

'Where have they gone?' Eunice demanded.

She shook her head. 'I don't know. They didn't tell me.'

'Where's Cecil?' Grandmother cried. 'We must find Cecil. They can't have got far.' She pushed past them both and proceeded down the hallway calling to Cecil.

Eunice looked at her. 'How could you?' she said, shaking her head in condemnation before she too departed.

Moments later the dinner bell rang out. It was not the usual three or four clangs, instead it went on and on, an urgent proclamation that something terrible was at hand.

She reached the front verandah to see Uncle Cec running across the lawn towards Grandmother, who was still ringing the bell, Eunice by her side. Della and Florrie were standing nearby watching with keen interest as Uncle Cec arrived out of breath.

'The Japs?' he managed to ask before leaning over with his hands on his knees, trying to catch his breath.

'Lydia,' Grandmother replied. 'She's run off with Claudio.'

When Uncle Cec had recovered from his sprint, he went into the house and returned with his shotgun. Emily had never seen him look so commanding. He seemed taller and had an unusual spring in his step. If he killed Claudio it would be her fault.

'You're not going to shoot him?' she said desperately.

'Not if he comes quietly. Womenfolk into the house,' he ordered, 'and stay there until I give the all-clear.'

Grandmother shepherded everyone inside. They heard the sound of the farm truck rattle into life and drive away. It was past seven o'clock and time for dinner, but nobody said a word about eating. Instead they stood around in the sitting room, and at some point Della and Florrie joined them there. Nobody said a word about this either.

Grandmother went to the marble-topped credenza and poured herself a glass of sherry, which she drank in one go. Then she poured two more and gave one each to Eunice and Della.

They were still standing like silent funeral guests when a distant shot rang out. Eunice shrieked and spilled the last of her sherry on the sitting-room rug. In the confusion that followed, Emily saw her chance. She left the room and hurried through the house, exiting via the billiard room. Once outside, she ran across the top lawn. The sun was sinking in the west, but there was enough light to see her way through the orchard. She did not know what she was going to do, just that somehow she had to save Claudio if it was not already too late.

She scrambled under the snake fence and ran towards the shearers' quarters. The truck was bouncing back across the paddock towards the yard gate. She saw it veer towards her and knew that she could not outrun it. Uncle Cec pulled to a stop beside her. One of his working dogs was barking and running up and down on the tray of the truck.

He leaned across and opened the passenger door. 'Thought I told everyone to stay inside.'

He motioned for her to climb into the truck, but she did not. She could hardly speak for fear that Claudio was already lying dead in a pool of blood.

'Claudio ...'

'Doesn't know a thing.'

'But the gunshot?'

'Snake. In the wood heap.'

Her legs felt suddenly weak. 'You didn't shoot him?'

'Shoot him? What the devil would I shoot him for? Fellow was cooking rabbit stew. By Jove it smelled good too. I told him he could teach Della a few –'

'But where's Lydia?' she rudely interrupted. She could tell that Uncle Cec was going off on a tangent.

'Searched the place from top to toe. No sign of her. Come on, you'd better hop in.'

She wanted to see Claudio, more than anything. 'Oh, don't worry about me, I'll walk,' she said, as if everything was quite normal and she was out for an evening stroll.

'Not on your nelly. In you get or your grandmother will have my head.'

She thought about making a run for it, but Uncle Cec was a step ahead. 'Giddy up. Unless you want a nip on the ankles from Clem.' Hearing his name, the dog in the back barked enthusiastically.

She got in. Uncle Cec revved the engine and they set off towards the yard.

'I'd say she's well and truly flown the coop. If you want my opinion, it's your grandmother's fault. Had her on too short a leash. If I was a betting man, I'd say she's headed for the bright lights.'

Ignoring the fact that Uncle Cec loved a flutter, she asked, 'You mean Melbourne?'

'Let's just hope it's not too late,' he said, with a nod.

She supposed he meant too late to bring her back, but she didn't really care. All that mattered was that Claudio was not dead, and that he and Lydia had not eloped, the implications of which were beginning to sink in. Perhaps they were not in love after all. Yet how to account for the mass of evidence upon which she'd based her earlier conclusions?

'Are you sure about Claudio, Uncle Cec? Perhaps they're going to meet up? She could be waiting for him somewhere.'

'No,' Uncle Cec said firmly. 'You're barking up the wrong tree.'

'How do you know?'

'A cove doesn't cook a rabbit stew if he's about to run off with his paramour.'

'But –'

'More to the point, how far would they get?'

'But if they're in love?'

'He'd be rounded up quick smart and spend the rest of the war in the lock-up. The man's no fool.'

They pulled up next to the tractor in the machinery shed. Uncle Cec took his gun from behind the seat and set off for the house with Emily trailing behind. As they passed the workshop, a pale strip of light was visible at the bottom of the blue door. She faltered. Was he alright? Should she …? No, she couldn't bear to face him. She hurried on, trying to catch up with Uncle Cec.

They entered the house together. When Uncle Cec turned into the sitting room, she slipped past and continued up the hallway to the white room. She wanted to be alone. Her head was filled with thoughts of Lydia and Claudio and William and how nothing seemed to make any sense, or at least not the sense that she had previously made of things. Lydia and Claudio had not run away together, and yet Lydia was missing all the same. She remembered how her aunt had said something about an escape fund. If they hadn't got sidetracked because Emily had wanted to escape too, which had led to Lydia saying the awful words *loony bin*, she might have found out where Lydia was planning to go. Was Uncle Cec right? Had she gone to Melbourne? In which case she must have caught the train, and yet who had taken her to meet it? With all her clothes gone, there was no possibility that Lydia had set off on foot.

A feeling of restless confusion propelled her around the room until at last she plonked herself down on the dressing-table stool and stared at her face in the mirror as if searching for answers in the familiar features that gazed back at her. She poked out her tongue. It did not feel like enough, and she twisted her face into a grimace. In the middle of her facial contortions her eyes snagged on a white rectangular object propped up against the bottom of the dressing-table mirror. A letter. She leaned forwards and stared at her name, scrawled across the envelope.

Opening it, her eyes skittered over the hastily written note.

Dear Emily,

I hope you will forgive me for burdening you with the task of delivering this news. I could lie, but I am sick of all the lies and deception. Ruth and I are in love and have gone away to be together. I have heard from Harry who is returning on leave. You know it is impossible for me to see him. It's all a mess and you will think me very weak for leaving you to tell Ma. We are going to Melbourne, but I can't give you our address

as Orm will hunt Ruth down. You can always send mail care of the YWCA. We intend to join the WAAAF and do our bit for the war effort. I am sorry.

Affectionately,
Lydia.

PS Look in your wardrobe.

She got up in a daze and opened the wardrobe to find Lydia's yellow silk dress hanging beside the pink gingham disaster and the outgrown church dress. She returned to the dressing table and read the letter through again. A fog had descended, and the familiar had become strange. Things were out of kilter. Lydia had run off with Ruth. They were in love, which meant that they must be lesbians – like Miss Maunder. Although she had not thought much about it at the time, she had taken Miss Maunder's lesbianism to be a euphemism for 'sexless' despite the dictionary meaning. Sexless, however, was not a description that fitted Lydia and Ruth, and she had a sudden vision of them doing the very things Fanny and Phoebe had done in *Fanny Hill* and had to force herself to think of the colour black in order to blot the vision out.

Once some semblance of mental order had been restored, she allowed herself to feel honoured that Lydia had entrusted her with the role of messenger. It was momentous news – she could not wait to tell William. But the thought had barely entered her head before she remembered the ruined state of things. There was nothing for it but to face the daunting task of telling Grandmother instead.

33

EMILY ENTERED THE SITTING ROOM to find the whole household still gathered there. Grandmother was pacing up and down or, to be more precise, around and around, dodging chairs and side tables as well as Uncle Cec, who was standing in front of the fireplace as if warming his bottom at the empty grate. Eunice was perched on the edge of a replica Queen Anne chair, and Della and Florrie had taken up residence on the couch. Grandmother was holding a handkerchief, twisting it with both hands as she paced.

'For heaven's sake, May,' Eunice begged. 'You're making us all dizzy.'

Emily took a deep breath. 'I know where she is.'

Grandmother pivoted on one foot, whirling around towards her with such speed that she almost lost her balance. Eunice rose from the edge of her chair, and Uncle Cec took a step forwards. With their bodies caught in the deep goose-feather recesses of the couch, Della and Florrie could only turn their heads.

'She's run away with Ruth. They're in love. It's all here.' She held up Lydia's note.

Nobody spoke, and she could see the shock in their faces.

'They've gone to Melbourne to join the WAAAF. They can't say where because of Orm.' And then realising it might not be clear, she added, 'In case he tries to hunt them down.'

Grandmother started to buckle at the knees, causing Uncle Cec to rush forwards and half carry her to the nearest chair where she managed to gasp, 'In love? Lydia and Ruth?'

'They're lesbians,' Emily said, unsure whether Grandmother had grasped the essence of it.

'But ... how? They can't be.'

'Of course they can,' Eunice interrupted. 'There have been Sapphists from time immemorial.'

'Like that Rita Frawley with the ferrets,' Della said knowingly. 'Called herself Ron.'

From the look Grandmother gave Della, the reference to Rita who called herself Ron was not welcome.

'Mind you,' Della went on in a more philosophical tone, '*In my Father's house there are many mansions.* John, chapter 14, verse 2.'

'Blast the girl,' Uncle Cec bellowed. 'What a damn fool thing, running off like that.'

'I can't allow it. She must come home at once,' Grandmother had found her voice again.

'Oh for goodness sake,' Eunice cried out. 'If they love each other, who are we to stop them? Who amongst us can live without love?'

Her *cri de coeur* seemed to go unnoticed by all except Emily, who had never imagined that Eunice would take such a stand for love. It was quite extraordinary; one more thing turned on its head, and when, a moment later, Eunice rose from her chair and rushed from the room, she caught a glimpse of shining eyes. She could not tell if it was the glint of tears or something more defiant and glorious. And though she couldn't yet forgive the brutal slap Eunice had delivered earlier, she knew that Grandmother's bridesmaid and helpmeet was not the person she had long supposed her to be.

With Eunice gone, the room began to break up. Grandmother left first, followed by Uncle Cec, muttering that he had to feed the dogs. Florrie struggled out of the couch and with Emily's help they hauled Della to her feet, only for her to shake them off with an irritated flick.

'Blinking couch. Nearly blinking suffocated. Come on, Florrie, get a wriggle on. The world hasn't ended.'

'I never said it had,' came Florrie's sulky reply as Della bundled her out.

Emily left the room last and returned to the white room. She did not know what else to do. She lay down on the bed and read Lydia's letter again. Her eyes closed. When she opened them, half an hour had passed and, despite everything that had happened, she found that she had not lost her appetite. There were sure to be leftovers in the kitchen safe.

To her surprise, when she entered the kitchen, everyone was already sitting at the table with bowls of soup and thick slices of bread and butter. Della was seated at the head of the table and, waving a spoon in her direction, indicated for her to come and sit down. She crossed the room and slid into a spare seat beside Florrie. That the family were eating in the kitchen with the servants was just one more peculiar thing to happen that day.

The supper progressed in silence except for the sounds made by each as they variously sipped and slurped Della's vegetable and mutton soup. Oddly – if anything could be said to be odd anymore when everything had become unpredictable – everyone seemed calm. She wondered if it were simply a temporary lull, or whether, after the fortifying effects of the soup, a plan of action would be devised to bring Lydia home.

'William.' Uncle Cec broke the silence. 'Poor blighter's had no supper.' His gaze fell on her. She felt her eyes slither sideways in a futile attempt at escape. She could not take William his supper given what had unfolded in the workshop earlier, but what excuse could she possibly give? She was still floundering for something to say when Grandmother intervened.

'If he wants to live like a hermit, he'll just have to go hungry. I won't allow Emily to go stumbling down there in the dark.'

She knew that if things between her and William had been different, she would have found a way to disobey Grandmother. She would have taken William his supper no matter what. Instead, she felt relief, even when it was clear that there would be no volunteers to take her place.

Upon issuing her edict, Grandmother looked around the table, silently calling everyone to attention. 'I trust that there'll be no gossiping about what has happened.' Her gaze lingered on Della, who did not say anything and sucked her tongue over her teeth, making an unpleasant slurping sound. 'Very good,' Grandmother continued, choosing to take this as a sign of agreement. 'In the morning, I shall telephone your father, Emily. He'll know what to do.'

Tell him to come and get me, she wanted to say, watching Grandmother push back her chair and rise stiffly as if her joints had seized up. How fragile she looked. Grandmother was still their leader, but the news about Lydia had taken its toll. *Tell him I want to go home.* It was on the tip of her tongue and yet the words remained unspoken. She did not know what stopped her.

The generator had been turned off. All was quiet, but Emily couldn't sleep. Her thoughts were flitting and jumping around like circus fleas. If only they would stop alighting on William. He would be hungry, she knew it. And angry that she had not come. Although, after what had happened he was sure to be angry with her whether she brought him supper or not. Too bad, she did not care. It was his fault. How could he be so cruel? She closed her eyes, hoping to block him out, but instead of black nothingness, she saw his crumpled body lying on the earthen floor. Perhaps he was … perhaps … no, she could not allow that thought. She tried to remember: had he groaned after falling?

A lifetime of penance stretched before her, and she made a vow that tomorrow, no matter what, she would volunteer to weed the top bed that was filled with soursob and had to be dug out, bit by bit, each tiny bulb sifted from the soil. She would do it willingly and in silence, like the Carmelite nuns who lived behind the high stone walls she had often walked past with her mother. *Poor little things, taken away never to see their parents again.* Whenever they passed, her mother would always say the same thing. Emily wondered if it were possible to join.

Unable to sleep she threw off the bedclothes and, sitting on the edge of the bed, lit the candle on the bedside table. She took Lydia's letter from the drawer. The contents were no less extraordinary on a fourth reading. The last line loomed at her – *PS Look in your wardrobe.*

Standing in front of the open wardrobe, she intended to take out Lydia's yellow silk dress but, instead, found herself staring at the dress from the *divine* little shop. For some reason it was this reviled dress that she now removed from the wardrobe. Shrugging off her pyjamas, she put it on.

A clown stared back at her from the dressing-table mirror. The pink-gingham puffy sleeves were as awful as she remembered and the lace collar framed her face like a hideous giant doily. She gave an experimental tug at the collar, then another, until at last, a piece of lace ripped free. Before long, the puffy sleeves joined the lace collar on the floor. She'd had to take the dress off and use her nail scissors with the result that the remaining inches of each sleeve were rather ragged. It was an act of wanton destruction but, instead of guilt, she felt quite elated. She had only wanted to get rid of the sleeves and collar but, looking at it now, she was seized by a desire to go further. With a snip of the scissors at bodice and hem, she grabbed hold of the material and tore the dress apart.

Bits of pink gingham littered the bedroom floor. She wondered if she'd gone mad and didn't care. If this was madness, there was a liberation to it. She went back to the wardrobe and, this time, took out the yellow silk dress. Had Lydia left it for her as a thank you for being the messenger and telling Grandmother? Or was it just because she was going off with Ruth, who had cupboards full of Le Louvre creations? Was it just an old cast-off, good enough for the little odd-bod? Thinking about Lydia calling her an odd-bod made her laugh. It did not seem to matter anymore. Lydia had left her the dress; there was no need to turn it into a tale of woe.

As she struggled to do up the recalcitrant zip, something tapped against the glass of the French doors, but she did not bother to look. It was sure to be a moth, attracted by the candlelight. She smoothed the silk material over her hips, twisting a little, watching the hem flare.

The tapping grew louder, and she turned to see a flash of torchlight. One of the French doors opened and William whispered, 'Don't scream. It's only me.' He manoeuvred himself into the room, shoving the torch in his pocket.

She watched him poke at the door with his crutch, pushing it shut. Her heart was fluttering like a trapped bird. *Speak*, she told herself. *Apologise*. But no words issued forth, and he was silent too, leaning on his crutches, staring at her in an intense way, and when a smile formed on his lips she felt a sense of dread about what was to come.

He gave a low appreciative whistle. 'You've turned into a beauty, Miss P.'

Without any warning, she burst into tears. Sobs forced their way up from deep within her and, although she wanted to stop, she could not. At least, not for some time. Throughout it all, William waited.

When the storm had passed, he bent down, picked up a piece of the gingham dress from the floor and handed it to her. 'Nose.'

She blew her nose on the puffy sleeve.

'I came to say sorry,' he began.

'No,' she interrupted, 'I'm the one who –'

'I'm a brute and I hurt you, and if you can't forgive me I don't blame you. But I want you to know that you can write. That's the important thing. Even more important than beauty. Although one shouldn't underestimate beauty.'

She shook her head. What was he talking about? Through bleary eyes she saw him pull something from his pocket. The letter! How could he?

'Listen. Don't say a word,' William said, cutting her off before she could object, and he began to read the part where she had described the fight between Claudio and Vincenzo outside the Catholic church. It went on for quite a few pages and, to her surprise, she got swept up in the action, almost forgetting that she was the author. When he had finished, William folded the letter up once more.

'See,' he said, 'you're a real writer.'

Again she shook her head. 'It's not even true – I didn't do anything. Lydia helped him, not me.'

'It's called fiction,' he replied. 'Sometimes writers have to steal what they need. You made it your own and whether it happened to you or not isn't the point. I won't lie to you: some of what you wrote was tripe. That romantic nonsense about the poor fellow's eyes and skin and so on. But it doesn't matter because you're going to get better and better. You just have to keep at it.'

There was a silence, and she could not look at him.

'Come on, Miss P. Forgive me.'

She raised her head and saw that he was smiling.

'Writers have to be courageous, you know. And ruthless too.' He held out the letter and she took it. 'I'm bloody starving,' he said. 'Some thoughtless brat forgot to bring down my dinner.' He laughed as he hopped across the room and opened the door. She listened to the squeak of his crutches and the sound of his 'dot and carry one' along the hallway, and it made her think of the evening he'd arrived and the shock of his missing limb, and how this was the first time he'd walked through the house since the day he had returned.

34

MORNING LIGHT STREAMED INTO THE white room. Cockatoos screeched as they flew over the house, waking her from a dream in which William had entered her bedroom in the middle of the night and she'd been wearing the hideous dress that she had mutilated with a pair of nail scissors. That was not all. William had told her that she was a real writer and had read out something from the Dorothy letter to prove it – not teasing this time – and the memory of his words of praise returned to her, lifting her up in a blissful bubble.

But then she remembered that her friendship with William was shattered; the bubble of bliss burst and she sat up. On the floor she saw pieces of the reviled gingham dress. She turned to the bedside table where a letter lay – many more pages than Lydia's note. She reached across and grabbed it. The handwriting confirmed that it was indeed the letter to Dorothy.

So William really had come to see her in the middle of the night and, according to him, she was a real writer. It was official. She let out a whoop. And hadn't he mentioned something about beauty? That she was turning into a beauty? She scrambled from bed, fizzing and bursting with an effervescent energy.

In the kitchen, Della and Florrie were already busy bottling tomatoes. It was an all-day job.

'Well, look what the cat dragged in,' Della said. 'What brings you here so bright and early? I suppose you want something to eat.'

'There's a lamb chop and bacon in the warming oven,' Florrie said and hurried across to the table with it before Emily could say that she wasn't hungry. Even if she was, the idea of eating a lamb chop for breakfast was almost as unappetising as kidneys or crumbed brains. And, in any case, her state of excitement was such that eating was impossible. She wanted to see William; she had to speak to him or, rather, she wanted him to speak to her, to say again the things he had said last night.

She could not stay sitting at the kitchen table and flitted across to the stove to put the kettle on the hob before returning to the table, removing the plate with the chop and taking it to the kitchen bench. The kettle was taking ages, and she moved it around on the hob as if hoping to make it boil more quickly. She didn't see Della behind her and bumped into the cook, who was unimpressed.

'Shoo, out the way. You're a blinking flibbertigibbet this morning,' Della said, giving her a shove. 'Go and sit down and let

Florrie make the tea.'

Knowing that it was foolish to disobey Della in her domain, she returned to the kitchen table. Florrie poured her a cup of tea, and she had begun to drink it when the telephone bell rang – someone was making a call. Grandmother must be telephoning her father, she was sure of it, and she jumped up.

Just as quickly Della pushed her down into the chair. 'You'll find out soon enough. No need to go getting under someone else's feet.'

She tried to rise again – it was urgent, she had to tell her father to come – but Della had a hand firmly on her shoulder. It felt like an age before Grandmother entered the kitchen.

'There you are. I've just been speaking to your father. He's arriving later today.'

'Today?'

'Yes. Just an overnight stay.'

'Am I going home?'

'Yes.' Grandmother looked disappointed. 'What a rush it all is. No doubt it's because of your mother.'

'How's Mummy?' The childish word slipped out, but she didn't care.

'On the mend.'

'What about Lydia?' Della interrupted.

Grandmother's mouth tightened. 'I do wish you wouldn't interrupt, Della. However, as you've asked: he thinks it best to let Lydia work things out herself. He's mistaken of course, but I can only wait until he's here in person. Really, sometimes I think the war has made everyone a little mad.'

Emily did not wait to hear anything more and rushed past her grandmother. The knowledge that she was soon to go home had brought forth a wave of longing for her parents and she wanted to begin packing immediately.

It took no time at all to stuff her clothes, willy-nilly, into the suitcase. When it was done, she sat on the bed and waited. How could she fill in the time until Father arrived? Even if he had left immediately after the telephone call with Grandmother, there were hours to go. Her thoughts returned to William.

The workshop door was open and, standing in the doorway, she watched William tying a leather strap around a bundle of rolled-up bedding. He noticed her.

'Miss P, come in.'

She reached the desk and had to navigate around a wheelbarrow filled with books. A little further on clothes spilled from an open trunk.

'What are you doing? Are you leaving?' She felt a quiver of alarm, forgetting for a second that she was leaving too.

'Rejoining the human race. Or what passes for it at Mount Prospect.'

'You're moving back to the house?' she asked, just to be certain. He nodded. 'Lydia's gone, did you know?' She had forgotten to tell him last night and now blurted it out.

'So I heard.'

'With Ruth. They're lesbians.'

'Yes.' William grinned, and she wondered if he'd known all along.

'I was sure she and Claudio –'

'Perhaps they were,' he said, before she could finish.

'In love?'

He laughed. 'Hardly. But Lydia's a flirt. I wouldn't put a dalliance past her. And the Italian's a man, isn't he? A hot-blooded Mediterranean. How long is it since he's held a woman in his arms?'

She tried not to flinch at the thought of Claudio with Lydia in his arms, but William was not deceived.

'No need to look so stricken, Miss P. I know you've got a crush on him, but it's not the end of the world. There will be others.'

She could not imagine that there would be others. Nor did she want others. But she wanted William to think well of her and attempted to rearrange her face into a less-stricken look. She'd been sure Lydia and Claudio were in love; a dalliance was shocking in a completely different way.

'What about giving me a hand,' William said, interrupting her train of thought. 'There's quite a bit to move.'

In addition to reclaiming his old bedroom, William needed a study where he could write and, with Florrie's help, the three of them cleared bric-a-brac from a spare room. The hours passed quickly as Emily loaded and reloaded the wheelbarrow, carting books to the new study, where she stacked them in piles on the floor. The bookcases had yet to be brought up from the workshop; Uncle Cec and Claudio were too busy with farm work.

She put down yet another armload and straightened up,

stretching tired muscles. In the middle of the new study, William was sitting on a chair, tying string around a parcel wrapped in newspaper.

'There's a pocketknife on the floor.' He pointed. 'Pass it here.'

She picked her way around tottering piles of books and found the pocketknife.

'What's in the parcel?' she asked, handing him the knife.

He cut the string and put the parcel on the floor, kicking it under the chair with his heel. 'What about a nip, Miss P?' he said, ignoring her question.

'Why do you call me that?' she asked, feeling thwarted on the matter of the mysterious parcel and needing to assert her right to ask something.

'Do you mind?'

'I just wondered.'

'You know the myth of Persephone?'

She looked sheepish and thought about lying. But, like Lydia, she was sick of lies and deception. 'Not really.'

Appalled at her ignorance, William made her search through the book piles until she found a volume on Greek mythology.

'That ought to give you the answer,' he said. 'In the meantime, there's a bottle of The Grouse over by the door.'

She took him the whisky and a glass, before sitting on the floor with the book of Greek myths. There was only one chair, and William had claimed it.

Persephone, she soon discovered, was the daughter of Demeter, and had been abducted by Hades and taken to his underworld kingdom of the dead to be his wife. But Demeter was grief-stricken at losing her daughter and mourned so much that all the crops failed. Something had to be done to bring Persephone back before everyone died of starvation.

'Where are you up to?' William interrupted impatiently.

'The Earth is on the verge of catastrophe,' she replied.

'Perhaps I'd better tell you the rest. That version is rather long-winded.' She agreed, for there were quite a few pages to go, and she was eager to learn the reason for her acquired pseudonym.

William explained that to avoid the catastrophe of mass starvation, Zeus sent Hermes to rescue Persephone. Hermes agreed on the proviso that she had not eaten anything in her time with Hades. On learning that she had in fact eaten six pomegranate seeds, Zeus had to find a solution. He decreed that Persephone could be united with Demeter for half the year so that the crops and harvests could flourish, and then for six months, the same number as the seeds she'd eaten, she had to return to Hades in the underworld.

'It was a way of understanding how the seasons came into being,' he said, pouring himself another glass of whisky. 'In the autumn and winter, Demeter grieves and nothing grows. Then in the spring and summer, when Persephone returns to the upper world, life returns to the earth, the crops all grow and the harvest is good.'

He tossed back the glass of whisky. 'So, there you have it. That's the myth of Persephone.'

She nodded, trying to disguise the fact that she still didn't understand. How could she ask him without seeming a complete idiot? She was continuing to ponder it when he spoke again.

'You see, Miss P, I was in the underworld, the kingdom of the dead, and you turned up like a breath of spring.' A shadow passed across his face and then he smiled. 'I thought you wouldn't come back, but you did.'

The idea that she had appeared to him that way gave her a pleasurable sort of pain in her chest. Like love, she thought, but there was no time to explore such a startling idea before the tooting of a familiar car horn interrupted them.

She flew out through the front door, skidding to a stop in front of her father. He dropped his overnight bag and embraced her.

35

IT WAS THE LAST MORNING of her visit. She had been awake for ages, listening to the familiar sounds around her. They no longer made her feel melancholy. It felt like years ago since Uncle Cec had collected her from the station and now, at last, she was returning home. She threw off the bedclothes and got dressed. It was time to leave.

The family had gathered for a goodbye breakfast in the dining room and her arrival in Lydia's yellow silk dress caused a small sensation.

'Excellent choice,' William murmured to her as she sat down next to him.

Her father, sitting in Lydia's usual spot, smiled at her from across the table. She knew he had not even noticed what she was wearing. Or perhaps he thought it was hers anyway, for as her mother so often noted: *We could walk around in sackcloth for all the difference it would make to him.*

'Hardly suitable travelling attire,' Grandmother commented. Eunice, of course, murmured her agreement.

But Emily did not care – she was determined to wear it. She took her serviette out of its ring and laid it across her lap. She did not want to risk a stain.

William touched her on the arm to get her attention, and she turned to see him holding the parcel from yesterday, wrapped in newspaper. In the background, she heard Grandmother telling her father that she was relying on him to send Lydia home. She did not catch his response because William spoke.

'Here,' William said, handing her the parcel. 'I hope you haven't read it but, if you have, it won't hurt to read it again.'

'For me?'

'The very same,' he replied with a smile.

She took the parcel and began to untie the string, but he put his hand on hers to stop her.

'No, later. When you're at home.'

'Thank you.' It felt inadequate, and she wanted to say more but William put a finger to his lips.

'Enough,' he said.

At the end of breakfast she gave Uncle Cec a farewell hug before he left to check the water troughs. He told her to come and visit them again soon.

Then she went to the kitchen, where Della and Florrie

presented her with a tin of homemade biscuits.

'Well, that's that then, you better get going,' Della said.

'Don't want to miss the boat,' Florrie added.

She put the biscuit tin on the kitchen table before throwing her arms around Della. Then she did the same with Florrie and they all bawled like babies.

'Can't see a blinking thing,' Della said, wiping her eyes with a tea towel.

'You shouldn't swear,' Florrie declared, and everyone laughed, including Florrie.

Now, standing next to the passenger side of the car, she watched her father loading the last few things into the boot. From a chair on the verandah, William watched too, smoking a cigarette. Grandmother and Eunice stood side by side nearby, from where they would soon wave goodbye.

All morning she had kept an eye out for Claudio. She had to say goodbye; she couldn't leave without a farewell, but there had been no sign of him. Time had run out.

Father closed the boot. 'Ready, my dear? Final goodbyes and we'll be off.'

Grandmother stepped forwards and offered her cheek. It felt soft and smelled faintly of Elizabeth Arden skin cream. 'You look lovely,' Grandmother whispered in her ear, 'even if it's not entirely suitable for travelling.'

She felt a huge lump in her throat and had to blink furiously to hold back her tears. 'Thank you,' she mumbled. 'For everything.'

'I'll miss you,' Eunice said, pecking her on the cheek then giving her arm a squeeze, and Emily knew that despite everything, she would miss Eunice too.

When Eunice had stepped back and re-joined Grandmother, she looked across to where William was lounging in the wicker chair. He'd told her earlier that he hated farewells, and that there was no need to say one because he was coming to Melbourne soon anyway. He had an appointment at the repat hospital for the fitting of an artificial leg. But she could not leave without saying goodbye. And, in truth, there was something else too.

She stepped onto the verandah.

William met her gaze. 'I told you, Miss P. No goodbyes.'

'I know. It's just ...' She hesitated. It was her last chance and she had to take it no matter how much it revealed and how foolish it made her appear. William knew all about it anyway. 'I wondered if you'd seen Claudio. This morning.'

'Ah.'

He paused, and her worst fears were confirmed. She never should have asked.

'You might try the stables. I heard Cec asking him to clean out the loose boxes.'

'Emily,' her father called from another universe.

She locked eyes with William. 'Tell my father to wait', and with that, she raced away.

Around the verandahs she flew, past the swinging seat, the red geraniums and the squatter's chair, past William's old punching bag and the hydrangea bed, leaping over the last bush and onto the gravel path. She ran down the path, through the gate and across the yard, arriving breathlessly at the open doors of the middle loosebox. She waited, catching her breath and then stepped inside.

Everything went dark, her eyes blinded by the sudden transition from bright sunlight to the gloom of the stables.

'Lydia?' His voice came to her through the darkness.

Of course, she was wearing the yellow silk dress. He was hoping it was Lydia; he didn't know she'd gone. The whole thing was a dreadful mistake. She stepped back, into the sunlight.

'Emilia?' Claudio emerged from the murk. He rubbed a hand over his face and through his curly black hair and bits of chaff flew out, glinting in the sun like tiny chips of gold. It was too late to run. She had to make the best of it.

'I've come to say goodbye.'

'Goodbye? Where are you going?'

She recognised the grammatical correctness of his enquiry and felt a glow of pride. 'Home.'

Claudio nodded but said nothing, and she knew that if she did not act immediately she would lose her nerve and moved towards him. Her mind was filled with fragmented thoughts: of Lydia, bold and brave even if she had run off and left Emily to tell the tale and even if she and Claudio had had a dalliance; and Dorothy, who was a bitch, but fearless in the face of authority; and Miss Maunder lecturing them on the virtues of restraint; and even Grandmother's odd phrase about bees to the honeypot. And most of all William, telling her that writers must be courageous.

And then there were no more steps to take, and she was face to face with Claudio. He looked a little startled, but suddenly she knew what to do. She moved her face towards his and their mouths met in a bumpy collision. With *Fanny Hill* as her guide, she had experienced her body in entirely new ways, but it was nothing compared to the shock of his lips against hers and the powerful sensations that flooded through her. She pressed against him and he moaned. She thought she might have too.

The car turned out of the Mount Prospect drive and onto the road. Her father preferred to drive in silence, and she was glad that it was so. She replayed the last moments of her visit over in her mind. She and Claudio standing opposite each other, her body tingling from the intensity of their kiss. The car horn had begun to toot, over and over.

'*Arrivederci*, Claudio,' she'd said.

'Goodbye, Emilia,' he'd replied.

The car picked up speed, and she gazed out of the window, watching the fence posts whizz past. On the back seat of the car was William's farewell gift to her – the book wrapped in newspaper. She wondered what it was and whether it might be *Jane Eyre*. She laughed. She did not think it was *Jane Eyre*. Her father glanced across at her with a smile.

'You see,' he said. 'I knew you'd enjoy yourself.'

She returned his smile and then looked out of the window again. As each post slid away into the past she felt part of herself sliding away too, sloughing off like a snake skin.

She was going home, and something new was beginning.